UNLIKELY PARTNERS

Is there no way of distracting him? She looks at him and suddenly kisses him on the lips. He tastes of ginger.

What are you doing, she asks herself. Didn't Tom read her that book about China and tell her how Victorian the Chinese were about sex? But this, she thinks, is not sex. This is something else.

Does she want to scare him all the way back to China? Make him the first person to walk all the way there on water, escaping this decadent Western woman, who, until this moment, has been notorious only for her prudery? Two prudes in a car, she thinks, one Eastern, one Western.

"Will you stop worrying?" she asks him, whereupon the Chinese prude bends over and kisses her.

"Eleanor," says her mother in her mind, "*think*. You drive people crazy thinking about why the sun rises and sets, and then you start kissing a perfect stranger without thinking about it *at all*. What do you think you're doing?"

But Eleanor, the totally preoccupied, has exercised her ability to suspend thinking.

"Eleanor," says her grandmother, "Scarlett O'Hara said she'd think about it tomorrow, and look where it got her."

Eleanor decides to do Scarlett one better and never think about it at all.

MAINLAND
SUSAN FROMBERG SCHAEFFER
bestselling author of
The Madness of a Seduced Woman and *Anya*

Novels by Susan Fromberg Schaeffer

ANYA
FALLING
LOVE
THE MADNESS OF A SEDUCED WOMAN
MAINLAND

MAINLAND

Susan Fromberg Schaeffer

BANTAM BOOKS
TORONTO · NEW YORK · LONDON · SYDNEY · AUCKLAND

The author would like to thank the John R. Simon Guggenheim Foundation for its generous support.

*This low-priced Bantam Book
contains the complete text of the
original hard-cover edition.*
NOT ONE WORD HAS BEEN OMITTED.

MAINLAND

*A Bantam Book / published by arrangement with
Linden Press*

PRINTING HISTORY
Linden edition published July 1985
Bantam edition / July 1986

ISBN 0-553-25805-2

Published simultaneously in the United States and Canada

*Bantam Books are published by Bantam Books, Inc. Its trademark, consisting
of the words "Bantam Books" and the portrayal of a rooster, is Registered
in U.S. Patent and Trademark Office and in other countries. Marca Registrada.
Bantam Books, Inc., 666 Fifth Avenue, New York, New York 10103.*

PRINTED IN THE UNITED STATES OF AMERICA

O   0 9 8 7 6 5 4 3 2 1

FOR NEIL

MAINLAND

N OT," SAYS HER MOTHER, "how one thing leads to another. No, in your case, it's how one scheme leads to another."

"What are you talking about now?" asked Eleanor, who is sitting in the middle of her antique oak bed, trying to look through a book of photographs of contemporary authors. If she isn't in the book, why have the publishers sent her a copy? She has recently developed cataracts and the world is in the process of sinking beneath a brown murk. She decides she isn't in the book and turns it over with exasperation, whereupon she sees something suspiciously like her own face peering up at her from the back cover.

"I never expected to find myself on the cover," Eleanor mutters.

"That's right, Eleanor," says her mother, "always expect the worst."

"If she expects the worst, she'll never be disappointed," says her grandmother.

"Expect the best, live through the rest," says her mother from the cloud she and her grandmother are now scouring.

To see the picture of herself on the back of the book, Eleanor presses one finger against her left eye (her right is under an eye patch) because that seems to bring things into better focus, while with the other hand she lifts the lid to let in more light. Cataracts, as the doctor explained to her, block the light. In that case, said Eleanor, I'm going blind.

"Well, yes," said the doctor, "in a manner of speaking." (A manner of speaking!) "But it's correctable."

Eleanor decides she really needs three hands for this maneuver: one to press against the eye, one to hold the lid up, and the third to lift the book closer to her. By balancing the book on her knee, she manages to bring it closer to her face, almost to her nose. Oh, yes, there she is. When her husband comes home, she must ask him whether or not it's a good picture of her. Meanwhile, she ought to find out what the caption beneath the picture has to say about her. She sighs and gets up to look for a magnifying glass.

"Everything should have a place," says her mother, who has just finished cleaning her cloud and is letting the dusty light of heaven burnish it.

"Oh, please," says Eleanor, rummaging through the things on top of her dresser.

"Do you really need all that junk?" asks her mother. "When I see clutter, I throw it out."

Eleanor finds the magnifying glass, which looks, to her, like a huge fish eye, and carries it back to the bed in triumph. She knows her mother throws things out; when she was a child, she was afraid to go to school because when she came back, most of her toys would be gone.

"They were dirty," says her mother.

As she sits down on the bed the sun comes out and the room is filled with a brilliant milky light. Eleanor sighs. It is harder to see in glare. It is impossible to use both hands to keep one eye properly open and at the same time hold the magnifying glass. Eleanor decides to try looking through the glass and squinting. It works. Ah, it works. She discovers that she is a famous author, a novelist, an essayist and a poet, that she has won many library prizes, and is Professor of English at a major university in Brooklyn. They have even included the name of her unfinished novel: *Getting Back.*

Apparently, thinks Eleanor, I am successful. But she does not feel successful. She looks around the room and her bed is like a raft lost in the brilliant white cloud which has invaded her room. She wants to tell her mother and grandmother how she feels, how it seems as if everyone and everything has floated off into the haze, how, though she knows everyone is there somewhere, she can't find them. The less well she sees the more distinct everything around her becomes. She hasn't been able to see her husband or her children clearly for some time now; the cloud moving closer in has swallowed them up. She has always had trouble believing in things she cannot see. Lately, she believes less and less in her family. They seem unreal, her husband, her two children, mythical animals about whom she hears frequent reports. But she is becoming detached from them, semivisible as they are. To them, she looks the same. For her, there is less and less to look at. She is adjusting to live in a world where things slowly disappear, and is perhaps preparing to disappear herself. She revises the phrase "ships that pass in the night" to "ships that collide in the night."

She gets up and peers at herself in her mirror. She can barely see herself. She moves forward until her nose is almost touching the cold glass. One eye has already been operated upon and is resting comfortably under a pink plastic eye patch.

"Don't worry," said the doctor. "When it heals and you get your glasses, you'll be able to see perfectly."

She doesn't believe him. Why should she? All she can see when she removes the patch is brilliantly colored unidentifiable shapes.

"Um," she says to her mother and grandmother, "I have something to tell you." She wants to tell them this: she is having an affair. But how?

"You haven't made your bed," says her grandmother.

"That," Eleanor says, "isn't what I was going to say."

"You're going to kill your mother," says her grandmother. "Isn't she, Frieda?"

"She is," says her mother.

"It's ten-thirty and that bed isn't made," says her grandmother. "Even a blind person can make a bed. You just feel for the corners and tighten the sheets. Look at your mother up here, crying. You won't give her a minute's peace. No one will marry you if you won't make your bed."

Eleanor points out that she's already married.

"Not for long," says her grandmother. "A man wants a woman who'll keep a nice house."

"There is something," Eleanor insists stubbornly, "that I want to tell you."

"I'll listen when the bed is made!" her grandmother says, "Not before! Nothing can be more important! Look at that mess! What an example you're setting for your children!"

"I really don't care," Eleanor murmurs, wondering why she spends so much time talking to the dead, especially when they're so unpleasant.

"She doesn't care!" says her grandmother, bursting into tears. "She doesn't care if she kills her mother!"

"That's not what I said!" Eleanor tells her.

"It's what you meant!" says her mother.

"It is!" her grandmother insists. "If she dies tonight, her death will be on your head!"

"Oh, God," says Eleanor.

Eleanor has a sudden memory of her grandmother's funeral. It was August and hot. She was sitting between her two cousins, all three of them trying not to cry, when her mind began to wander, and suddenly she saw her grandmother sit up in the coffin and point to her, saying, "She did it! That's the one right there! She did it! With her unmade beds and her long hair!"

No wonder Eleanor so hates going to funerals. She always feels as if she has dispatched the unfortunate person in the box. No wonder she now believes her failing eyesight is a punishment for something. What? She doesn't know. But now her father, permitted a rare cameo appearance, chimes in: "If you don't know today, you'll find out tomorrow."

They are all crazy, she thinks, starting to smile.

"If you're laughing now, you'll be crying in a minute," says her father.

Eleanor lies down, turns on her side, and stares out the window. Why are the crones allowing him to talk?

At her mother's funeral, an old man came up to her and told her he remembered the day she was born. He was there, in the hospital, and her father was waiting in the hall when her grandmother came to tell him he had a girl, he said, "A girl!" and walked away in disgust.

"He always was a fool," says her grandmother.

Lying on her bed, Eleanor asks herself: Can't I do anything right?

"All right, credit where credit's due," says her grandmother. "Children and animals love you. Everyone loves you. You can be so sympathetic to a stranger's troubles. But we know what you're really like."

I'm a good mother, Eleanor thinks, a good wife. Or I was. Before I got caught in this cloud.

"It's not a cloud," says her mother, back from a celestial dusting trip, "it's dust."

Eleanor, who still has something to tell them, decides to wait until they've become rational again. Perhaps later, after the housekeeper has come and made her bed. She falls asleep wondering why they always took everything she said so seriously, so literally.

"Drop dead!" she said one day, half out of her mind after an argument over an unvacuumed rug.

Her grandmother collapsed on the couch. Her mother ran over to her grandmother, who would not speak, but lay on her back clutching at her heart.

"To wish her mother dead!" her grandmother said at last. Then she stared at Eleanor as if at a seven-year-old murderess caught in the act of stabbing her own mother. Eleanor, who was horrified by her grandmother's reaction, kept staring at her mother to make sure she was still alive. The expression on her grandmother's face clearly indicated the presence of her beloved daughter's body in the middle of the well-scrubbed floor.

Is it any wonder, thinks Eleanor, falling asleep, that I only trust in what I can see? Which, these days, isn't much? Is it any wonder I don't like words, that lately I don't even want to speak? Not even to my husband? What is there to talk about but this endless blurring, and if I talk about it much, everyone will get terribly upset. What's worse, everyone may come down with the same thing. You know that's nonsense, she tells herself, but nevertheless she fears it: the contagiousness of her condition, her character, the danger she poses to everyone around her.

TWO

WHEN SHE WAKES UP, the house is absolutely silent. The housekeeper has gone to meet the children at the bus stop. Eleanor gets up and wanders into a room she has filled with stained glass and beaded bags, sits on the couch and tries to remember what they used to look like.

She looks up at the ceiling and says, again, "I have something to tell you."

"If it's about the bed . . ." says her mother.

"Oh, Mother," she says.

Those words, *Oh, Mother,* fall backwards, as if caught in a draft not quite of this world, an undertow always there in the air, until they reach the bottom of her own personal sea. She can see them now, like the emerald necklace dropped into an emerald lake by the first of her fictional villainesses, whose antagonist, her heroine, was to receive great acclaim and gratitude from a formerly unappreciative family when she retrieved it. But the story stopped there because Eleanor could never think of a stratagem which would permit its discovery, and so the emerald necklace still lies there, the little detective (looking so much like her) in her pink dress peering out of her rowboat into the emerald waters, befuddled: where could the treasure be?

And to tell the truth, Eleanor herself has forgotten just where in the water the villainess dropped it, and so this childish mystery from her ninth year goes on and on. There are so many lessons to be learned from this alone, most of which she has not learned. Certainly she subscribes to the view that life is a muddlement, but is that enough?

Perhaps not, when those two words, *Oh, Mother*, fall like two smooth stones right to the bottom of the sea (to the right or to the left of the still-missing necklace). Does it matter if she dropped the necklace in an ocean or into a lake? It would to some people, careful people, but she's always in such a hurry to get on with things. The details don't matter. Where does it come from, this conviction that she'll die young? Too late to think about that now, when those two words, *Oh, Mother*, have fallen into, are trapped inside a small apartment on Bedford Avenue and Avenue U.

Everything is painted white there. (Where are the surgeons? The nurses?) In a back room, her grandmother, her long gray hair braided, the braid pulled down over her left shoulder ("I don't like it swinging like a horse's tail") is patiently erasing Eleanor's pencil marks from her white-painted plaster wall.

Her grandmother and mother are both wearing cotton housedresses. Don't let anyone think they are made of anything as fragile as material, mere cloth. No, they are so thoroughly starched they shine like metal pots. She ought to remember those dresses. She bought each woman two every year, one for birthdays, one for Christmas. Oh, she knows those dresses, soft when she buys them, starched stiff after one wearing, emblems of chastity, of propriety, all the virtues. Next to them, the unicorn is an untidy beast. What husband wouldn't be secure seeing his wife in a stiff, shiny garment like one of those, covered as they are with beautiful hothouse roses, big, thick, overripe red petals like lips too red and waxy from lipstick; a hint.

But how can that be? Everything is pure in Brooklyn, place of security so absolute even nightmares enter grinning and guilty, saying, "Joke, joke, you know it's a joke; no need to take me seriously. No one's frightened by me. Of course, it's different in other places. I guess I'll be off then. We nightmares have our jobs to do, too."

In the past, nothing ever changes. In Brooklyn, nothing does either. It's not so much a place as a vale of time, which is perhaps why Eleanor can never leave it for long, although she escaped once, to Chicago, for nine years. But she can barely believe she lived anywhere else, living as she does now ten blocks from the house in which she was born.

"Oh, Mother," she says, "why can't I wear my new dress?"

"Because," says her mother, "it's your birthday and you'll show off."

Eleanor protests that she never shows off. It's the truth.

"There's always a first time," says her mother. "You'll be punished."

Nevertheless, she wears the dress to school, shows off, and is astonished to find herself standing alone in the corridor staring at the door to the first grade class, currently decorated with drawings of seals, penguins, whatever they have seen on their trip to the aquarium. Punished on her birthday. The sixteen-paned window is about to be opened by the second grade teacher, a Miss Wimpole, who wears wool whatever the season. She comes down the hall with a long pole, a brass hook on one end, reaches up, puts the hook into the brass loop screwed into the window top and pulls the window down. A cool breeze ruffles Eleanor's skirt.

"You're out here again?" she asks Eleanor, who nods and mumbles and blushes. She is seven years old. Inconceivable to be punished on her birthday. It is a pink dotted swiss dress with cap sleeves, tied at the waist by a satin ribbon, its skirt so starched she might have been wearing crinolines.

Is her mother always right? Is every transgression followed by punishment?

"But Mother," she says now, "it began so innocently."

"Doesn't everything?" asks her mother.

She waits for what her mother will say next. In that house, in her family, silence is a void to be filled with words.

While she waits, she asks herself why the past and present are interchangeable, why the past seems, lately, so much stronger than the present, elbowing it aside with sharp bones as her grandmother used to elbow through a crowd in front of the sale tables at Klein's.

"For an intelligent girl, to have so little common sense."

"It made sense in the beginning."

"Everything always does," says her mother.

Why is she constantly talking to the dead? Because they are so predictable. They are beyond change, as she once thought she was. When she reached forty, she told her husband: "The advantage of aging is knowing what you're going to do next. You see your emotions coming around the corner in old clothes. They never surprise you."

"Those whom the gods would destroy, they first make

stupid," says her grandmother, walking out of the mirror, holding a pencil with an eraser top now worn down to the gold metal band.

"Have you any idea how many erasers I've worn out on your walls? Enough erasers for all the starving children in Europe."

A great reader and great moralizer, her grandmother, but she never got anything straight.

"You're not that old, Eleanor," says Tom, her husband. Surely he must tire of talking over these endless voices which hover just below the ceiling.

"Amen," says her grandmother.

"I *am* that old," she insists, forgoing, for once, a display of her gray hairs, a recitation of the endless physical ills she is more than entitled to mention.

And how, she asks herself, did the present get to be such a jumble? It's no longer continuous. It is, she thinks, a shattered glass, first one shard, then another, presenting itself to her attention.

"And look how old you can get and still have no brains," says her grandmother.

"Oh, none," says her mother, who continues ironing, one of the few people in the world who finds such an activity soothing. When Eleanor irons, her attempts look like maps of despair, predictions of the ills of the flesh, the wrinkles, the burnt places, charts which show the goal and the many obstacles to getting there.

She thinks, Mother, Grandmother, how to tell you this? Perhaps if she puts it this way: I had an affair.

Her grandmother won't know the meaning of the word. When she died, affairs were bar mitzvahs and weddings. Later, they were also sweet sixteen and naming parties.

Instead, she says: "I committed adultery."

"I knew it!" says her grandmother.

"How could you do this to me?" asks her mother, bursting into tears. She has turned toward her daughter, the iron still hot on the white shirt sleeve, not replaced on its safe metal triangle: this must be important. Her mother is about to cremate an article of clothing, purchased, as she has so often told her, with her father's blood. All those years waiting for him to whiten and it never happened. Perhaps some people had more blood than others.

"Mother," she says, "I don't know how it happened. It was the Year of the Mouse. It was *my* year. I should have been safe."

"Year of the Mouse?" asks her grandmother. "What are you talking about now?"

"The Chinese year," she says.

"And that explains everything?" asks her grandmother. "The Year of the Mouse?"

"You know her," says her mother. "She always goes crazy when she's upset."

"Chinese? Mice?" says her grandmother.

"If you ask me," says her mother, "she's been talking to Jane again."

"I haven't talked to Jane in five years," Eleanor says indignantly.

"You've been talking to her," says her mother, "you never could live without her. You lived in her house more than you lived in ours."

"Mother," says Eleanor, "that was in high school."

"People don't change," says her mother. "Does Jane still sleep all day? Whenever I called the house, I woke her up, even at dinner time. She had more absences than the rest of the school put together. Did Jane tell you to commit adultery? You always said she'd end up with married men, she was so crazy about her father."

"There's nothing wrong with Jane," Eleanor says automatically, although there is: Jane cannot take too much of the world. She's skinless. When too much happens to her, she retreats. "Jane," says Eleanor, "is very funny. She's the only person I knew who had a sense of humor."

"She considers adultery funny?" says her mother, beginning to sob.

"Maybe," says her grandmother, "it was that other one who put her up to it. Gloria. The one who ate up all the food we brought Eleanor when she was too sick to come to Cedarhurst for Thanksgiving."

"No one," says Eleanor, annoyed, "put me up to anything. Leave my friends out of it. You never liked my friends. That's why I never brought them home."

"One thing you have to say for Jane," says her grandmother, "she was certainly a beautiful girl. The type who loses her looks by the time she's twenty."

"Enough!" cries Eleanor.

"Why can't you have normal friends?" asks her mother. "Normal ones would give you sensible advice. Jane's in another world. I'm surprised she can cross a street by herself. And that Gloria. What do you need with her? She's a leech, a bloodsucker. What do you need with her?"

"Another one of Eleanor's stray cats," says her grandmother. "She sees something hurt, she has to take care of it even if she gets eaten when it gets better. She can't get rid of anything. Even if it's a poisonous snake, she's got to be loyal to it."

"Adultery," says her mother, sobbing softly. She is sitting in the deeply ribbed, fern green upholstered chair she drags into the kitchen when she irons.

When Eleanor's mother moves to a new house, she will paint the walls dark green ("Green is my color," she

will say, dismissing the rest of nature's spectrum), pick out
dark green wall-to-wall carpets and tint the ceiling green
so that the entire first floor will appear to be somewhere
deep beneath the surface of the sea. Intact, clean and lux-
urious, but the bones, the skeletons in the closet falling
from the surface of Eleanor's life, litter the perfect cleanli-
ness. Even the rooms of the past are not safe from a
daughter's doings.

"Don't tell me Jane had nothing to do with it!" says
her mother. "A sixteen-year-old girl who saves up her al-
lowance to have tucks taken in her thighs is not a normal
person. Someone who uses up all her energy dieting and
gets too tired to support herself isn't normal."

"I should never tell you anything," says Eleanor.

It is the night of their Junior Prom and she and Jane
are at a movie—far from home so that no one will know
they have no dates.

"Do you think it's because I'm too fat?" she whispers
to Eleanor, who ignores her.

"Do you?"

People in back of them whisper in annoyance.

"No," says Eleanor. Jane pokes her in the ribs.

"What, then?"

Eleanor considers. "We don't fit in," she says.

The two of them stare at the screen, not wanting to
look at each other.

"Do you think I'll get married? Ever?" Jane whispers.

"Of course."

"Don't you want to? Get married?"

"No," says Eleanor, who believes that even should a
man be foolish enough to marry her he'd live to regret it.
Within a week.

Then why did she marry young when Jane never
married at all?

"Because," says her grandmother, "*you* took a married man away from his wife. You're lucky you didn't lose your job. You're *both* lucky you didn't lose your jobs. But," says her grandmother, turning it over, "what did he want with a woman who couldn't make her bed?"

"*Wouldn't* make it," says her mother. "Wouldn't."

"She's made her bed now," says her grandmother grimly.

There's no comfort in the past, thinks Eleanor sadly; I should stop returning to it.

Confusion, she thinks, is her element now.

And what is confusion but an absence of trust?

But how can one trust a world whose image flickers on and off like a face on a bad television screen?

I can't, thinks Eleanor, who tries to resign herself to the way everything, all her certainties, seem to shift and move and disappear as if in a heavy fog.

THREE

HOW LONG can she stand at the window, looking out? Everyone in Chinatown seems to be wearing lavender down-filled jackets, with pointed hoods. Every time she walks to this small borrowed apartment, she sees the coats, still new and shiny, unlike hers, heaped outdoors for sale on big tables whose surfaces are unfinished wooden boards and whose legs are sawhorses. She looks down through the thin curtains of snow—the clouds are hanging between her and the crowded street—and supposes she ought to wear hers also. Anything to be less conspicuous. The coats are made for the Chinese, she thinks, the exiled mainland Chinese, who still expect to be rusticated and sent to the frozen north. The hoods fasten across one's mouth and cover one's nose. All you can see is the eyes.

Anonymous and warm. That's why he wants her to wear the one he's bought her—not out of possessiveness, so that when she comes here even her clothes will belong to him. Somewhere, she's read about a custom like that, the bride going naked to the house of the bridegroom, and so it is impressed upon the bride that she belongs where she now is and to return would be shameful and dangerous: particularly in a cold climate. Oh, he is possessive, although he does not think so, but she does not want to think about questions of possession, and so she wears the coat as if it were not an article of clothing at all, but a thin tissue of invisibility.

She takes the curtain's edge between her fingers. It's stiff fabric and cheap, but from a distance it looks like delicate lace. The light, she sees, is turning it yellow just as light yellows her old manuscripts. Suppose she wanted to write "Help!" on the frosted window. She knows how to write two Chinese words: tree and forest, half the accomplishment it might seem since the symbol for tree, written twice, means forest. She traces the ideogram for tree on the window, thinking that perfectly sensible people do not walk into forests about which they know nothing. She turns to look at him. He was watching her before, but now he's fallen asleep, his black hair startling against the white pillowcase whose fabric is so thin that beneath it the lines of the pillow-ticking show through, making it seem as if he has fallen asleep against a large pad of school paper. One strand of his hair has separated, and slashes across the white fabric like the stroke of a calligraphic brush. She wonders what words could be formed around that line.

His eyes open and he sees her watching him and he smiles. What does she want to say? That it is preposterous for him to spend time with a woman her age? He's only twenty-seven. But here her thoughts veer off into the new incandescent silence she's only recently discovered. It was that kind of thinking that brought her here: he's only twenty-seven, I'm old enough to be his mother ("A young mother, an unwed mother," her grandmother whispered, but she didn't listen).

She smiles back. That narrow hospital bed, painted white, the white chipped off through the years, perhaps chipped off deliberately and obsessively by a child trying to sleep, each chipped place like a region on a map. Every time she lies in that bed with him she wants to learn their shapes, piece them together, retrieve the true shape of the world. He looks like a child in that bed. She smiles and moves toward it. She is in love with that face which might be, no, is, the face of the world. The two crones, her mother and grandmother, snort just over the ceiling of the room. *Here* they are crones. When she is home, they wear velvet robes and hold golden scepters and pound their scepters all night long against the floor above her. Yesterday morning, she woke up and saw the cracks in her bedroom ceiling and thought, no, it's not my imagination. They're really there, the two of them. Now she thinks: whether they're there or not, the cracks are only cracks; they can still be plastered over.

"Do you still want me to wear that parka?" she asks him.

"I think so," he says.

"I'll wear it from now on."

She picks up her pocketbook and starts looking for her keys. If she's lost them, she won't be able to get into her own house. Everyone's gone today.

He laughs and points to her pocketbook. Everything disappears inside it, it's so very large.

"Another cow's stomach," says her mother, observing it from her empyreal perch, shaking her head. Eleanor is forever searching through it, trying to find her keys.

"Where are you going with that thing?" asks her grandmother. "Russia?"

Disapproval falls from the air.

Queens have died young and fair.

If only there were as many doors in the world as there are keys on her ring. She sits down on the bed and slides under the three woolen blankets which once must have been peach-colored, but are now, except in the folds, a dunnish color. Separately, the blankets are useless against the cold. Together, they are warm.

FOUR

BUT IT DID BEGIN so innocently, because otherwise it could not have begun at all. Not to her, happily married creature that she is, determined guardian of Family Circle morality, not because she is innately moral, the whole world knows she isn't, but because immoral behavior complicates. And she has long ago learned that there is something in her gaze that will complicate the most simple situations, or, more precisely, will search out the intricate balance of complexities which pass for simplicity, the mistakes canceling each other out: love, for example, and hatred, like two colors which, when mixed together, form an off-white the color of fog with sun behind it, the color so often mistaken for peace.

No, immoral behavior is for people who see the lake is iced over and presume they can walk, at least right now, on water. No such mistakes for her, whose grandmother pointed out repeatedly that one could drown in a teaspoon of water. For years Eleanor turned this problem over: how could it be done? And last year, it occurred to her—one could swallow the water the wrong way and choke on it and that would be a form of drowning. A solution. Very possibly the right one, but not very satisfying, not as satisfying as imagining the various ways one's body could contort, could manage to fit itself into the bowl of a spoon. A mind like hers, one that will work tirelessly on the most innocent comment, the least interesting riddle, wearing itself (and everyone else) out in the process, is not meant for immorality. Such a mind does not suffer from an excess of virtue but, at the end of any given day, a lack of energy.

Then how can she explain what she's doing?

She can't.

She's often asked herself what she would do if something happened to Tom, her husband. Would she continue living? Would she want to live? She doesn't think so.

"Of course you'd go on," says her grandmother. "You have two children to live for."

"Let's hope," says Eleanor grimly, "they'll be old enough to take care of themselves." She ignores her grandmother, who is raving about what an unnatural mother she is. To want to die because of a *man!* Eleanor, who remembers how her grandmother treated her grandfather, shakes her head and stares at the blurring window.

She remembers driving up to the country soon after she was told she'd need eye surgery.

"Why do we have to go *this* weekend?" wails her ten-year-old son, David. *"This* weekend we want to stay home and ride our bikes."

"Go to sleep," says Eleanor. They never fall asleep until they are three miles away from their destination, no matter how far away that destination might be.

"We're not turning around," says Tom.

"I only wish I'd had a country house to go to when I was a child," says Eleanor. She shudders. She sounds just like her mother.

"You can go to the one you have now," says her daughter, Julie. "You can leave us home with the house-keeper."

"Will you go to *sleep?*" Eleanor demands, her voice rising several octaves.

Silence in the back seat. She slides closer to Tom and rests her hand on his thigh.

"Mo-ther," says Julie.

"Don't bother your mother," Tom says automatically.

"What?" asks Eleanor.

"When you die, can I have your snake bracelet?"

Eleanor doesn't answer immediately. "Is that all you want?" she asks finally. "Not my collection of antique dolls?"

"Your mother," says Tom, clearly upset, "is not going to die so fast."

"Yes, she is," says Julie, who is six, "that's why she's going to the hospital next month to have her eye taken out."

"Julie," Eleanor says, turning around, "I'm not going to the hospital to have my eye taken out. They're taking out the cataracts in the eye. Not the eye. You know what a fly looks like when you squash it on a window? You can't see out that spot? That's what a cataract does. You can't see out through them. That's why they're taking them out."

"A squashed fly!" says David. "Yuk!"

"No," says Julie. (What a stubborn child! Where does it come from? *"Where* does it come from?" her mother asks, incredulous.) "An old lady on the block said you didn't get cataracts until you were very old and were going to die soon anyway."

And to think, Eleanor muses, I was afraid she'd never learn to talk.

"You," the child says, her tone accusatory, "got old all at once."

"Your mother is not old," says Tom.

"I am not old," says Eleanor. "I am not dying. They'll cut a little slit in my eye and cut out the cataracts. I think they have some kind of machine that slurps them up with a straw. Something like that."

"Yuk," says David again.

"She is dying," she hears Julie whisper. "Alison told me."

"Alison doesn't know everything," says Eleanor. "I'm not dying. I'm only going to get my eye cut open."

"That's all, Eleanor?" asks Tom.

In the back of the car, Eleanor's precocious daughter considers. "When you do die," asks Julie, "can I have your snake bracelet?"

"Yes."

She waits for David, also known as Davey, to ask what he can have, but mercifully he doesn't. Perhaps, miraculously, he's fallen asleep. She looks at Tom, who doesn't seem to want to look at her. Perhaps he too is afraid she'll go into the hospital and won't come out. Why shouldn't he think that? She does.

She stares at the rain, beading on the glass and then snaking down like liquid mercury. Her mother was a great one for threatening everyone with her will.

"If you keep up that behavior," she tells Eleanor, "I'm going to leave all of my ivory collection to your brother." "Slam the door once more and I'm going to change my will. Your brother will get the china."

Eventually she and her brother had an idea. They conferred and told their mother that when she died, they would disregard the will and decide who got what. Her mother never mentioned her will again. When her mother and father were killed in a car accident, she and her brother divided things up. Her brother got the china,

Eleanor remembers, smiling. It was meant for her. She never liked it.

She feels, she thinks, like a widow, or someone about to be widowed by the world, which is so quickly fading from her sight. At other times she feels like a ghost, haunting the site of her old life.

Tom keeps driving. The rain lets up.

"You were right," Eleanor says picking up the thread of a conversation they had three days ago. "I shouldn't have let *any* ex-student stay at the house. But I thought Tina would take good care of it. She loves the country."

"Maybe," says Tom, "she did take care of it. Maybe one of the other people who stayed there didn't."

"Other people?"

"Oh, come on, Eleanor. You didn't expect her to stay there alone."

Eleanor thinks this over.

"If only she hadn't thrown out my scale. I've had that scale for fifteen years. It was completely tame. It never scared me with sudden gains or losses."

"Scales," says Tom, "have been known to make their way back home across countless miles. You'll wake up in the middle of the night and hear it scratching at the door."

Eleanor starts to laugh. "You think so?" she says.

He nods. After a while, he says, "What's more mystifying than the scale is the hair dryer. What made her put it in the woodshed?"

"Never mind that," she says, "how did Tina manage to scratch a floor with twelve coats of polyurethane?"

"Maybe," says Tom, "one of them killed another one. We should check the closets for bodies."

"You can't *open* the closets," says Eleanor, sighing, sliding down in the front seat. She's never as happy as she is when she's alone with Tom, which, since the birth of the children, seems a rare event. Most of the time she is not sitting close enough to him to see him clearly. Lately, he seems to be erased by the mists of her failing eyesight. And, thinks Eleanor, I am adjusting to his disappearance. Even though he's not going anywhere. When he gets sick, she threatens him.

"Don't you dare die," she says. "You'll leave the children orphans."

"You'll still be here," Tom points out.

"Oh, no," says Eleanor. "If you go, I'm going too." She means it. It may not be a perfect marriage, thinks Eleanor, but it is often an ecstatic one. Lately, however, she drifts.

"Then stop drifting," says her grandmother. "What are you? A rowboat?"

"Drifting?" asks her mother.

"My *eyes,*" Eleanor says, tired.

"Everyone *I* knew had cataracts," says her mother.

"Mother," says Eleanor, "you were *at least* seventy years old."

"What are a few years, one way or another?" her mother asks.

Eleanor sighs and tries to sleep, but she is wide awake.

Where is her pink scale? Why is everything around her deliberately disappearing? She thinks back, again, to how it began.

FIVE

FOUR TIMES THREE is what?" she asks her son, who is working his way through his homework as though through a Siberian tundra, as if balls and chains were attached to his ankles and wrists. "No, it's not sixteen," she says. Two more mistakes and she'll lose patience entirely. "What are we up to?" she asks her son.

"Five, Mother," he says. "Can't you see?"

No, she can't. If she rubs her eye, if she gets more sleep, she'll see more clearly. But when she rubs her eye it hurts.

"I think I'd better see an eye doctor," she tells her husband, who, behind her, is cooking lasagna for support.

"Keep going," she tells her son and gets up to show Tom her eye.

"Look at my eye." She asks him, "Is there anything in it?"

He puts down the wooden spoon and rinses his hands under the faucet.

"Pull up the lid," she says.

"No," he says, "I don't have to. It's bright red."

"Bright red! Let me see."

"Let me see!" says her son, jumping up from the table.

"You sit down and work," she tells him. "I can look at my eye by myself."

In the morning, an eye specialist is looking at it for her.

"An inflammation?" she says. "Not an infection?"

"Not an infection," he says.

"That's good," she says. But she doesn't like his expression. "Isn't it good?"

Apparently, it isn't. An inflammation, he tells her, can be worse than an infection.

"How long will it take to clear up?"

"In some people, weeks. In others, months."

"Months!"

She jumps in her chair. He steps back.

"I have so much work! Everything," she tells the doctor angrily, "is foggy."

"That's because of the drops."

"Then I'll see normally when I stop them?"

He begins fussing with some instruments on the tray at the side of her chair.

"Actually, no," he says. "Part of the treatment is keeping the eyes dilated."

"Oh, God," says Eleanor, "it's the end of the world."

"It's not the end of the world, Eleanor," says her husband, usually known as Tom. In crises, such as this one, the seriousness of which he always fails to appreciate, he acquires a more appropriate title: The Idiot. "You'll sit around, rest, you'll think of things to do when your eyes are better. You work hard, you're entitled to a rest."

"What about you?" she asks. "Aren't you entitled to a rest?"

"That's something to slam a door about?" asks her grandmother, "because you have a husband who says he'll take care of you? He's too good for you."

"Right," says Eleanor, pulling the covers over her head. When upset, she sleeps.

This, then, was the innocent beginning. When a person's senses take leave of her, she is not responsible for what she does. Her eyesight flew out the window first. Then she caught a cold and lost her voice along with her sense of smell. She calls her Aunt Lucy in Arizona, her mother's sister, who hangs up. She thought the graty, whispery voice belonged to an obscene caller. Nevertheless, Eleanor goes off to the college four blocks away from her house and teaches her graduate seminar and is puzzled by her students, who are answering any and all of her questions in barely audible whispers. Have they gotten it through their heads that a person with a cold cannot tolerate loud noises? Then they stop whispering and begin moving their lips, whereupon Eleanor realizes that she has lost her hearing. In time her voice returns, and whatever has been blocking her eardrums drains, and she can hear.

Her eyes, however, remain dilated and red. Street lights and street signs disappear behind the haze which has rolled in like mist from the sea. People, too, are disappearing. The eye doctor, whom she has long since dubbed The Maniac, tells her to have patience. It will all clear up in a short time. Time flies, after all (Oh, yes, she thinks: on Icarus's wings), and eventually, one year later, he pronounces her eyes cured.

"Two brand new eyes," he says, beaming.

So new that they have not yet learned to work as well as her old ones. She finds it harder to see in glare. The outlines of people blur when she looks at them. A person approaching her is faceless until he is less than two feet away. Week by week, the world fades.

"It's nothing," says the eye doctor. "You're getting older. More farsighted. It happens to everyone."

"In one week?" she asks him. "People get so far-sighted in one week?"

He beams at her.

He's worse, she thinks, than a lighthouse. At least a lighthouse beam sweeps back and forth, or goes on and off, she's not sure which. The eye doctor beams like some kind of perverse sun that refuses to go down. The man must be miserable, thinks Eleanor, to smile so much.

Still, it doesn't occur to her to go to another doctor. And why doesn't it, since Eleanor is not brain-damaged, and is, at the moment, enjoying a great deal of attention in academic circles for her essay on the myth of adult-hood? She doesn't go because she, Professor Noseybody, has become obsessed with doings in the doctor's office. The doctor is a religious man, married, possessed of at least three children, all of whom think nothing of march-ing through their father's dimmed examining room on their way to the street.

"Children, they're so adorable," says his receptionist whenever they go by, from which Eleanor deduces that the receptionist-assistant hates the doctor's wife.

"She's a nothing," the secretary tells her during one of the four-hour waits to see the eminent doctor. "She likes to drive in that big car with the M.D. plates. Who knows where she goes with it? Where does she have to go? Around and around the block."

It is clear to Eleanor that the secretary, whom they call Challah, is waiting for the doctor to see through his wife, whereupon he will walk around her three times and his first act as a free man will be to propose to the glorious

Challah. The secretary is four feet ten inches tall and does
not wash. She is twice her proper weight and in fact resembles the loaf of bread after which she appears to be
named, and she braids her thin, oily hair into a long rat's
tail which she skewers to the top of her overly large head.
Patients' consultations with the doctor are punctuated by
Challah's interruptions: she has no one to take her home.
The area she comes from, they found a dog murdered in it
yesterday. Couldn't he tell the next patient he has an
emergency and go out the back door for the car and come
back after he dropped her? They'd never know he was
gone. They're used to waiting. He says he can't. Soon he
starts to whine: I can't, I can't. The word "can't" suddenly
has four syllables.

Eleanor is put into something like a closet adjoining
the waiting room while her eyes dilate. On the other side
of the wall, she can hear Challah taking her revenge. Suddenly, she can fit everyone in.

"An emergency is an emergency," she says. "Come
right over. Such an emergency, you're going to walk? Call
the car service."

In ten minutes, Challah discovers ten such emergency
patients. Eleanor is sent out to wait in the outside room.

"With emergencies, it's all or nothing," Challah says,
lifting her protruding blue eyes to the acoustical tile ceiling. Eleanor asks her if the doctor won't be stuck in the
office until all hours.

"What can he do?" Challah asks with a resigned
shrug. "He's the best. If people need him, he's here."

"So," Challah says, putting on her coat, buttoning it
with one hand, switching on the answering machine with
the other, "I'm going. You don't know what to expect
when you get off that train and the sun's shining. In the
dark, even God can't see you."

As she gets ready to leave, the first of the emergency patients walks in. Eleanor asks her what's wrong with her eyes.

"I think I need a new prescription," the woman says. "I thought: get it over with. I call up and Challah says it's an emergency. Why should it be an emergency? I've needed new glasses for two years, three. You think they're not telling me something?"

No, says Eleanor; she doesn't.

"So, Eleanor," asks her mother, "this is a good reason to go to an eye doctor? You want to find out about how the story of Challah and the doctor ends? It's cheaper to watch a soap opera."

But Eleanor is staying to see the end.

"You always sat through movies twice," says her mother, disgusted.

She returns for a checkup after the summer, and lo, there is Challah looking almost human (if a fish with braided hair can look human). She is wearing a blond acrylic wig (the sort advertised in *The Enquirer,* Style No. 6, "The Cleopatra") and she has dressed herself up in an outfit from the fifties so that she now looks almost modern.

"Married?" Eleanor asks her.

"Oh, yes," says Challah, "a wonderful man, a scientist. He can't work right now, he just had back surgery, I was there every minute. I didn't go home at night, I slept on a chair, the doctors couldn't touch him without my knowing about it. Of course, we don't have much room in our apartment, it wasn't meant for two people, it wasn't meant for even one. Before the operation, he met me at the subway, you know it isn't safe where I live (the whole world knows it isn't safe where she lives) but now he says, walk fast. Well, what can you expect? His back hurts him.

Yesterday the doctor and I did three operations on cataracts. Of course, I help; I'm the one who pumps the foot pedal for the gas to freeze the cataracts. But my husband, he's getting restless about my long hours and I tell him, what can I do? He's the best doctor there is, people come from all over the world to him, even from Queens. You can't turn people away. Still, I'll be glad when he starts earning money again."

"Who, the doctor?" asks Eleanor, wanting more of this diatribe, staring at Challah, trying to conjure up a picture of the operating room, the poor patient ("Doctor! Doctor! Save my eyes!") semiconscious while this walleyed, deep-sea creature in an acrylic Cleopatra wig pumps away at the foot pedal, talking ceaselessly: "So put down the knife for a minute. Tell me, you can't take me home? This hospital could be in a better neighborhood. Last night two patients on the third floor were raped by a man from Georgia. He came all the way here to get to this hospital. No, keep your money for a car service. I'll call my own. At least I know from those drivers. If you can't be bothered, you can't be bothered. If that's it, that's it, finish up the operation already. The man's starting to talk. Soon he'll be ready to walk off the table. Leave the bleeding alone. It stops by itself."

At last, knowing the end of Challah's story (the wretched woman has taken a physicist captive and is slowly torturing him into insanity and hypochondriasis), Eleanor is free to go to another doctor. By now she is also sure that, between them, Challah and the eye doctor are blinding half the cataract sufferers in Brooklyn. But by the time she arrives at a second eye doctor's office (This man is competent. He has two efficient secretaries who do nothing but type and answer phones. What a boring place it is.) she learns that she too has cataracts, induced by the medication the first doctor gave her for approximately one year too long.

"You have," says the new, sane doctor, "baby cataracts."

"Cataracts!" says Eleanor. "They blind you!"

"Unless you do something about them," says the doctor.

"What can you do about them?"

"For the moment, nothing. We wait and see if they grow. We try to correct your vision with glasses. Yours don't seem to be correctable. Usually cataracts grow very slowly," he says, fidgeting with his pen. "Sometimes they take twenty years to grow."

"I can hardly see now," says Eleanor. "I can't tell the difference between red and green lights. When I drive, I watch the car in front of me and see how long it takes to disappear into the murk. It doesn't take long. This only started a year ago."

"When you have drug-induced cataracts," says the doctor, "they often grow very quickly."

"Drug-induced!" says Eleanor. "The other doctor *induced* them?"

"If they get any worse," says the doctor, staring at a spot over her head, "we'll have to do something about them."

"What?"

"Operate."

"Operate!"

She has turned into a demented, frightened echo of herself.

"What," she asks at last, "is the operation like?"

"Oh," he says, "it's nothing much. We give you a local anesthetic and take out the cataracts. You can be back at work the same day."

"Nothing much!" says Eleanor. "An operation!" She resolves to get a third opinion.

"I would think," says the doctor, "you'll be ready for an operation in three months."

When she goes to see the third eye doctor, it is four months later and she is not surprised to hear she is ready for an operation. After all, it's not easy, driving when you can't tell the color of the traffic lights. Or when you enter a tunnel, can't see anything, and drive hugging the wall. She has a morbid fear of turning into a lane and finding a car stalled in front of her. She'll know it's there when she crashes into it; she can't see far enough ahead of her to stop in time.

The third doctor is less cheerful than the second. It's serious surgery, he tells her; things can go wrong. Detached retinas, hemorrhages, total blindness. It's surgery, after all. These things are not likely, but they happen.

"Is it painful?" asks Eleanor.

"The shots are."

"Can I talk? Ask questions?"

"You have to lie perfectly still. No smiling. If you smile, you move the facial muscles. Do you think you can lie perfectly still for an hour?"

"Yes."

"Yes?" asks her mother. "You can't keep your mouth shut for ten minutes. You'll want to get off the table to take a look around the operating room. Be sensible. Get knocked out."

The eye doctor calls her family doctor, who tells him that Eleanor is very high-strung and he doubts if she can lie still for five minutes.

"I think," says the surgeon, "we'll give you a general."

"Oh, no," says Eleanor. "I know all about general anesthesia. It's dangerous. I'll lie still."

The surgeon regards her dubiously.

"No," Eleanor tells her husband the day before the operation on her right eye, "don't stay here while they operate. They never do anything on time. Come back here tomorrow afternoon. Around three."

"Why three?"

"They said they'd be finished at one. They're usually only two hours late."

When he leaves, Eleanor, who is familiar enough with hospital routine, takes off her wedding ring. She remembers her last surgery. The worst part of the operation is, according to her, giving up your wedding ring. The first time they took her rings, she was sure the doctors were trying to tell her, subtly, that they didn't expect her to survive. "But Eleanor," said her internist, "people don't die of hysterectomies."

"Should I have made a will?" she asks him.

"Of course you should have made a will," he says. "Everyone should have a will."

Eleanor starts to cry. The internist is not impressed by tears.

"This is elective surgery," he says. "We wouldn't recommend it if we thought it would kill you."

"You have to take off your nail polish," says a nurse coming in with a bottle of nail-polish remover.

"My nail polish?" Eleanor asks, incredulous. Next, they'll be asking her to remove the dye in her hair. She glares murderously at the nurse.

"Eleanor," says her doctor, "they take off the nail polish so they can see your nails."

"They *can* see my nails."

"They need to see their color. If they turn blue, they want to know."

"Why?"

"It means you're not getting enough oxygen."

They are only an hour late coming to get her this time. David Bowie's "Modern Love" is playing on the hospital's version of Muzak. She lies absolutely still while they slide her onto the trolley. "You can move around now," says the nurse. "You have to lie still later."

"Um," says Eleanor, "when does the tranquilizer shot start working?"

"Isn't it working now?" asks the nurse.

"No."

"I'll tell the doctor."

The doctor decides the medication is slow to take effect on some people, and tells the anesthesiologist, who agrees with him. "It will work soon," they tell her.

The doctor's assistant arrives and tells her he's going to give her the shots she needs. "Relax," he says, to the boardlike patient on the bed in front of him.

"I am relaxed," says Eleanor, "can't you tell?"

He gives her her first shot and Eleanor screams.

"Don't *do* that," the doctor says, shaking.

"You didn't tell me the shots went right into the eye," Eleanor says.

"Do you want a general?" he asks her. "You can still have one."

"How many more shots?" she asks.

"Three," he says. And sighs.

It takes five shots.

"Anesthetics don't work well on me," says Eleanor.

"So I see," the assistant surgeon says grimly. "Is the tranquilizer working yet?"

"No," says Eleanor.

During the surgery on her right eye, Eleanor concentrates on remembering the words to "Modern Love." She would, she thinks, ask the nurses if they remember the words, but she's not allowed to make a sound.

"Don't worry," says the surgeon, "we're just cutting your eyelashes."

Fine, thinks Eleanor, one bald eye.

"When," she asks, "does the shot start working?" She hears them mumbling together.

She sees a wash of red.

"We're beginning now," says the surgeon. "Did it hurt?"

Eleanor doesn't answer. She knows she's not supposed to talk. She lies still, rigid with fear. It's cold. The cuff on the blood pressure machine inflates and squeezes her arm. What if it doesn't stop doing that? Will it cut off circulation entirely? Will she end up having her arm amputated? The cuff decompresses. She watches the bright light above her. Hands waver down toward her right eye. It is not glamorous in here; in fact the operating room bears a distinct resemblance to an automobile garage. Her arm begins to hurt but she's afraid to move it.

"Are you all right?" asks the doctor. Eleanor, who assumes he's talking to someone else, the anesthesiologist perhaps, doesn't answer.

"Are you all right?" he asks again. No answer. He taps Eleanor on the head. "All right?"

"Who, me?" she asks, surprised to find she's still alive.

"We're almost finished," he says.

She doesn't answer.

"Done," he says.

"Can I talk now?" she asks.

In the hall, they leave her for twenty minutes while they work on an emergency case. She tries to let the terror bleed from her body into the sheets. She thinks of the little room where the doctor came to give her her shots and starts to cry.

"Don't cry," says the nurse, "it's not good for your eye."

"She can cry all she wants," says the doctor, appearing suddenly. "It won't hurt her. Just don't blow your nose," he tells Eleanor. "And, when you get back to your room, don't bend over."

Eleanor, who cannot imagine crying without blowing her nose later, stops. When Tom comes at three o'clock, she is just being returned to her room.

"Where's my ring?" she asks the nurse.

Tom smiles at her, his face close to hers so that she can see him. He touches the pink plastic eye patch taped over her right eye. His wife starts to cry.

"What am I going to do now?" she asks; "I can't blow my nose."

As long as he's there, she doesn't worry about anything. When he leaves (the children, the work he's brought home from the office) she stiffens. But she should be used to this kind of fear, she tells herself. She tries watching television, but her eye hurts when it moves.

"You brought this on yourself," says her mother. "All that reading in the dark."

When she was a child, her father, a powerful man who liked to sit in the chair which blocked access from the kitchen to the living room, used to hit her when she passed behind him.

"What did I do?" little Eleanor wails.

"You must have done something," says her father.

Such a complacent man, with a knack for casual cruelty.

"You'll understand why when you have to support a family," he says.

She is not complacent. Naturally not, with a father like that. Perhaps she's being punished for something she hasn't done yet. It's possible. This is one track of the long-playing record of self-pity and self-accusation, alternating bands, which plays in her ears all day long.

When the nurse comes, she asks for a sleeping pill.

She keeps prying up the corner of her eye patch, trying to see if she has any sight left in that eye.

"Don't do that," says the nurse.

"Don't do that," says the doctor when he comes to examine her and removes the eye patch and turns around to see her covering her good eye and trying to peer through the recently operated upon eye.

"I can't see anything," says Eleanor. "Only a gray soup."

"You'll be able to see when the blood clears out of your eye."

"Blood," says Eleanor, "is red. Not gray."

"Tomorrow," he says, "you'll see fine."

Eleanor pretends to agree. No point in alienating the surgeon, not when she still has one eye to go. The instant he leaves, she calls a high school friend who is also an eye surgeon and asks him if her doctor's telling the truth.

"When you tried to see through your eye," he asks her, "did you try covering it up and taking your hand away?"

She did.

"What happened?"

"The light got dimmer when I covered it up. When he shone a light in my eye, I could see the pattern of the blood vessels."

He tells her her eye will get better by morning.

"You have to trust your doctor," he says.

Why should she? She doesn't trust anyone. She doesn't trust the world. Why would anyone trust a world full of operating rooms?

"Why not?" asks her grandmother.

"You're asking me why not?" says Eleanor.

The next morning, she can see brightly colored shapes. So they were not lying after all. She curls up on her side like a snail, trying to get as far from the world as possible.

SIX

THAT WAS HOW IT BEGAN. Innocently. Somewhere on her cloud, her mother snorts. That her daughter should even use the word innocent! And the way she keeps repeating it, the way a condemned man says "I'm innocent," over and over again, so often that everyone's convinced he committed the crime.

After the eye surgery, Eleanor cannot drive, but her husband won't let her on the subway. They live at the end of the line near the college, and her students are perpetually staggering up the subway steps, shaking, having just been attacked by gangs of little boys who run through the cars hitting passengers with their bookbags, which contain rocks as well as books. Old ladies emerge dripping blood, necks red where necklaces have been ripped against skin. When class attendance is down, no longer does anyone wonder if it is because of illness or the weather. No, the students haven't arrived at class because there has been a riot on the train.

Besides, says Tom, Eleanor sees so poorly she'll get on the wrong train and he'd have to get her in New Lots, wherever that is. When he was a teenager, he had enough of driving all over New York trying to locate his senile grandmother. Eleanor is likely to walk right off the edge of the platform and onto the third rail. No, no, he has it all thought out. He is placing an advertisement in her college paper for a driver.

Eleanor keeps insisting she can still drive. If she can't tell whether a light is green or red, she'll just slow down and wait to see what the other cars do. If she drives herself into Manhattan life will be much less expensive.

"Mother," says David, who has been listening, "you can't drive. When we were in the country, you drove the babysitter home and we almost fell into a cornfield. Remember I said that funny thing? I said we liked corn on the cob, not corn on the car?"

"Shut up," says Eleanor.

"What's he talking about?" asks Tom.

"Nothing," says Eleanor. "I couldn't see because I couldn't find the switch for the headlights. He's talking about the weekend you left us in the country. I had a rented car, that's all. I can see *fine* with one eye."

"No," says Tom.

"Good," says Davey. "She's a drunken driver."

Eleanor may be forty, but she has not forgotten how to sulk. She sulks now. She *likes* to drive by herself. When else is she alone? She *thinks* when she drives. She doesn't want to put up with another person for an indeterminate number of hours a week.

"Don't worry," says her husband, "no one's going to answer the ad. You'll take cabs. We'll find a way to afford it."

But two days after she comes home from the hospital, someone from Eleanor's college does answer the ad: a young Chinese student just enrolled in the graduate school of chemistry. By now, Eleanor, who has bumped into every doorjamb and dresser, is a study in black and blue. Her husband doesn't have time to take her anywhere and she goes into Manhattan, for meetings, or lunches, or to readings, two or three times a week. She has a horror of turning into Challah, calling him up at the office, saying "So give the director a piece of cake and a cup of coffee, he'll hardly know you're gone."

When she has to return to the hospital for her weekly checkup, her husband's complaints fill the air like furies. He has, however, decided against hiring the Chinese student or anyone else. If he does, he says, he'll never see his wife or the car again.

"Hire the student," says Eleanor.

"You always said no one could teach a Chinese to write a sentence," says her husband.

Eleanor points out that the Chinese person will not have to write up reports of their trips in the car, and besides, it was her friend Gloria who said that, not her.

("So innocent, Mother!" Eleanor cries. "Such a long way from the beginning to the end."

"People never talk about innocent beginnings unless there are evil endings," says her grandmother.)

Eleanor calls the student herself.

Tom insists on taking him for a test drive.

"How do we know he can drive?" he asks. "Not many people have cars in China."

The Chinese student arrives with a map of the city. Eleanor has never before seen a map of the city in which she was born. She finds her way about in the city just as she finds the books she wants in the library: she stops people and asks them where things are. Eleanor looks at the map, sighs, and glares at her husband. Three routes into Manhattan already inked in. Alternative routes.

"Toe," she asks, "like these?"

She points to her five toes hidden inside her thick

boots. She is afraid to go out now without her snowmobile boots, which make her, everyone says, look like the Abominable Snowwoman.

The young Chinese student laughs.

"Not Toe," he says, "Toe."

Oh, fine, thinks Eleanor, he's crazy.

"T-O-H," says Toh, spelling it out.

"To?" she asks.

"No," he says, slightly annoyed, "Toh."

"As in towing a car, Eleanor," says her husband. "Toh."

He is standing beside Eleanor, inspecting the criminal who is about to make off with the car and his wife, for both of which he has licenses. He has already inspected Toh's driver's license.

"Oh," says Eleanor. "Toh." She is no longer looking down at her boots. Everyone laughs with relief.

Eleanor tells the student she always drives into midtown Manhattan along the F.D.R. Drive because it's prettier that way.

"Oh, very pretty," agrees the Chinese student, nodding violently.

And, says Eleanor, she likes to pass the magnificent trompe l'oeil painted buildings.

"Oh, very pretty," he says.

Now she is sure of it. He doesn't understand a word she is saying. Her husband finds this momentarily amusing but then begins giving instructions: here is the windshield wiper, there is the brake.

"Stop acting as if you'll never see me again," says Eleanor. "I'll be back by three."

He tells her to call him at the office as soon as she gets back. He wants to know how it went.

"Me or the car?" asks Eleanor.

"The car, naturally," he says.

He watches his wife waver across the icy sidewalk to the car. She looks, he thinks, as if she expects to step on the ground and feel her foot going through it to thin air beneath. Nothing he can say will make her feel more secure in the world. Whatever he says she interprets as his well-intentioned effort to make her feel better. He loves her. He is not, after all, a neutral party. He has never felt more useless.

SEVEN

I WILL NOT LIVE through these drives into the city,"
thinks Eleanor, who, despite the alien creature sitting next
to her, has decided to pretend she is alone in the car and
think, the way she always does. She has spent too long
worrying about detached retinas, hemorrhages of the eye,
and has decided that worry is not a form of thinking at all,
only a state of boring vigilance in which she checks her
eyes every three hours for signs of danger.

What's more, the magazine which published her article, "The Lie of Adulthood," is becoming ever more his-
trionic in its requests for her replies to the several hundred
people who took objection, by letter, to all its points,
major and minor.

She wonders about them frequently, these letter writers ("All grown up in Georgia," "Tantrumish in Toronto"), especially the ones who write the anonymous,
hysterical notes. Those, of course, are the ones she wants
to answer, but Mr. and Mrs. Anonymous are rarely careless enough to leave their addresses. Those who sign their
letters Professor, Major Department, Major University,
Quaint Campus, Well-Known University Town, Any
State, puzzle her not at all. There are so few rewards of an
egocentric sort in academic life, one takes whatever one
can get. A letter to the editor, published in *The Times* is
something to show around the Faculty Lounge, not, how-

ever, without the de rigueur complaints about how the
newspaper altered the lovely, platonically ideal structure
of one's sentences and committed atrocities of punctua-
tion of which even a freshman would not be guilty. Eventually, if these professors are up for tenure, they will duly
list their letters to the editor under that section of their
vitae called "publications." To a tenure candidate, even a
letter to Mum is a publication.

In *her* article (which ought to be, she thinks, considered a letter to Mum), all she did was contend that the
idea of an adult was as much a fiction as, and perhaps
more a deliberate hoax than, the idea of God. She went on
to wonder which of the two ideas—the idea of an adult or
the idea of God—was the more dangerous. Perhaps, she
concluded, it was the idea of an adult.

"As everyone knows," argued Eleanor, "adults are
nothing more than collections of artifacts and circumstances, perspectives and contexts (laboriously acquired,
at one mental rummage sale or another) arranged about
them just as mental filings are artfully arranged by a
magnet around the true center. The true center is the im-
mortal baby, the insane baby, who believes every disappearance is a death, who believes his cries control the
rising and falling of the planetary faces over the rail of his
crib, who lies wrapped, not in clouds of glory but of fear,
and who will soon discover the grown-up, that mythical
beast who seems to feel no such terrors but instead seems
to spend his time controlling the easily controllable
earth."

Eleanor looked inward and decided she could find
herself in no way superior to any child—which was, perhaps, why she got along with them so well.

"Perhaps?" asks her grandmother.

Adults, claimed Eleanor, are only old babies who en-

courage the child to believe there is more separating them
than years, more separating them than the exact manner
of wrinkling (because the newborn is wrinkled too), more
between them than an unalphabetized encyclopedia of
knowledge, randomly collected to no particular purpose.

Adults wave their hands; they smile, they perform the
dubious acts of magic for which they were born, not out of
selflessness, not to protect the new, blue-veined infant, but
out of selfishness. They smile, they wave their hands, all
for the baby they always carry inside them, howling and
blue, so afraid it won't open its eyes. They carry on with
their superior magic until the infant inside them falls
asleep and they appear to be all that's left in its stead,
saying: "Look! A true metamorphosis! Look what I've become! Calm. Permanent as a statue. Wise. Rich in under-
standing of the earth upon which I walk."

Whereas, something with the right sort of eyes, perhaps the cockroach or the beetle, all set, so they say, to in-
herit the earth after the bombs go off, would look around
and say: What I see is a collection of babies, some large,
some small, some in bassinets, some in double beds, some
erect, some crawling, all screaming, all blue with terror,
all blind and stumbling in the dark.

And I, wrote Eleanor, taking her usual plunge into
autobiography, am a particular collection of artifacts:
Chinese rugs, china cabinets, stained glass windows, Victorian furniture; a collection of circumstances: a teacher, a
writer, mother of two children, a wife, custodian of a
housekeeper, possessor of enough money to preclude serious financial hysterics, at least for three months at a time.
Also a particular collection of perspectives acquired from
random events, primary among these the belief that life is
dangerous, nothing lasts, there is nothing more fragile

than human life. Glass animals survive hundreds of years, but their makers do not. The body and the spirit are always at war, and it is safe to say that the body usually wins, wins by taking things back—the mobility of joints, one's senses—so that finally the well-worn face of the world begins to sink beneath dirty water. The face of the world begins to disappear altogether, and finally the spirit begins to suffer starvation for that face, and the slow, invidious conviction that the world is leaving, never to return, begins to take hold. There is the slow wearing down of memory, of the artifacts that constitute the self, contexts, perspectives, circumstances, until all that remains is the child, the child with its small but essential knowledge pulsing at the top of its skull, that ocean of blood always threatening to break its boundaries and sink back into the earth ready to receive it, the coming union of blood and earth which the child fears so instinctively, its own dissolution. The simple knowledge of the child: survive. And the adult is only the larger one who knows the stratagems for survival. Under certain circumstances, Eleanor wrote, the adult can always be broken down into the child.

What a depressing article, Eleanor thinks now. No wonder she has so many letters to answer.

"Who didn't you outrage this time, Eleanor?" Tom asks her when he sees her glumly staring at her stack of unanswered mail. "Which discipline did you fail to attack? You write things like that and you're going to get complaints."

Then should she not tell the truth? As she sees it? (Or saw it?)

"People who tell the truth," says Tom, "do not win popularity contests."

"But even so," says Eleanor.

"Even so, what?"

His wife doesn't answer him. He studies her. A quiet Eleanor is an alarming animal.

"Do you still love me?" she asks.

"Why not?" he says.

She gets up and hugs him. He is always surprised by how frightened she is, how she cowers at what she has done and then insists on doing it again. He hugs her, hard. She takes a deep breath, collapsing against him.

Have *I* been broken down? Eleanor now asks herself, staring out of the window, refusing to look at the Chinese driver. She sees herself stumbling through her Victorian house, over her beloved antique chairs, all of them with claw feet. At night, she imagines the furniture running around the house on those feet, while she stumbles up the stairs because her new glasses make the steps look higher than they are. She takes circuitous routes, avoiding mirrors, in which, with her thick lenses, she resembles the ordinary housefly, so inhumanly do the lenses magnify her eyes. She sleeps, as commanded, on one side only, a plastic eye patch taped over her eye at night lest she poke herself while sleeping. She is convinced she is being punished ("See?" says her grandmother, "I may not see what you do, but God does. You see? You skinned that knee because you didn't do your homework.") and observes, with horror, her adult self rising as vapor rises on those ghostly country mornings when the night fogs begin going up, spirit by spirit, back to their appointed place, so human in their movements, their hesitancies, they convince the walker abroad in the damp that they have souls, have appointed places.

But, thinks Eleanor, things are not so serious. Really, she is doing very well. She has found someone to drive her into the city even though what she most wants to do is sleep (how can such a small incision in one eye produce such a need for sleep?). Although she is constantly frightened, she cannot complain; that, too, is normal. She has frightened her family enough by having an operation. It is not fair to burden them with further fears of her own when they are still frightened themselves.

She tries to pay attention to the children but she cannot resist sleep. Outside her door, she hears them arguing with the housekeeper, trying to persuade her to wake her up:

"Leave that mother in peace," says Emmeline. "You want to wake her up to tell her what? Julie had another bite more of a cookie? Your mother, she thinks about you day in and day out. Let her sleep, man."

Inside the room, Eleanor tries to persuade herself to get up; the children don't care about cookies. They want to see her. But she stays where she is and eventually falls asleep. Her bed is like a small boat, drifting farther and farther out until the children are dim figures waving frantically from the shore. And as they wave, they dim.

She has long since concluded that it is easier to be the one operated upon than the one who watches someone else undergoing the procedure. At least, she thinks, if the surgeon is operating on you, you know what's happening; you are not waiting in an echoing hall, waiting to hear if the patient, without whom you do not want to live, has survived.

There are moments when she suspects that her intellect, which she has always regarded as a small if not insignificant integer in that larger entity, her mind, has become disengaged from it, but no one seems to notice and so there can be no harm in it.

She continues to walk to school, to teach, to check her children's homework (using a huge magnifying glass) but she does not write. She stares gloomily at the manuscript of a novel she finished before the eye surgery and wonders if she'll revise it. Everyone tells her not to worry. Naturally she is not writing when it is painful for her to move her eyes.

But it is not really painful; that's not the reason she avoids pencil and paper. Only when she writes can she find out what she truly thinks and now she has no idea of what she thinks. Even if she does, she has no desire to know. But is that so bad? Few people seem to know what they think. She's always wanted a chance to stop thinking. Here's her chance. It's not a chance she wants right now, but of course no one's asked her.

Eventually, it seems unimportant to think. Certainly Eleanor does not reflect upon her willingness to give up thinking, her continuous pastime since she first learned one idea could be connected (maddeningly) to another. Eleanor, the one-track minded, is indifferent to her mind's new habit of running along no track at all. At times she wonders if this is, perhaps, a nervous breakdown. Most of the time she does not wonder. She concentrates on not falling up the stairs, on reacting semicalmly to the strange, fluorescent blue shapes which sometimes float in front of everything, just as she reacts semicalmly to her suspicion that nothing will ever be the same again. She notes with amusement how the walls balloon outward and away when she approaches, how all familiar faces seem abnormally lined with age as if twenty years had passed while the surgeon operated upon her eye.

"It's distortion caused by the glasses," says the surgeon. "No one is older. Don't worry. I hear the same story from everyone."

The customary clear wrap that holds her world together—family, house, lawn and tree—tears, and when she looks inward she sees nothing, perhaps a page, white and blank, not lying on a table but standing up straight, stiff, like a wall.

Occasionally, she asks herself what will happen next, but she doesn't try to answer that question. It's too large. There are the stairs, so much higher than she thought. This will never end. Wasn't it always this way? Nothing interesting ever happens to her. She is only a housewife afflicted with a mysterious aptitude for writing. She falls up the stairs once more. Still, she is adjusting well, all things considered.

EIGHT

ELEANOR FINALLY LOOKS over at her Chinese driver, Toh. She is squashed over to the right, practically perched on the door handle. She resents Toh's presence. Five or six blocks later she has gotten off the door handle and moved closer, because she has noticed, to her astonishment, that Toh has a habit of going through red lights. Also a habit of braking too late so that they have narrowly avoided making the intimate acquaintance of seven or eight dangerous characters who would not like it if her car installed itself in the trunk of theirs. Who am I to criticize him, thinks Eleanor; first of all, I hardly know him, and if I upset him, he'll crash into a wall, and second of all, he drives as well as I do, or did. So she sits still for another mile or two, a goldfish in a large fish tank of self-pity.

She tries to avoid looking at red lights, which, in any case, she can barely see. Through the operated-upon eye, she sees brightly colored, fishy shapes. Through the "good" eye, the once-normal swims through brown muddy water.

The good eye is waiting to be operated on. "Attacked," says Eleanor to her friend Gloria, whenever Gloria pauses to take a breath, which is not often. As soon as the first eye heals well enough to tolerate a contact lens, they'll have at her again. She sits still thinking, I must have done something.

They have gone through another red light.

"Um," says Eleanor to Toh, "where do you come from?"

"Come from?" repeats Toh slowly. "What means come from?"

"Where," says Eleanor, speaking slowly, "did you live?"

"Oh, live," says Toh, starting to laugh.

Apparently, notes Eleanor, Toh is pathologically cheerful. She resents that. In her current state she would prefer one of the pathologically depressed. Someone who would drive and weep, drive and weep. Then she would feel right at home in this car going through red light after red light. Before the eye surgery, she cried so often and so copiously that she wanted windshield wipers fitted to her lids, little, tiny ones that would fit right under her eyelashes. What had she been unhappy about? Who knows.

"Oh, live," says Toh. "On Coney Island Avenue."

This will kill me, thinks Eleanor; I have no patience. No resources at all.

"I meant *before*," Eleanor says, "in China."

"Oh, in *China*," says Toh. "Peking."

"In Peking," Eleanor asks cautiously (she doesn't want to offend this seventeen-year-old hysterically cheerful person; her husband won't give a second person a chance), "do people go through red lights?"

"Oh, sure," says Toh, "no problem."

"*Here*," Eleanor tells him, "it's against the law to go through red lights."

"Law says no?" asks Toh.

"Law says no," Eleanor repeats.

"Ooooh," says Toh, taking this under consideration. He very seriously thinks this over. For blocks. Miles.

Eleanor decides he must be stupid. She asks Toh how old he is. The same routine begins again.

"Old?" says Toh. "I not old."

Desperate, Eleanor asks him how many years he has. She did not study Spanish for nothing.

Oh, Toh says laughing; he has twenty-seven years.

Here I am, thinks Eleanor, three-quarters blind and caught in a Groucho Marx film. Obviously, he's lying about his age. The blur with whom she converses cannot be more than seventeen years old.

"You no believe?" Toh asks, turning toward her.

She must have moved much closer to him, because now she can see his face clearly. What a nice face. What odd teeth, straight and white, but four of the top teeth slant inward. He has a high forehead, high cheekbones, Mephistophelean eyebrows, a smile that says: I am not in this world to hurt anyone. But everyone is, thinks Eleanor. Everyone is here to hurt everyone else. He does not seem embarrassed by this long inventory she is taking of his face. His ears are flat against his skull and long, pointed slightly at the top. His hair is exactly the color of hers: black.

No, she says; she doesn't believe he's twenty-seven.

"No one does," says Toh.

Some time passes. The Brooklyn Bridge looms, its stone supports buried in mist. What, wonders Eleanor, is so beautiful about this bridge? Would anyone think it so beautiful if he didn't know it was the first one to span the water between Brooklyn and Manhattan? Of course, to her it is beautiful, encrusted as it is with memories. She cannot go over it without remembering shopping for school clothes in a huge store, so large that two sections of it were connected by a bridge over a street. Was that Macy's? There was no point at all in going to that store

unless one crossed that bridge. Such adventures in spring
coat land. No one wears spring coats anymore.

"I drive good now?" asks Toh.

"Oh, very good driving," says Eleanor.

What, is she now losing her ability to speak her own
language?

"Very good driving," she says again.

He tilts his head and nods with satisfaction.

"I have confidence," says Toh slowly. "That is right?
I have?"

"Right," says Eleanor.

"So I should learn. To speak English. You tell me
when I wrong."

"Right," she says. "I will."

He is taking her into midtown for a business lunch.
When he asked her what she was going to do in the city,
he didn't seem to understand her explanation. After a
while, he seemed to form some idea of her mission. She
imagines he is now picturing a fancy table with typewriters between the dishes, carbon paper under the nap-
kins.

There is something about him, something far away.
Far from home. Where does it come from, that line? It takes
her quite a while to remember. From a book she used to
read to her children. *Whose Mouse Are You? "Where is your
mother? Far from home. Where is your brother? I have none."*

Toh turns and smiles at her. Evidently, he has sensed
a change in her mood. She smiles back but doesn't say
anything. It has been a long time, really, since she has
thought about anyone but herself.

When they pull up in front of the restaurant, Toh insists on escorting her out. Fine. In China, people are cour-
teous to the old and the demented. But then Toh grabs
hold of her arm and steers her across the sidewalk and

does not let go until he is sure she knows where she is going. Eleanor is mortified. No one takes such care of her.

"You can take care of yourself, Eleanor," says her mother. "You need a college degree to find your way around a restaurant?"

Her editor and the head of the art department are already seated at a table overlooking The Coconut Court, wonderfully situated for viewing the five coconut trees shivering outside, whispering to one another about founding the first Society to Prevent Cruelty to Tropical Trees, The SPCTT, whose first project would be to knit five sweaters, one for each of the trees. She can hear the ghosts of the decorators: "Keep it simple, all white except for the wood. We'll finish that dark, of course, and all the greenery will be alive. White and green and vases of colored flowers at the tables." What a wonderful concept it must have seemed, she thinks, except that the restaurant now looks just like a hospital, but furnished with tables and chairs instead of beds.

The three of them begin the usual futile discussion about what kind of cover they ought to put on her new book. In the middle of it, Eleanor finds her mind wandering off to Toh, sitting in her car, waiting for what could be two and a half hours. (No, he says, he doesn't mind. He has studying to do. He points to his book. *Chemical Engineering.*)

She thinks about his face, its odd, pointed eyebrows. Suddenly, it is not a face at all, but an enormous plain, half the surface of the earth, more and more of it coming into view as she walks across it. At first it seems an arid plain, but that proves to be an illusion. It all depends, she sees, on the tilt of one's head: just right and there are wonders. What will they be like? She doesn't know. They are too tiny for her to see just now, but she will see them. Ah, lovely. They exist as in a childhood story about a world that existed between the spaces left by the solid objects of this world, invisible to almost everyone, that second world providing the power for this one, permitting this one to exist.

"But Eleanor," says the art director, a little earnest woman with short dark hair cut like a monk's, "red letters won't show up well against the beige. White will."

Art directors, thinks Eleanor, will say anything.

She reminds the art director that the white letters on her last book jacket didn't show up at all. Not *at all*.

"Maybe yellow, then," the art director says thoughtfully.

Success is measured in such small things here, thinks Eleanor. Yellow instead of white, both disastrous, one less disastrous than the other. She says that omitting the title altogether might be just the thing. Imagine all those people picking up this mysterious beige book, possessed by a desire to know what it could possibly be.

The two women are staring at her, and no wonder. She is becoming openly sarcastic, even nasty. This is how a woman writer gets her reputation for being difficult. A difficult woman is soon pronounced hysterical, then irrational. Then they've got her. Irrational. She's irrational. No need to listen to her, that raving maniac. Whereas her friend Tom Peters, darling of the publishing industry, throws furniture. Very expensive furniture, whatever he can lift, usually chairs, although once he tried to pick up a Danish modern couch, and when he couldn't move it, had to content himself with slamming one end of it up and down against the floor. Do they send for the little men in white coats? No, no, they rush about doing his bidding, even if he doesn't yet know what it is. What would happen to her if she picked up this thick, round, glass ashtray,

saying in red blurry letters, *Coconut Club,* and smashed it
down on the tablecloth? Help, police! Call the zoo! Get a
tranquilizer gun! A wild animal! A lunatic!

Ah, her hero, *malchik* Khrushchev with his shoe,
shouting, We'll bury you! If only Margaret Thatcher
would take off one of her high heels and split open someone's head! What freedom she would give Eleanor, sitting
in a straightjacket in the Coconut Club. What an example
she would set for little girls everywhere! But on she goes,
ruling a whole country in her ladylike way. A bad example, that woman, no role model at all. What do they call
her? The Iron Lady? Also the name for a chastity belt.
Some blood under the fingernails, Margaret! Throw out
that hairspray and tear your hair!

And what of *Queen* Lear? Would she be allowed out in
the rain, raving on the heath? Come inside, Queenie!
What you look like! Comb that hair! You want the neighbors to see you like this? And later, when the poor thing's
asleep: She thinks she's going to divide up the land? Let
the old bat do what she wants. The will won't stand up in
court. An old crone like her, the judge will throw the case
out. Let her write what she wants. We'll divide things up!

Oh, Eleanor, what's wrong? Not distracted enough
by what goes on around you since you can't see it? Becoming a bitter feminist, is it? Go home and call all your
friends who criticized you for not reading *Ms.* Call them
up and say I have seen the enemy and she is everyone. Tell
them about these two nice women sitting in The Coconut
Club, running things, who don't care what other women
think.

Eleanor, she tells herself, pull yourself together. And
she does. When in doubt, gossip.

"I have a driver until my eye gets better," she says.
"A Chinese student. He can't understand a word I say,

but he opens the door, he pulls my hat down over my ears if it's cold." (That's right, exaggerate, embroider, look how friendly they're becoming. Perhaps they'll consider changing the lettering to red after all.) "He brushes the dust off my coat." (That last was true. When she first got in the car, he reached over and dusted her off. "Salt," he said, his voice severe, such a deep voice for a child.)

"Oh," says her editor, a very small woman who looks young enough to be endangered by men who might want to take her over a state line (why is she now surrounded by grown-ups wearing infant suits? When she first met her editor, she called her agent to ask him why a child would want so much responsibility): "Keep him. Keep him forever! If my husband and I ever get divorced, the only thing I'm going to ask for is the chauffeur."

"I can't keep him forever," says Eleanor. "I only hired him because I couldn't afford to take cabs into the city. From my house, a round trip is over forty dollars."

They mustn't think she has too much money. She'd never get an advance again. Quite a problem, this, keeping her editor, whom she is beginning to know well, thinking she has just enough money to remain independent but not so much money that the woman becomes envious. But this is an old dance. She knows the steps.

The editor and art director are greedy for details. Where did she find this Chinese paragon? But irrational Eleanor is now infuriated by their questions. What business is it of theirs?

"There's an article in *The New Yorker* about China," she says; "have you seen it?"

How can they have? This particular issue won't be on the stands until late afternoon. So convenient, having students who free-lance everywhere and know all kinds of things, such as the contents of next week's magazine. Now they'll change the subject. All editors like to think they've read everything.

"I must have missed it," says her editor, brow wrinkling (at last: guilt, guilt), "but we're just sending out galleys of a book on China. It's a beautiful book. Would you like a copy?"

Eleanor says she would love the galley. She is quite pleased with herself. She knows how rare galleys are. Knows, too, that there is no earthly reason for her to get hold of this one.

Let me out of here, thinks Eleanor.

She is amazed to find herself so eager to get back in the car with Toh, that complete stranger for whom she has been feeling, or so she has assumed, nothing but hostility. She wants to see him. When did she last want to see anyone? God knows where he is, she thinks, smiling at the art director. If thoughts could kill, that woman would be in the middle of all that nouvelle cuisine, her face in that green pie, kiwi, whatever it is. They won't find her until they clear the table, and by then irreversible brain damage will have set in. White doesn't show up against green; everyone knows that.

He doesn't know anything about parking regulations. They've probably towed him off to one of the city lots and she's going to spend the afternoon stumbling through the city trying to liberate both Toh and the car. Why should she expect him to be there after two and a half hours? He's probably given up and gone home. That's where her car is: in her driveway. Toh has resigned. Good for Toh.

But when she walks out and hesitates under the canopy, she feels someone's hand on her arm.

"Car here," Toh says.

She tries to tell him it's all right, she really can see

well enough to find the car, she can even read if she holds the page right up to her good eye, but he ignores her.

Oh, well, she thinks, he doesn't want me to break my neck. Then he wouldn't have a job.

Such a charitable soul you are, Eleanor.

"Everything okay?" he asks her.

Apparently he has that phrase down pat.

"Oh, fine," she says.

He looks more closely at her.

"No problem?" he asks.

"No, everything's all right. Everything's fine."

He looks troubled, but turns the key in the ignition. The motor starts immediately.

If everything's so fine, Eleanor asks herself, why am I staring out of the window so no one can see me cry? Dumb, stupid tears.

"Don't say dumb," says her mother, "say stupid."

NINE

THEY SAY LITTLE on the long drive back to Brooklyn. Eleanor cannot imagine burdening Toh with the problems of cover design. He wouldn't understand anything about it and she has decided to avoid "getting involved." ("If you wouldn't get personally involved with people in business, your life would be so much simpler," says her agent, who gives up in the face of her absolute incomprehension.) However, traffic on the F.D.R. Drive is heavy. Cars are falling into potholes or stalling where construction has narrowed traffic to one lane and Eleanor finds herself pointing things out: "Look at that ship coming down the river. It's an old-fashioned schooner."

"Oh, very nice," says Toh.

"Look at that building," she says, pointing to it. After the Chrysler building, it's her favorite one in the city, painted so that it appears to be a row of European shops.

"Oh, very . . ." says Toh and then hesitates.

"Strange," says Eleanor, finishing the sentence for him.

As he drives, he conscientiously repeats the word: strange, strange, strange. Evidently, he is serious about learning the language. Too bad. She has no intention of giving in to her usually irresistible urge to teach anyone. What she needs to do is keep quiet and think. About why she doesn't like to talk to anyone lately, especially people who ask her how she is, why she won't watch television (she knows why: inside that box, people are incessantly talking), why she'll only listen to music and not much of that.

She is also disturbed by her habit of talking to the old dead, the long gone, as well as by her recent discovery that her principal emotion is anger. Is that behind her recent appetite for silence? Are the people around her the wrong people? And if they are wrong, wrong for what? Ten minutes of her children's chatter and she starts screaming in a high-pitched voice which is not hers but her dead Aunt Frieda's. Of course she screams. The children are impossible. If there's one raisin in the house, she has to get out a dissecting microscope and cut it in half for them while they measure their portion with calipers. However, last month they were just as bad and were not impossible. She is, she thinks, growing increasingly intolerant of words, even though she knows nothing else to work with. She is especially intolerant of her own.

"I'll be up soon," she tells the children. "I'll play with you when I get up." But she doesn't.

"Today," announces Davey, "I'm going to be Cyndi Lauper. Julie, punk up my hair."

Julie wets Davey's hair and combs it into spikes; Davey turns on his tape of "Girls Just Want to Have Fun," and they start singing and dancing.

One more minute of this, thinks Eleanor, and I'm going to start screaming. Still, she stores the scene in her memory. When this period of lunacy is over, she will relive it and enjoy it. Really, she is not *here*. Who can trust what she says?

"I hate words," she says aloud, and is startled to realize she has spoken.

"No, don't hate words," says Toh.

Who is he to tell her what to do? Then she understands. He thinks she said *he* hated words.

"Not you, me," she says, thinking, it took three words
to say I hate words. Indispensable things, aren't they, like
the bacteria which break everything down, making room
for the next growth. Some words, however, are not biode-
gradable. She must give that idea more thought, should
she ever think again.

"Oh," says Toh, and laughs. "You," he says, pointing
at her, "not me."

So cheerful. He even laughs at his own mistakes. How
will she put up with such cheerfulness three or four times
a week? Eight hours of cheerfulness, a challenge to which
she cannot possibly rise.

It has long been her theory that cheerful people are
secretly psychotic. Look at the world, standing there, a
skull in one hand, a sword in the other. That's something
to be cheerful about? Her husband will find her cold and
stiff in the chair. Coroner's report: death caused by over-
exposure to good cheer. An allergic reaction. Good cheer
in large doses can be dangerous to your health: a slogan to
be printed on the T-shirts of all abnormally cheerful Chinese students. Side effects: death, depression, biblical
plagues. One mustn't tempt the gods with displays of
one's good humor. Didn't his mother teach him anything?

Still, as they sit there in the car, looking at the gray-
blue stones of the Brooklyn Bridge, there is a sadness in
the car. She can feel it, something white and whispy between her fingers, occasionally gritty, like the fine beige
dust left by a wood stove. *Far from home.* Is he homesick?
The sadness becomes a sound. What is that sound,
Eleanor? She has long believed you can hear emotions.
She rarely tells anyone these things because she knows

how useless it is. People smile and think she's eccentric. Artists are supposed to be eccentric. She has learned to wait until her beliefs turn into the symbols of her prose and poetry. They are safe in there, in those intricate, mazelike structures.

Amazing pyrotechnics, but empty, said last year's reviewer.

She feels about writing (about everything) as physicists must feel when sending coded messages into outer space. Of course, there will be no answer. The trick is not to care when it comes.

She thinks of the astronomers she has known, patiently sending their messages out. They know they will be long dead, gone, erased when an answer comes. Do they think the answer, when it arrives, will somehow resurrect them? Once, when she was pitiless, she used to ask such questions. The usual answer: a shrug. One of the astronomers said maybe. And why did she bother asking? She knew what they hoped for.

She looks over at Toh. Definitely sad. For once, she tells herself, mind your own business.

"Everything okay?" asks Toh, looking over at her.

"Oh, fine," she says, looking at him driving in his blurry brown cloud. Can he tell what she's thinking? Impossible. It is one of her first axioms: no one knows what Eleanor's thinking.

"Tomorrow," he says slowly, "day be more blue."

Is that possible, she asks herself: more blues, darker blues?

"The *sky*," he says. "Many, many more blue. Tomorrow."

Well, this is alarming. He has an idea of what goes on inside that addled egg she calls her mind. Eleanor the Inscrutable. *He* is supposed to be inscrutable, she thinks, annoyed, yet there he sits, so obviously sad somewhere deep beneath the cheerful manner. Learn inscrutability, she advises him silently; then I won't have to be bothered by you. He looks at her and smiles. Sad. A sad person can get anywhere with Eleanor.

TEN

W HEN ELEANOR WAS in public school, her mother used to say that she spent more time inside the school talking to her daughter's infuriated teachers than her child spent in the classrooms.

Eleanor was not, she now admits, a model child. She was, however, a tall one, and her inability to do any kind of math problem went unnoticed for some time because she was always sent to the blackboard with a very short boy whom she would threaten to beat up if he didn't do her problems in very tiny numbers at the bottom of the board so that she could copy them, whereupon she benevolently allowed him to erase her problems and get on with his own.

The incident her mother always remembered had to do with a composition assigned after one of the holidays. The topic was "What I Know About Life." When her mother asked her if she'd written her composition, (in other families people said good morning, hello, see you tomorrow. In hers, they asked, "Have you done your homework?") she said she'd already done it, and the next day Eleanor brought home a note asking her mother to come in and see the teacher and discuss the child's unsatisfactory composition. (Which teacher was it? Perhaps Mrs. Greene, who always stood with her back to an open window, even in winter, as if at any minute the children would force her to jump through it to safety.)

Her mother went to see the teacher, came home, reported to her father, who dutifully whipped her. They showed one another the composition, snorting in disgust. Her Aunt Lucy, who had stopped by, found it funny and was sent by her grandmother to the bathroom until she regained control of herself, which she evidently did not do if one could judge by the whoops of laughter issuing from behind the white-painted door with its faceted glass knob.

Eleanor's entire composition consisted of one sentence: "Nothing remains the same."

She still likes that sentence, which continues to sum up all she has learned about life, and is retrospectively proud of herself for getting to the heart of things so quickly and adorning her discovery with internal rhyme.

It is a lesson she keeps learning over and over. It is a sentence whose wisdom is inexhaustible. What, then, were they so mad about? The teacher hadn't specified a length for the paper, though Eleanor suspected hers might be a bit shorter than papers the other students would hand in. And what had her Aunt Lucy found so hilarious? Wasn't that the day she had found out she was pregnant? Eleanor thinks it was. Still, what was so funny about it? Sooner or later, that text swims up from beneath whatever is happening around her. The variations on it are endless: everything emerges or disappears. Everything moves forward or back. Nothing stands still.

This is the first truth Eleanor came upon on her own, a frightening one, but no matter how she struggles with it, it wins. And so she trusts it. Trusts it to upset balances, trusts it entirely. But now, it is not so much a slogan as an image and a memory: there is the white bathroom door, painted so many times there are hairline cracks in the paint like cracks in fine china cups. There is the faceted glass doorknob, pear-shaped, there are the whoops of wild laughter emerging from behind the door. Given this fundamental *unter image*, there like a watermark beneath the sheets of her daily life, it is a wonder she manages to take things so seriously. Perhaps I only appear to take them seriously, thinks Eleanor.

In the weeks following her first drive into the city with Toh, they begin to speak to one another more and more. For a while, Eleanor believes they will never talk about anything but Chinese food. (Food and the price of food are the two constant subjects of conversation in the Faculty Cafeteria, that hall of learning to which she once so seriously aspired. Food, shoes, and pensions.) Eventually, she understands that Chinese food is not one of Toh's favorite subjects, but given her lack of knowledge of anything else Chinese, he has been putting up with it.

No food, he says, is as good here as it is in China.

He becomes irritable when she asks him (again) if people eat bread in China. Eleanor has trouble believing in a country she has not seen.

"I told you," he says, "in China, main food is rice."

Would he like to come with them to a Chinese restaurant?

"I don't like," says Toh.

She is sitting next to an upset person. The doctor has removed the patch that had covered her right eye and the light bothers it. She sits in the car, her hand over her eye, sure that Skylab II intends to fall right on the little wound under her eyelid. If, when the sun is bright, she sometimes wears two pairs of sunglasses at once, Toh does not comment. A strange American custom, no doubt.

"Would you like to come to an Italian restaurant?" she asks.

His face changes, a veritable face-lift of pleasure.

"Oh, wonderful," he says. "Anything but Chinese."

"I like Chinese food," she says thoughtlessly.

"Everything here Canton or Szechuan," he says angrily. "How they represent all of China?"

"Well, of course they don't," says Eleanor, looking over at him.

Who, she asks herself, is the stupid person in this car? Why doesn't she just ask him to list, item by item, everything he has left behind in Peking? She is making him homesick.

"If you like," he says, "I cook some dishes and bring them to you."

"That would be good," says Eleanor, who is trying to be as bland and unprovocative as possible.

"What you like?" he asks her.

They begin a long conversation, the point of which is to convince him that she, her husband, and her children will eat anything, even fried vacuum cleaner, if he goes to the trouble of making it. He is frowning. What's the matter now?

"I want you like what I cook," he says. "I eat Chinese food all the time."

But she does, she does, like everything, eat everything. She does not, however, want to argue all the way home.

"No like beef?"

"I like beef."

"Which you like best?"

Oh, Lord, thinks Eleanor, another stubborn mule. Of course he would have to be stubborn, iron-willed, to come to this country in the first place. Without relations, without money, unable to speak the language. She is beginning to admire him.

"Chicken," she says. Chicken is cheapest. He can't have much money.

He nods and narrows his eyes. Good. He likes chicken, too.

As the weeks of driving continue, he becomes the one fixed, clear object in her world. Slowly, he begins to be adopted by the family. He offers to fix any electric appliances she may happen to have around shooting sparks into the air or starting fires behind wallboards. ("In China, I was electrician. Also drive the truck for electricity.")

At the moment, all of her lamps are working, but she resolves to cut off a plug and fray the wires so that he can fix it. She sees that he needs to feel useful, although he ought to feel useful enough, driving her about all week. She understands, finally, that it is not a question of usefulness, but of belonging. Which must be why he can tolerate her company eight hours a week. He wants to belong to someone, to belong somewhere.

Eleanor believes that anyone can get along with her provided they don't have to see her more than once every two weeks. Whenever anyone asks her how she can manage a career and a marriage, she says it isn't hard: she and her husband hardly ever see one another.

But what about summers, her friends ask. In the summers, you're together for months. In the country.

"Summers?" asks Eleanor. Oh yes, the *summers*. When it's hot. When Tom's computer business slows, he turns his company over to its vice-president, and she and her husband do nothing but swim and walk and talk to each other and pick the kids up from camp and then go out at night. Always together. Perfectly happy. How resolutely they reject offers of friendship in the summers.

"Summers don't last long," says Eleanor.

No wonder people sometimes ("Often, Eleanor, often," says her mother) think she's crazy.

"But what," asks her friend Gloria, "do you talk to him about?"

"Anything," says Eleanor, who wonders why she talks to Gloria every day, as once she used to talk to her mother, even after her mother retired to Florida and the daily long-distance conversations presented her with a phone bill the size of the national debt.

"What?" asks Gloria.

"About China. About what it means to get things through the back door. It's not the same as our black market. About the weather."

"You were never interested in China before," Gloria says suspiciously.

"I only get interested in things through people," says Eleanor, which is true.

"Are you falling in love with him? You're always falling in love with someone, and then the next week you forget they existed. Probably," muses Gloria, "you are. What else have you got to do?"

"I'm not in love with him," says Eleanor, "but he's a very impressive person," a comment she knows will annoy Gloria, who will take it to mean that *she* is not impressive.

"What's so impressive about being penniless and not knowing how to speak the language?"

"He's the only grown-up I know," says Eleanor; at least, he's the only grown-up with whom she now has much to do. Tom is busy; his company is planning to merge with another, smaller one and he is occupied hiring and firing. The sight of her eye, as Eleanor knows, saddens and frightens him. And so she draws away from him. She does not want to harm him because she has been harmed.

"Let's change the subject," says Gloria, snappish.

As if, thinks Eleanor, I'd come out with it and *said* she was a case of arrested development.

"It was pouring this morning," says Gloria. "You can't imagine what it was like."

No one can ever imagine what things are like for Gloria.

"Oh, yes I can," says Eleanor. "I went into the city this morning and on the way back the car wouldn't start."

"So Toh rescued you?" Gloria asked. Sarcastic and bored.

"Let's change the subject," says Eleanor.

When she came out of the doctor's office, she found a distraught Toh standing under an umbrella. The streets of the Upper West Side had been drained of all color and now resembled an old etching of themselves. On both sides of the canopy the rain poured down in mercury-colored streams. Poisonous city, thinks Eleanor.

"Car will not start," says Toh. "It is my fault. I keep radio on."

"No," says Eleanor, "it often doesn't start in this weather. I'll call my husband at the office."

"Call husband!" Toh exclaims, astonished and outraged. "No call husband! One man here, one there, little difference. *We* solve problem."

Eleanor thinks for a minute and understands what he means: in these circumstances, a man is a man. He can do just as good a job as anyone else.

"You'll have to call AAA," she says. "Tell them where we are and what's the matter. They'll come for us."

"I saw phone at corner," says Toh. "You get in car. Rain water dirty. Your eye stay clean."

Eleanor ventures the opinion that it may be hard for him to explain where they are over the phone.

"Not hard," says Toh, impatiently. "If it hard, I find someone."

She begins searching through her pocketbook for a quarter, but Toh puts his hand over hers. "I have quarter," he says, and disappears into the rain.

He returns but the tow truck does not come. "Um," says Eleanor, "maybe I should call again."

"Truck lost," Toh says, adamant. "I go out and look for it." Before she has a chance to protest, he is gone.

She is sitting in the car thinking, I knew it, he couldn't possibly make himself understood, we'll be here all day, when the tow truck pulls up and Toh jumps out.

"Truck lost itself," he says, laughing.

Five minutes later they are on their way home.

"I never thought we would get back," says Eleanor.

"Still," says Toh, "we are back."

"I was sure we'd be there all day," says Eleanor.

"But we are not there all day," says Toh.

"No," says Eleanor, looking over at him, wondering why dangers averted remain to terrify her long after the occasion for fear is gone.

She thinks about it now, as Gloria talks on and on: his absolute confidence, his belief that life presents a series of problems which need only be solved, his conviction (which she will never have) that life itself is not a problem, but something he was born to enjoy.

I can learn from him, thinks Eleanor. I have to learn from him.

"Are you still there?" asks Gloria suspiciously. She is in the middle of a long recitation of her landlady's transgressions.

"I'm here," says Eleanor, who is not sure she is. Only when she is in the car with Toh does she seem to know where she is. She listens to Gloria, thinking, for me, there's a thin line between admiration and love. But he will not be her driver forever. Temporary situations, temporary emotions.

"Eleanor," her grandmother asks her, "haven't you learned anything yet? What isn't temporary? While something lasts, it's permanent."

"Gloria," says Eleanor, "I'll call you back later. I'm going to sleep."

ELEVEN

SHE AND TOM invite Toh to come with them to the Brooklyn Museum and, to her surprise, she finds that Toh likes children, so much so that he is willing to carry her daughter on his back for hours until she orders the child down.

"But I'm tired," whines her daughter.

"Walk," Eleanor commands her.

What is the child trying to do? Kill Toh?

The five of them go to see the miniature houses, glass box after glass box containing miniature rooms, every detail scaled down and perfectly reproduced, a tiny world in the spaces of this one.

"You like the little things," Toh says to her, laughing.

She has shown him her dollhouses at home. She rarely shows them to anyone outside the family, especially if they are over twelve. Intellectuals are not supposed to play with toys. She notes that Toh is speaking English much better these days. She also notices how angry she becomes when the children take him away from her for too long. She is becoming protective and possessive. But, she tells herself, there's nothing wrong with it. It's all perfectly normal. So what if she's coming to believe that he's been sent by God or the fates as compensation for what's happened to her eyes? She's old enough to be his mother. That thought, she realizes later, ought to have been the danger signal, but Eleanor believes in ignoring danger until it's over. Then it's safe to react with fear and trembling.

They come out of the white stone museum, blinking in the white stone light.

"Snow soon?" asks Toh.

Eleanor shrugs. She stares back at the gray-white buildings, pinking as the sun sets, at the terra cotta figures, Medusa faces, cornices, parts of roofs, carved lions that have lost their cement teeth, and fluted pillars that decorate the museum grounds. She doesn't want to part with him.

"Your eye hurt you?" Toh asks her.

She shakes her head.

Her husband looks at his watch, a twin to hers, a digital Timex. Matching rings, matching watches, clearly a marriage meant to last.

"Let's go to dinner," says Tom.

Tom, Toh, the same name except for the final letter.

"Looking for trouble?" asks her grandmother. "People who look for it usually find it."

So what if she's old enough to be his mother? In the backwoods, you *only* sleep with your mother. Or father. Why is she thinking about incest? Confused, she turns back to the museum. The little rooms. Where the dead souls go, the smart ones, who want to be warm and safe and find chairs just the right size for them. Why wear their wings out for no reason?

"Can we go to Chinatown?" her son Davey is asking Toh.

She should have known better than to take her eyes off that child for a single second.

"I've never been to Chinatown," David continues, the same child his teacher tells her looks like a Botticelli angel. Perhaps his teacher has never adequately studied the paintings of Hieronymus Bosch. There are some excellent likenesses of the child in those, too.

Disaster. Toh will never say no to a child. Still, she has told her husband about Toh's dislike of Chinese restaurants, how gloomy they make him feel. Her husband will rescue them all. *Far from home.* How well Tom knows that line. Between them, they wore out the book, reading it first to one child, then another.

How can she be standing here, thinking such contradictory thoughts?

Alas for her, her husband's love of Chinese food wins out.

"I'd like to go to Chinatown," he says, oblivious to the many daggers Eleanor is enthusiastically plunging into his back.

And now her daughter chimes in: she also wants to go to Chinatown.

Eleanor tells Toh he doesn't have to go to Chinatown. *They* don't have to go, unless he wants to. *Say no,* she prays.

"Why not go?" he asks. "I show you where to shop for spices."

"No, no, no," Eleanor whispers to her husband, "this will be awful."

He doesn't hear her, suffering as he does from the intermittent deafness of the long married. He wants to go. Since childhood, he's had a love affair with everything Oriental. Then why isn't *he* involved with Toh?

Toh volunteers the information that parking in Chinatown is practically impossible.

Eleanor sighs. Her husband could find a parking place in the middle of Yankee Stadium.

They have no trouble parking the car.

"Pick a place," her husband is telling Toh, "where they serve food Peking style."

Ah! He knows he has done something wrong and is trying to make up for it. Idiot. If the streets were less slippery—to get out of the car they have to climb up and then slide down a gray-black barrier of ice—she'd cross the street and pretend she didn't know any of them.

"Let's walk and look," says Toh.

And they set out, her husband holding on to her arm or the four layers of clothing covering it: long underwear, V-necked shirt, pullover sweater, and finally the quilted blue coat. Ever since her eyes began acting up, she's been hopelessly cold.

In the dark, she's practically blind. Approaching cars seem preceded by two enormous neon signs in the shape of light bulbs. Traffic lights are huge red or green hoops of light. She is living in a surreal world which she fears describing to anyone. What she needs is a support group composed entirely of the Aged and the Decrepit, although she doesn't imagine she'd get much sympathy from them, to whom this flagrant rebellion of the senses must be almost routine. A nice idea, that aged and decrepit support group, but they'd only resent her for being young. Only to an eighty-year-old is a forty-year-old young.

She wonders, many times a day, if her family is surreptitiously looking for an ash-heap on which to deposit her: so many physical ailments in one middle-aged person. If only the doctor would give her her bifocals now, but he won't. He seems to think she'll get too attached to them. But why shouldn't the semiblind be attached to their glasses? Instead, she has to wait three more weeks until her eye heals. Now she slips and slides.

For blocks. For miles. It appears they are going to walk around all of Chinatown at least forty times before

Toh is finally prepared to reveal which restaurant serves food Peking style. Toh breaks down and points one out, Eleanor has not said a word for some time.

She insists on sitting next to Toh. She knows what's coming. It is only a little worse than she expected.

Toh, brow wrinkled, arched eyebrows almost touching his hairline (no one, thinks Eleanor, would describe him as cheerful now), explains the menu to them. This, he says, is the only restaurant in the city where you can find eel prepared the Peking way.

"Eel! Yuk!" shouts her son.

Eleanor tells him to shut up or wait outside.

Toh also recommends the sweet and sour fish.

"Fish!" scream both children. "Eeeeeyou!"

"What joys they are to take places," says Eleanor.

She tells Tom to order spareribs and dumplings immediately or they'll all be thrown out. Out of the corner of her eye she sees the waiter coming closer.

"Haven't decided yet," says Toh. "Come back."

Discussion ensues. Such etiquette. Such courtesy.

"But do *you* like it?"

"I like."

"Then order it."

"But not everyone like it."

"We like anything."

"Maybe you want some meat, not two fishes."

The waiter has evidently called the manager, who puts a pad of paper in front of Toh, and tells him to write down what he wants when he makes up his mind. Meanwhile, a line of people waiting to come in is winding out the door and onto the crowded, icy street. No final decisions have yet been reached. Negotiations still in a delicate stage.

Eleanor is no diplomat. This is too much. They have

taken this pathologically cheerful person and in short order turned him into a wreck fit to live in their own family.

"*You*," Eleanor says to Toh, "order what *you* like to eat. We *insist* on taking your advice."

Toh, who looks as if he has just received a telegram from the Chinese legation describing the death of his entire family, turns around and calls the waiter. Thank God he orders in Chinese: eel and sweet and sour fish. The children don't know what's been done to them. Time enough for them to learn when the dishes arrive. When they do, unexpected good fortune: her son likes the eel.

"Eat it," Eleanor tells her six-year-old daughter. "It tastes just like hamburger."

Her daughter gives her the scornful looks she deserves and takes another sparerib. She gnaws on the bones like a rat. A very funny looking rat, since she is missing all her front teeth.

"These are the dishes Toh ordered," she tells Julie, who clearly adores Toh. Eleanor is not scornful of big passions in little breasts, but that does not prevent her, as a mother, from trying to make use of them when necessary.

"Then let him eat them," says her daughter. "They're *all* for him."

Her daughter's passion is not grand enough to persuade her to open her mouth for a spoonful of eel. Julie looks at her and shrugs, looks at Toh, and nuzzles up to him. The rest of the meal actually proceeds pleasantly.

Later, when she is putting her daughter to bed, Eleanor says, yes, Toh is a student. Yes, he is Mother's driver. Yes, he is our friend.

"Daddy's too?" asks her daughter.

"Of course, Daddy's too."

"I don't think so."

"Why not?"

"He looked annoyed because of Daddy."

"What are you talking about, because of Daddy?"

"Because he's *there*," says the child.

"Nonsense," says her mother.

She starts to close the child's door, but her daughter begins screaming. What's the matter now? Eleanor forgot to kiss her (and Garfield, the Cabbage Patch Kid, and the other eighteen essential stuffed animals) goodnight.

Disaster that it was, Sunday's outing has changed Toh from a driver and sometime friend to a part of the family, so much a part of it that Eleanor spends one afternoon away from her precious tape recorder, with the help of which she is trying to retrieve what were once perfectly clear thoughts, while around her, Tom resurrects the old pool table; everyone hunts through the cluttered double garage for the Ping-Pong table top that fits over it, scurries to stores to find paddles and Ping-Pong balls, runs in and out, cleaning up the front porch, carrying cartons from the porch to the sidewalk because tomorrow the garbage man comes, an event of no small importance to a family of four, one housekeeper, and one adopted twenty-seven-year-old Chinese student.

This house, Eleanor thinks, must be a lot messier than I've realized. Wait until I get my eyesight back! Three cartons to take out!

And after the cartons, Eleanor tells them to take the shocking-pink crib outside, the crib she used first for her son and then her daughter.

It turned shocking pink just before her daughter Julie arrived. That was when she decided to decoupage it with pictures cut from a ripped Richard Scarry book, *Busy,*

Busy World. (Eleanor is very good at decoupage. She likes cutting out the pictures, likes applying the shellac, a mix of white and orange, watching the pictures turn sepia under it, instant aging, instant preservation, everything floating in a sea of brownish-gold, a confounding of time and perception.) The same crib that got her into so much trouble with her colleagues when her friend Gloria (eleven years ago, when she first came to teach at the college, she was a new friend; now she's no friend at all but something inevitable, like a terrible relative) came over to congratulate her on the birth of the new baby.

She could tell from Gloria's expression what she was thinking: Why doesn't Eleanor raise vegetables? They're so much quieter, and at least in the beginning, so much nicer to look at.

"What a darling, darling child," Gloria says over and over, and then she asks: "Is it a boy or girl?" Of course, it doesn't make any difference, but if Gloria had been a boy, her father would never have disinherited her just because she moved out at sixteen, because boys are allowed to do anything.

Tom comes in and sees the two of them looking at each other like animals in opposite corners of a cage.

Gloria, dear birdlike Gloria, with her hunched back and her little beaked nose and her voice which swooped up and down the room so that you wanted to tell her, Pull back your sleeve and let me see the feathers. All those frantic motions: see how charming I am, so vivacious, so entertaining. So vivacious indeed that when she prepares to leave one wants to ask her, Do you prefer to fly out the window or are the stairs good enough? Birdlike Gloria, in whom the metaphor has been made flesh, whose constant refrain is "I want to be bone-thin," and she is. If she

stands in front of a bright light, her skeleton is silhouetted
on the wall behind her. It is Gloria who once confessed to
Eleanor, "At my age, you have to stay thin or no man
wants to bother with you. So what if I lie about my age?
So if I say I'm ten years younger? I can get away with it.
People throw you away like a bone if they find out you're
forty and haven't gotten anywhere. When you're in your
thirties, there's still hope you'll do something. Oh, I've
heard them talking. They say, well, she's forty and if she
hasn't become a principal dancer by now, she never will.
Why should I give them that satisfaction if I can get away
with it? If I'm bone-thin, everyone thinks I'm thirty-one.
Why shouldn't I do it? I'm not married like you are; no
one wants to put me in the center of a stage."

Eleanor tries to inject a word here or there, but the
bandages on Gloria's soul are too thick; the needle bends.

It's no use saying, "The worst thing about lying is
that you lie to yourself. You never know where you are.
Soon nothing will seem real. I don't lie, not because I'm
good; I just want to know where I am in the world."

"Oh, if you were single you would," says Gloria.
"Then it would be another story for you. Of course, you'd
have to lose weight to get away with it."

"Oh, I don't know," says Eleanor, meaning, Don't
you ever shut up? Is there only one hole in your garden
wall to look through? Gloria is the only person on earth
who would maintain year in and year out that the sea was
the size of a blue button because, after all, that's what it
looks like to her.

Of course Eleanor, who believes certain people
(Gloria) are in this world to punish others, while others
(herself) are in this world to be punished, does not say,
Gloria, they believe you're thirty-one because you say you

are. Your face is a ruin. I see little archaeologists climbing it now with ropes and pitons. What they think is, look how quickly some people age. The pity of it! I hope that doesn't happen to me.

And just then Gloria catches sight of a shocking-pink crib in the bedroom, the decoupaged crib, and screams, "A Gloria Vanderbilt crib! They cost a fortune."

Oh, thinks Eleanor, she's gone crazy at last. Who would have thought a crib would push her over the edge?

"What?" she says politely.

"A Gloria Vanderbilt crib!" Gloria shrieks (vivaciously, charmingly). "Her decoupage is a rage. She's decoupaged floors for the richest people in Manhattan."

Eleanor makes the mistake of saying she's thought of decoupaging a floor. If she did, she'd do the floor in the baby's room. It's the smallest.

And out the window Gloria flies to tell the faculty that Eleanor has a Gloria Vanderbilt crib and must have made a fortune on her last book.

"Don't bother correcting them," says her grandmother from Cloud Nine, where wives of retired doctors are allowed to sit. "The more you deny having money, the more they'll think you have it. Don't say a word. Let them eat themselves up."

After that, things change at school. Of course, everyone still discusses the price of shoes and where to find the best egg-salad sandwich in New York, but now they look at her and say, Oh, you wouldn't be interested in bargains.

She has, according to them, gotten rich working on the same premises where they toil, making so little. How has she gotten so well known when they haven't? How has it happened when they weren't looking?

Oh, well, thinks Eleanor, let them suffer. They didn't mind her being the center of attention when her success was only literary. But financial success! Intolerable.

There goes the last of the cartons down the red cement steps.

Now Toh and the children are setting up the net and for the rest of the afternoon, she and her husband hear the little white orb traveling, puk, puk, puk. She was once such a good player herself. The only one she couldn't beat was her father, but then nobody could. He held the racket in such a strange way, straight down. He hit everything so that it spun crazily and then bounced off in unpredictable directions. But she is a good player. She wants to play, and when she puts down her tape recorder her husband looks up at her and says, I was wondering how long you'd be able to stand it.

And when she comes out on the porch in her blue parka (it's early December and very cold), she sees Toh, holding his racket straight down. Davey starts shouting, "Let Mamma try! Let Mamma try!"

Even though the Ping-Pong ball bears more of a resemblance to a dandelion gone to seed than the things Eleanor remembers hitting back and forth, once she and Toh start playing, they don't want to stop. Toh says it's a long time since he's played Ping-Pong and then he misses one of Eleanor's serves. Everyone does. That was the only way she got a point from her father, by learning to return a ball so that it just cleared the net and hit the table near the edge, just inside the white line. To reach it you had to have rubber arms or fall down on the table and go after it. No one could get it. After that serve, Toh looks surprised and plays harder. They are playing better and better.

In the background, the children are complaining, It's my turn, it's my turn, but no one listens to them. No one

notices when Tom comes out and sits down, watching the
two of them, and when they're finally finished, Tom says
to her, I didn't know you could play Ping-Pong, and
Eleanor says, Oh, I told you.

Tom looks over at Toh and smiles. A game is no
game to Eleanor, as he has long ago discovered. When she
plays, she plays to win.

Outside, the children are calling to their friends
down the block, You should see my Mom play Ping-Pong.
Eleanor calls out to them, Keep quiet, you don't have to
advertise everything that goes on here.

It isn't the best of neighborhoods. She doesn't want
anyone breaking in to steal a Ping-Pong table complete
with paddle and balls. Every day, she thinks, she sounds
more and more like her mother, or a parody of her
mother. Her husband puts his arm around her, but she
doesn't look up at him. She knows Toh is not looking at
them, or is trying not to, but she doesn't say anything to
Tom. What is she supposed to say, after all? How can you
be so cruel as to hug your own wife in front of this now
not-so-total stranger?

And she thinks, as the days pass and he comes more
often, playing Ping-Pong with the children, playing Ping-
Pong with her on the porch, under the aquamarine ceiling
she and Tom painted to resemble the color of the sky:
Now I am safe. He's a friend of the family, of the children,
of my husband. Now he won't be lonely. He'll stop saying
he can always go back to China. Those other stray and
stupid thoughts are irrelevant now—annoying, but without force of consequence. He's a family friend.

How stupid can you be, Eleanor?

TWELVE

ELEANOR TENDS to ignore history, on the ill-considered theory that since everything repeats anyway, she'll catch all of it the next time it comes around. Nevertheless, she has a dim awareness of how giant motions set little wheels, such as the clock wheel of her own little life, into unexpected frenzies of motion, but never before has her life been so directly affected by an historical event as it is when the premier of mainland China comes to the United States.

He has, of course, nothing to do with her, but the brief sunshine of good relations caused by this visit allows more Chinese out of their country and into hers and one of those to benefit from the premier's visit is Toh's uncle, who promptly collects his visa, his tickets, and goes immediately to the Peking airport where he sleeps overnight. In China, political winds shift suddenly and Toh's uncle has been trying to leave for five years.

Still, thinks Eleanor, the premier's visit alone would not have been sufficient to set things on end. No, it is the combination of the premier's visit, an unexpected blizzard, and one minor hoodlum, New York style, that is to blame. They, or history, are to blame for sending her to a small, unheated apartment in Chinatown, furnished with a single iron bed and one suitcase and, of course, Toh.

"Blaming history, are you now, Eleanor," asks her grandmother. "What will you stoop to next?"

Eleanor, who never pays attention to current events which will be old hat in the morning. Oh, Russia's been invaded by giant scallions? Why didn't someone tell me about it?

But Eleanor, the papers have been *full* of scallions and you can't turn on the television without seeing scallions climbing all over the Kremlin.

During the Cuban missile crisis, her mother called her at college, and proceeded to relate a long list of vault numbers "just in case." ("Get a pencil, Eleanor. I know you don't have one.") She didn't write the numbers down. If they were going to be bombed, they would be bombed and she wouldn't care much then about those boxes. How passive I am at times, she thinks.

"Not passive," says her father, allowed in, once more, by the two crones. He's holding a black Ping-Pong paddle, perfect to spank her with. If she hasn't done anything yet, she will. "Not passive. Stupid."

Why are all of her thoughts so angry? Except when she is in that little room, painted white, on which the gray dust has settled unevenly, so that, even at noon, twilight seems to leak from the plastered-over cracks in the walls. And why can't she think long about this affair?

Her mind refuses admittance to that word: affair. But it is a strong word, isn't it, and it crawls hand over hand up the bricks of the building. A clever word, it picks the locks on the doors, and here it is. It looks like the ghost of Lady Macbeth's father. It also resembles Lady Macbeth herself.

"You are not a sexual affair," Eleanor tells it. It rattles its bones at her. It makes motions as if it were washing its hands.

"You can't stay here," Eleanor says to it, "not when I can't think at all."

The word backs away, unplugged.

But the affair exists, and this is how it came to exist:

Eleanor gets up and looks out her bedroom window. An icy gray sky signifying snow. She switches on the radio; the announcer is predicting six inches of snow. Good. She and her arthritic elbow are never wrong. She calls Toh, who lives three blocks away with four roommates, and tells him it's going to snow: would he mind leaving earlier than usual? She hates to be late for a meeting.

"What does it mean," Toh asks as they drive through the thickening gauze, "beef up?"

"To make larger. Or stronger," says Eleanor. "Beef up what?"

"In school paper, it say president going to beef up tuition. I look it up in dictionary. Nothing about tuition. All about cows. President putting cows in the college?" he asks, starting to smile.

"No," says Eleanor, starting to laugh; it's enchanting, the image of cattle wandering up and down the halls of the school buildings grazing happily on green dollars. "No, it means he's going to raise tuition. Charge more money."

"Ooooh," says Toh, whistling softly, "that bad news for my uncle."

"Uncle?"

"My uncle coming from China."

"That's wonderful," she says. "You must be excited." What she means is, good, now you won't be so lonely, no more threats about going back to China. At the same time, a sharp pang: now you won't be entirely mine. And surprise. Until then, she hadn't realized what she wanted was total possession.

"Isn't that what all women want?" asks her mother. "Isn't that what all *men* want? Think about *that*, Eleanor."

Eleanor ignores her.

She hasn't realized that she would resent sharing her magic rescuer who gently went through her pocketbook when she couldn't find her keys, who zipped her coat when she couldn't see the recalcitrant zipper. Just courtesy, cultural differences.

"Can I take the car away?" asks Toh.

"Take away?"

"To get my uncle. At airport."

"When?"

"Wednesday. Not this week, next one."

Eleanor and Tom have few rules. One is never to lend anyone their cars, blunderbusses so jerry-rigged only they can drive them. But this car, given her by her parents just before they died, white outside, baby blue inside (all it needs, Eleanor thought when she first saw it, is pink tires) is in good shape.

"Yes," she says, "you can take away the car."

The afternoon before Toh is to get his uncle, who is arriving one week before the Chinese premier, the television and radio have forgotten about the large unpeaceful world and all talk exclusively about the blizzard they expect Wednesday morning.

"No problem," says Toh. "Rainman always wrong."

"Weatherman," she says, automatically correcting him, looking at the sky. That is a Chicago sky, the color of leaden glass, resting heavily on the spires of Manhattan. It's going to snow.

By the time they get home to Brooklyn, the side streets are covered by snow, and beneath it even Eleanor can see the dangerous shark-gray gleam of ice. She tells

Toh to stop the car. Has he ever driven in snow before? He hasn't. Eleanor explains, clearly, theoretically, what to do if a car skids. Toh is very intelligent and understands. Theoretically.

"All right, start the car and brake in the middle of the block."

"Break?"

"Brake. Step on the brake," says Eleanor, pointing at the pedal. "Step on it hard."

He does. The car skids.

"Don't touch the wheel," says Eleanor. "Wait until it starts to come back."

The car is traveling first in one large *S,* then another, from sidewalk to sidewalk.

"Now stop it," she says.

Toh is terrified.

"*That's* a skid. If you go tonight, you have to be careful."

"Still, I have confidence."

"No one can control a car on ice."

Still, he intends to go. They spend the rest of the afternoon calling each other. Pan American's clerk informs Eleanor that the airline plans to divert their flight to Montreal. Eleanor calls Toh and tells him there's a good chance the airport will be closed. He doesn't think so.

Miraculously, the airport is open for the Chinese flight. When Toh comes to get the car keys, Eleanor sends him off with a huge thermos of herb tea. Suppose he gets stuck on the side of the road? In this weather, you could freeze to death. When she sees the white car turn the corner, blurring into the white snowflakes, she wishes every evil she can think of upon Deng Xiaoping, whose visit to the United States has unstrained diplomatic relations, made it possible for Toh's uncle to leave China, and sent Toh out on the road to get him on a night like this.

"You shouldn't have let him go," says Tom.

"No."

"Why did you?"

"He wanted to go so much."

"What kind of reason is that?"

"If he didn't take our car, he'd borrow one from a friend. They're all wrecks. The last one he borrowed didn't have brakes."

Tom shakes his head.

"He *had* to go. He knows how terrified his uncle will be. He hardly speaks English."

"It would have been better," Tom tells her, "if we'd given him the money for a cab."

"He wouldn't have taken it."

Tom looks down the street and shakes his head. "Come on in," he says, putting his arm around her. "It's cold."

"Damn," Eleanor says softly. "I wish *you* had said no."

"He's your friend."

"He's *your* friend, too!"

"Don't start blaming this on me," says Tom.

Eleanor apologizes.

"Don't stay up all night listening for the car," says Tom.

"I won't. I'm going to sleep. I can't stand it."

She falls asleep immediately, Eleanor the catatonic, whose eyes close when her accountant confers with them about taxes, who could not sleep while she sat in the hospital corridor waiting for news about her father.

"Come to bed with me?" she asks Tom. But he has

work to do, a pile of contracts to read. She gets in bed, still lying on her left side only because her right eye is still healing. No sleeping on that side for another month. She thinks of the gray ice under the car and cries.

She wakes up suddenly. A thin gray light is coming through the windows. She jumps out of bed, goes out onto the sun porch which adjoins her bedroom and looks down into the driveway. The car is there. She goes back to sleep. Someone will wake her later.

They wake her in plenty of time to get dressed. They wake her in time to build a small pyramid before it's time to leave for a meeting with a visiting literary critic. She sits, waiting for Toh, in the leather wing chair, in the living room, staring at the stained glass window she bought fifteen years ago from an electrician with whom she had struck up a conversation, a man worried about how much the insuring of the windows was costing his church.

She wound up with five gigantic stained glass windows, one a rose window. On the one at which she is now staring, a white dove dives out of a calla lily floating above purple-veined storm clouds, the sky beneath him bluer than any human sky, bearing in his beak a long, thin scroll unwinding across the sky: *In my father's house are many mansions.*

"That's a nice sentiment," says her father, chewing on his green cigar, his round belly puffing up under his light blue shorts. "That's a nice window."

"Mmmm," says Eleanor.

Thank God he never read the bible. Thank God he didn't ask her what part of the bible that nice sentiment came from.

"After your grandfather died," he says, the smoke

from the cigar curling through the room, around the head of the marble lady on the mantle, making her seem, not stone, but a momentary presence, one which could, in an instant, turn back into smoke and disappear, "maybe two years after, I found myself dialing a phone number. I call him. His old number. Well, you never know they're gone until you need them. You never know at all, even though they tell you often enough." He seems to be talking to the bird in the window.

Her eyes fill. Lately, she feels like a pendulum clock, one slightly off balance and likely to stop. She cries and then stops crying, stopped by a feeling of peace the color of the snow outside, an unfamiliar emotion. Little scenes from the past hang in the room like figures painted on wind chimes. There are the children, held up, one under each of the housekeeper's arms, who is presenting them to her to kiss. It becomes a ritual. A wise woman, her housekeeper, who knows better than to rely on words: "I'll be back soon. I love you." An action. Lips against lips. The children go back in quietly, wave smiling from the windows.

Once, in the country, she and Tom are about to drive away when a little figure bursts out of the door in its red snowsuit, howling. "A kiss! A kiss!"

"I'm sick of this kiss business," says Tom.

"So am I."

They were wrong.

How seriously her own family took words!

When Eleanor had the measles, she said she wished her mother had them. She could have blinded her mother, said her grandmother, *would* have blinded her if she'd said it again. She remembers being locked in her room for two days, her meals left outside her door, allowed out only to go to the bathroom. But if words are so powerful, what was her mother doing, still healthy, still seeing perfectly? It was a puzzle.

It has become the central puzzle of her life. Her contempt for ordinary conversation has made her something of a hermit. She would as soon listen to people on the phone as see them. In either case, they're not really present. Most of what they say is a kind of signboard painting, cozy scenes word-painted on billboards made to stand in front of dangerous caverns of emotion and impulse which they cross safely, daily, only because they remain unaware of the danger they are in. She thinks of the abysses of passion which exist in her own house, the murderous ravines of jealousy and hatred and love over which they dance like acrobats, safely, because long ago they were taught not to look down, one foot in front of the other, until finally they believe nothing's there, no depths at all. She shudders. Snowflakes can fall far and land safely, not people.

"You only have use for paper," says her mother. "You don't care about your own flesh and blood."

More words. Which mean nothing but can do infinite harm.

When she writes she uses the one true language, the words that mean what they say. It isn't that she has little use for people, but she is tired of trying to talk to them. They will be talking about the weather, or what they will do this summer, and she thinks: What do you mean? What are you talking about, really?

Whereas she always knows what Toh is talking about, even when he's silent. She trusts him: that's it. When she writes, as she is again beginning to do, printing her poems in huge, black penciled letters, she pretends she is writing them as letters to him.

She waits for him to ring the bell. The dove is still flying down from the clouds. *In my father's house are many mansions.* Which ex-New Yorkers, like her parents, apparently took to mean the condominiums of Florida. The entire United States, she thinks, could be taken hostage if someone sealed off Century Village. The parents of everyone she knows live there. The phone rings. It's Toh.

"You made it!" Eleanor says.

"No."

"No?"

"I have accident. You saw car?"

"Not yet. Not really. Tom just brought it back. He took the kids to school. What do you mean, you had an accident? What happened to you?"

"Not to me. To car. On the way to airport, I stop for light and car stop for light, but then slides into parked car."

"You weren't hurt?"

"No problem with me. I pay for car."

THIRTEEN

O N THE PEBBLED SIDEWALK in front of Eleanor's house, Toh begins babbling something about taking the car to a body, while Eleanor, in her blurry way, peers at the white car trying to see if any new dents have been added to the spectacular one she inflicted on the car two days after its arrival in New York when, distracted by the children's fighting in the back seat, she inched out of the driveway and hit the already thoroughly dented jalopy across the street. While she looks, she realizes Toh is trying to tell her he will take the car to a body shop where the car will be fixed and where he will pay for repairs.

"No you won't," says Eleanor. "It's my car. It was my fault for letting you take it. You could've gotten hurt. I'm not worried about the car."

Under her auspices, cars disintegrate, until, careening along the road, they seem pulled along by an invisible tow truck. Toh, however, insists. He is going to take the car to a house of the body.

"Body shop," says Eleanor, looking at him closely. "Get in. You're not in your right mind today."

All the way into the city, all the way to the surgeon's office on West 165th Street, Toh does nothing but talk about the accident. He wasn't going too fast. He had stopped for the light when the car skidded. All night he felt as if a ghost was around him. When his uncle finally came in, five hours late, his luggage was lost. His uncle had nothing to wear, such bad luck, he couldn't understand it.

Wonderful, thinks Eleanor, he is becoming more and more like her. Soon he too will be known as a wall-to-wall worrier. Now fix this.

She patiently explains why it wasn't his fault. Did he put the ice on the road with his own two hands? No, he couldn't pay for it. He was her friend. He always sat in the car for hours, waiting for her. Forget it. Will he forget it? He doesn't answer her. She gets out and goes into the doctor's office.

When she comes out, two and a half hours later, following the thick yellow line painted for those with eyesight as bad as hers was before the surgery, Toh is still sitting in the car, waiting for her in front of the main entrance.

"I found body shop," says Toh, "but it close itself."

What, Eleanor wants to know, was he doing, driving around the cliff-strung streets of the Bronx looking for body shops?

He wanted to find an estimate.

Eleanor tells him to park the car, which he does.

"I've been thinking," she says. "It wasn't *your* bad luck yesterday. You got caught in your *uncle's* bad luck. *His* plane was late. *His* plane almost went to Montreal. *His* luggage was lost. *You* were lucky. All you did was dent the car."

Inconsolable. She puts her hand over his.

"It's all right," she says.

No answer.

"I think," he says, "when I hit the car, I go back to China."

He looks at her and looks away.

Go back to China! What should she say now? Without taking her hand from his, she slides over in the seat until they are pressed together.

"Come here," she says, putting her arm around his shoulders. She is surprised at how warm the rough, waterproof material of his parka is. It reminds her of summers, of warm gray rocks heated by sun, large enough to lie on. He looks at her, terrified, and then relaxes. He smiles, hesitantly. She nuzzles her head into his neck and with her left hand pulls his head down on top of hers. They stay that way for some time, his thick black hair against hers. Then Eleanor picks up her head, and pulls away. She begins stroking his hair: rough, like the hair of an animal. "It's all right," she says again. Finally he sighs, as if he were exhaling a ghost.

"All right?" he asks.

"All right," she says.

They sit still. Elderly people, walking with canes, supervised by middle-aged sons and daughters, stop every few feet, stare down at the iced sidewalk, gain the courage to go further on, and proceed slowly up the sloping street.

"Are you still worrying?" she asks.

"I never have accident before."

"I know."

Is there no way of distracting him? She pulls back, looks at him, and suddenly kisses him on the lips. He tastes of ginger.

What are you doing, she asks herself. Didn't Tom read her that book about China and tell her how Victorian the Chinese were about sex? But this, she thinks, is not sex. This is something else.

Does she want to scare him all the way back to China? Make him the first person to walk all the way there on water, escaping this decadent Western woman, who, until this moment, has been notorious only for her prudery? Two prudes in a car, she thinks, one Eastern, one Western, parked across the street from a hospital.

"Will you stop worrying?" she asks him, whereupon the Chinese prude bends over and kisses her. On the lips. They're chapped, thinks Eleanor; I should put something on them.

The two of them are in shock. That's it. People in shock ought to keep warm. Their arms are around one another's shoulders. They move closer together. What an excellent way to treat misery.

"Eleanor," says her mother, "*think*. You have a split personality, Eleanor. You drive people crazy thinking about why the sun rises and sets, and then you start kissing a perfect stranger without thinking about it *at all*. What do you think you're doing?"

But Eleanor, the totally preoccupied, has now exercised her ability to suspend thinking under certain circumstances.

"Eleanor," says her grandmother, "Scarlett O'Hara said she'd think about it tomorrow, and look where it got her."

Eleanor decides to do Scarlett one better and never think about it at all.

"In China," says Toh, "I had girlfriend, but school said I had to give her away. Grades in whole school were down, so government said no boyfriends, no girlfriends. In Communist country, things go that way."

"Oh," she says, kissing his cheek, stroking his hair, "I wouldn't have liked that."

"It makes no difference. When government say do, you do."

"I would not be here to tell the tale."

"Tell something to a tail?"

She explains: tale as in story.

"Your husband," asks Toh, looking at her (there are puffy pouches beneath his eyes, just like her daughter's), "he would approve?"

"Of what?"

"This kissing?"

"No. He would not."

"You kiss other people before?"

"Never."

"Never?"

"My father. My grandfather. My uncles. My son. Otherwise, never. I'm old-fashioned."

"I, too."

They stare out the window. An old man and an equally old woman are laboring up the hill.

"Your husband," Toh asks, "should we tell about this kissing to him?"

"Absolutely not." Is Toh an idiot after all?

"Then it is wrong?"

"Probably it is wrong."

Toh considers this.

"I don't care," he says suddenly, starting to laugh. "You know," he says, "I never know woman before." Again, nervousness, misery.

"Well, you know one now."

"Eleanor," asks her grandmother, "what do you think you're doing? The surgeon could come out of his office and see you."

Eleanor tells her grandmother the man wouldn't recognize her with her body on. To him, she is one disembodied eye.

"Eleanor," her grandmother persists, "you know right from wrong. Is this right?"

"Right? I don't know what that means."

It seems to her that all this is taking place within the great golden arch of her wedding band, although that seems impossible to explain to her grandmother or to anyone else. Safe under the arch.

"What you are doing is wrong," her grandmother says.

"Wrong," says Eleanor.

They begin the drive home.

Eleanor is not surprised by what has happened, any more than she is surprised by how happy she is when Toh asks her, several weeks later, if she has some time. When she says she does, he tells her he wants to show her something. That something turns out to be a one-room apartment in Chinatown he has borrowed from a friend.

When she goes into the room, she recognizes it as one recognizes something seen in a dream many times before. It is not a room but a world, a mainland, cut off from all other land not by water but by a zone of time. The room floats, bobs gently, like a boat on water. As she walks into the center of the room, the rest of the world ceases to exist. Actually, thinks Eleanor, it has not existed for a long time.

I feel, she thinks, as if I am starting school, not an affair. How have they grown together like this? In the car, they have only each other. She loves him, but it is an odd love, precious but odd, and if someone asked her what kind of love it was, she could not say. All the same, it is love, however improbable, however incomprehensible, however indefinable. Its indefinability gives it its strange power.

She sees herself reflected in a pitted mirror, a tall, slender woman, long black hair hanging straight to her hips, a face heart-shaped and pale. Who is that woman? Why does everyone say she's beautiful? What does she have to do with her? She turns her back to the mirror, and stands at the edge of the bed.

She takes off her clothes slowly and then she stands, naked, hugging her breasts with her arms because she's cold, she is always cold. Toh finally removes his shirt, folds it neatly, and places it over the back of the wing chair. An odd pattern on the fabric of the shirt: black twigs against a white ground. Brought from China, part of a two-years' supply of clothes. So much cheaper there than here. He gets in bed beside her, still in his jeans. She reaches for his hand, which she clasps tightly. She smiles.

"I am funny?" he asks her. She doesn't answer. "With many women," he says, "I have been close, but not like this."

Where has it come from, her newly acquired capacity for silence? In real life, in her other life, she would be jabbering, comforting, explaining. In this little room, the metal bed frame icy against her shoulders, she says nothing.

"I think," he says, "I will disappoint."

Now she laughs, an odd, low laugh she has not heard before.

"Not possible," she says.

"Very possible," he says. Almost angry.

"No," she says, "it is not."

His eyes are scanning her face: for what?

"You have confidence?" he asks her.

She nods her head.

"I have not," he says. And starts to cry. Is there a better way to break any woman's heart, especially that of Eleanor of the Stray Cats? To make her pick up her own inhibitions and guilts and throw them, like a bundle of sticks, out the window, utterly careless about the heads upon which they will fall?

"Well, then," she says, stroking his cheek, "why don't we wait until another time?"

She kisses his hairline, his eyebrows, the wet tip of his nose, his chin.

"Sometime next week?"

She kisses the side of his throat. She feels him swallow, nuzzles his chest, pretends not to notice how his breathing quickens, that he is now holding her by the shoulders, tighter, that his face has contorted into a grimace which makes him look so much older than he is. She pulls back slowly and begins stroking his hair, thick and rough. Oh, she knows him well. Whatever he starts, he finishes.

He gets out of bed and begins unbuckling his belt.

Back in bed, his arms lock around her back, hers around his neck. Something has happened to her body. It is gone, it's outline left behind, sensitized to touch as a film is to light. She, who has spent years worrying about getting pregnant, so many years that she still worries—even after the hysterectomy—now doesn't worry at all. Doesn't care.

His lovemaking is violent, even angry. Angry and far from home, thinks Eleanor, before she stops thinking altogether. Later they lie in bed, on their backs, trying not to notice what happened. Which, surprisingly, they find very easy to do. For Eleanor it is as if her life in Chinatown, which has now begun, takes place in one crystal bead of a necklace, her life in Brooklyn, in the next, separate bead. She has no desire to break the string that holds them together.

FOURTEEN

I T IS SEVERAL MONTHS later, and Eleanor's eye has healed enough to allow her to drive herself—with glasses on. She is not used to them and shudders whenever she passes a mirror. She also notices a new inexplicable tendency to retrieve friends from the past.

She began by getting in touch with her ex-fiancé, a man she had not seen for nineteen years. The reason for this: a dream she had convincing her that disaster had befallen him. If she hadn't been so intent on ingratiating herself with her ex-fiancé (for his own good, of course), would she have become so interested in Toh so fast? Her ex-fiancé's fourth wife was an expert on China, and her ex-fiancé told her his wife was going to China and didn't know anyone there.

"I know someone from Peking," said Eleanor. "Maybe your wife could call his family. I'll ask him about it."

To her ex-fiancé's astonishment, Eleanor knew something about events taking place somewhere beyond Passaic, New Jersey.

From her ex-fiancé, she proceeded to move backwards into high school. Finding one's high school friends might have been a great, even daunting project for some. Not for Eleanor, who had liked four people in her eleven years in Cedarhurst.

One of them is now an adviser to the President, a man who has managed mini-celebrity for himself by disagreeing with everything the President says. She sees his pictures everywhere, advocating, in little paragraphs, limited deterrence. Lately, sane deterrence. Now that his name is in the paper, she knows where to find him. She calls The White House and is amazed to find that, one, the place is real, two, no one threatens to arrest her for impudence, and three, she can actually speak to the nouveau celebrity.

They talk. She discovers he's as unpleasant as ever. How reassuring. She is worried about people's tendency to mellow with age. Soon she will be the only one in captivity with a sharp tongue and a thirst for vengeance. To end one's life as one began: the worst one in the room!

Her friend, the President's adviser, is also having trouble with his eyes. What can that mean? Is eye trouble visited upon a particular sort of person? Is it a punishment after all?

She calls her second friend, Eric, a failed screenwriter living in California, where, according to her, people go to become stupid—not a bad ambition since she's never known anyone to fail at it. But, according to him, he has gone there to write a novel. He couldn't possibly come back to New York.

Why not? Does he think only Los Angeles has sockets for electric typewriters? Oh, pardon me, word processors.

Well, perhaps he can't come back, not when he was the most handsome man on campus, the one they all dreamed about, his red hair, his crinkly smile. They were so ignorant then. They didn't know there was more to dream about. The famous Fifties, shading off into the infamous Sixties, innocent and quiet, everyone reading books, going to the movies, making noise in the movie the-

ater, trying to get thrown out, planning for sweet sixteen
parties, inventing boyfriends in college to annoy the other
girls and (with luck) to make some of the boys jealous. If
there was a Fonzie, he lived in a world they never thought
to look for, safe as they were in their Long Island cocoon
of mild wealth, mild terror over SAT scores, waiting
peacefully to hatch like so many eggs, knowing just when
they would: when they unpacked their bags in their college dorms.

Eric, the screenwriter, is not married. What astonish-
ments there are in the world. Eleanor stays on the phone
talking to him far longer than she should. The whole time
they talk, she feels as if *she's* come home. After all, she sat
next to him for seven years, planted as they were in the
good soil of alphabetical order. She begins to tell him the
story of her eyes (why can't she talk about her eyes to anyone in her own family?) and he tells her to call Jimmy
Bergman at once. He's an excellent eye surgeon. Of
course, that's all he's interested in. Eyes. If you were Oedi-
pus and did a stupid thing like put your eyes out, he
wouldn't consider treating you or talking to you; he'd call
the police. Anyone who offends against an eye is, according to him, a war criminal. Jimmy's office is only four
blocks from your house. Call him.

She does. His name was next on her list.

They spend hours going over the history of her eye
trouble.

"Are you sure your vision's twenty-twenty?" he asks
her. "That surgeon you have isn't as good as I am."

She makes arrangements to meet him at his office
since he can't think of a time when he *isn't* there. He may
not be in his office some Sundays, but then he's probably
in the O.R. at the Harkness Pavilion. Emergency work.
What, are all her high school friends demented

overachievers? Is this what comes of seating them in alphabetical order? Did they all start out this way, or did they all catch the disease from one carrier?

"By the way," says Jimmy Bergman at the end of their fourth run-through (By now, the discussions have become quite technical. "If you're going to talk about something, you might as well get the terms right," he says.), "how's Jane?"

"Jane," says Eleanor. "I haven't talked to her in the last few years." Five years. She stopped talking to Jane when her beloved childhood friend, at whose house she'd slept on weekends for ten years, began flirting with her husband—that was tolerable. She knew Jane could not resist married men, no matter who their wives might be. But it was not tolerable when Jane, who always drank (even in the Fifties, even in high school), began calling later and later when she knew Eleanor would be asleep and kept her husband on the phone for hours at a time, rambling her way into a thicket where no one else could or would follow her. Eleanor was not afraid that Jane would seduce her husband, but that she would exhaust him: talk him to death.

But now Jimmy Bergman has mentioned Jane and she wants to talk to her. Jane, she tells Jimmy Bergman, was still living in Cedarhurst, when last heard from was still a psychologist, still unmarried.

"Who does she find to treat?" asks Jimmy. "Cats and dogs? We were all brought up to believe that no one in Cedarhurst was neurotic. We were too fortunate to be neurotic. Still in Cedarhurst," marvels Jimmy, and then they both fall silent.

Oh, those long afternoons in Cedarhurst when there was nothing to do. How endlessly she and Jane rode their identical maroon bicycles, Schwinns, with thick tires, all over town, under the thick canopies of oak leaves which met overhead, little gold rags of sunlight slipping under their rubber tires as they rode, as if many princesses had torn up many gowns and in a fury tossed the scraps back to earth.

How carefully they inspected all their classmates' houses, with the precision of insurance agents. A house on the horseshoe shape of Rugby Drive meant you had more money than God. A house on a tree-lined street which permitted only small patches of sun to litter the well-swept ground meant you were in high standing with the mysterious city gods of finance and so had to be reckoned with. Off to Blenheim Court, where the daughter of an editor of the *New York Times* lived, and so you had to like her.

So little to do that they were all expert bike riders whose pastime was watching one another. She and Jane could ride alongside each other and talk as they slowly moved from block to block.

She remembers weekends when Jane was out of town, when she was reluctantly pried by her parents from her own bed at eleven o'clock; when she was so bored she used to lean her head against the elephant-skinned trunk of the oak tree in front of her house and count the hours until she could go back to sleep again. Was she bored? Oh yes, she was. Depressed? Did any of them know that word then? The feel of the trunk is still there, against her cheek. Some yellow gum is oozing from the trunk just above her eye. A lone ant is making its way down a jagged groove. The trunk is gray and black and the sky is the same blue the sea turns on a sunny summer day, and the lawns are well trimmed and brilliant green. If she stays here long enough, staring at the tree trunk, she will see her brother running back from the house across the street carrying the family dog, who has just stolen a lamb chop from the cat whom they all dislike. The cat is too big and goes after the dog. The dog refuses to relinquish the lamb chop. Her brother has to carry the dog home, lamb chop and all. Whenever she talks to her brother for more than half an hour, he brings it up: Remember when Biff stole the cat's lamb chop? Such monotony, such security, such high ambition, silently growing.

Yes, she wants to talk to Jane. If she hadn't found her soon after her family had moved to Cedarhurst from Brooklyn, she would have expired of an inexplicable misery beyond the reach of her parents' willingness to understand, smug as they were in the face of what they had accomplished, the move to the suburbs. Now the children had to be perfectly happy; how could they not, after their parents had gone to so much trouble?

She calls Jane and leaves a message on her office answering machine, which means that she deliberately did not copy her home number into her new address book. She must have intended to break with her permanently. Now she hovers around the phone waiting for Jane to call back. Of course she will take her time. It's taken Eleanor five years to return *her* last call.

Is it a form of senility, Eleanor wonders, this calling of one's old friends? One's older and older friends? Soon she'll call her dead mother in Florida and ask her what the name of the child was who lay in the carriage next to her in Prospect Park. She'd like to go back there, too.

She wants to call Jane, or have Jane call her back, before Tuesday, when she again goes to Chinatown for the afternoon. Jane does.

"Can I come over?" Eleanor asks her.

Silence.

"You haven't asked to come over in twenty-three years," says Jane.

Silence from Eleanor.

"Sure you can come over," says Jane. "If you can't, who can?"

"How about forty minutes?" Eleanor asks.

"Forty minutes from *now?*"

"Right," says Eleanor.

"Oh, boy," says Jane.

FIFTEEN

THE DRIVE TO THE ISLAND is soothing. It is wonderful to be able to drive again, although if she had the slightest excuse, she'd still have Toh driving her. She's thought of using nervousness as an excuse, but no one cares whether she's nervous or not because she gets everything done that needs to be done. Farfetched fears—Alzheimer's disease, Parkinsonism—all appeal to her but she dismisses them. Thinking about things makes them happen. So the Chinese say and so Eleanor believes.

She takes her own peculiar route from her house to the highway. No matter what her starting point, her path never varies. She drives to the nearest corner of Bedford Avenue, turns right and drives until the street ends at Sheepshead Bay, first passing her grandmother's red brick row house, or what used to be her grandmother's house. The new people in it have changed nothing. Even the pink metal awning is the same.

How well she remembers the inside of that red brick row house with its steep steps up, dark, dark, dark, its two side walls windowless, what windows there were covered with heavy velvet drapes so the plush velvet sofa and chairs would not fade. It was always so silent in that house, except of course when everyone was shouting at everyone else, which only happened on festive occasions when attendance was mandatory. Eleanor still dreads holidays.

She wonders if the newcomers have done anything to the tiny bathroom on the first floor, the one just inside the front door. Does it still have its seasick blue tiles? Does the door still open with a bang against the knees of the unfortunate sitting on the toilet seat? And what about upstairs, where everything was painted dusky pink, and what about the big rose bush in the backyard?

"Eleanor," says her mother, "even rose bushes grow old and die."

Whereas she, some maniacal kind of Penelope, madly unweaving the strands of the day and reweaving them into the tapestry of yesterday and the day before, wants everything as it was.

Nothing stays the same. She knows that but does not believe it. She thinks about the review of her last book:

Her great talent and her great obsession is to demonstrate how art provides a bulwark against all forms of loss. In her latest book, however, this impulse has gone slightly mad and begun collecting the past with the indiscriminate and appalling energy of a Manhattan bag lady.

She passes the playground they were sent to explore while the family held their interminable family councils on the front porch of the row house, passes the street which led to her own grade school, P.S. 206, past her Aunt Lilian's house, Lilian now long dead, mentally waving, hello, hello. Eleanor has no need for graveyards, doesn't understand them, the thing to do is return to the place where everything happened. Goodbye, Grandmother, park, Lilian, goodbye, all.

Eleanor sighs, turning left and driving past what used to be Lundy's. Was there a child in Brooklyn who wasn't dressed up in patent-leather shoes to eat fish there on Sundays? How could anyone permit such a landmark to close? The oxidized copper roof, all those family dinners, solemnly cracking lobsters while sitting in one's best dress under a paper bib: gone, dreadful, some people have no sense of tradition.

At least the boats are still there, bringing in loads of slippery silver fish, signs nailed to their rails offering to take the bolder people on excursions out to sea, or the more timid to Rockaway. She rolls down her window, and the sharp, fishy smell floats on the cold air, the smell of women who have made love to men or have gotten old in homes where there are infrequent baths.

What has she lost that she should so miss it? And did it seem so wonderful at the time? No, in those days she tired quickly of famous outings and soon learned to turn green in the car, so that when the family went house-hunting (how she hated that word), driving down Bedford Avenue on their way to the Island, the same route she is taking now, they would have to stop the big green Hudson and send her up to her grandmother's. Although it was not her grandmother she wanted to see, but her grandfather, who would take her for walks, to the kosher butcher, the bakery, her grandfather, who would ask her questions and carry her home groggy.

And Toh has always been so good to her, from the first day. When she sprained her ankle (that was before it began—"Say it, Eleanor," says her grandmother, leaning over the edge of her cloud: "the *affair.*") he came to the house and carried her from room to room. Did her husband do that? Of course not. Her husband is exactly her age. He aches and twinges and strains his back. She wouldn't *permit* him to pick her up. How carefully Toh laid her down on the bed, all under the watchful eye of her housekeeper, the astonished looks of her children, who thought only they were small enough to be carried.

Three weeks after her first visit to the little room in Chinatown, she was sitting in the eye doctor's office, reading an antique copy of *Time* magazine, when Toh came in and sat down next to her, and while they were both reading magazines, he suddenly said he didn't have enough time to study. Would she mind if a friend took over the driving for the next two weeks? She was so stunned she didn't say a word all the way home.

Never give them the satisfaction of seeing you cry, says her mother.

She refused to cry, staring out the window, gloomily observing the Brooklyn Bridge, looming up solid gray in a light gray fog, the sun behind the clouds making what was left of the stone buildings float in an iridescent silver light, as if the whole city rested on a bed of mother of pearl. What a horrible drive home it was.

"It was too sudden," Toh says later. "I should have told you about me not driving more slowly."

"Oh, no," says Eleanor, "you need to study."

If he wants to study, he's going to study.

"I drive just once more?"

"No," says Eleanor. She knows when she's been rejected.

Somehow, he maneuvers her into letting him drive her again. Once again, there is a tension between them. For several weeks neither of them mentions the room in Chinatown, but the cat, stuffed back in the bag, is trying to get out.

She likes to think about those first days in the room, how natural it was to lie down on the small bed, how thoughtlessly she patted the mattress next to her. He lay down and they both were lying on their backs, faces to the ceiling, stiff as two figures on a catafalque. Of course she was the one who first turned on her side and kissed him as if everything was innocent, as if nothing would have consequences, and his cheek was ice cold and his eyes wide open and frightened.

"Women! Women! Women!" wails her grandfather, tearing his hair. (Is the entire family up there on that cloud? Is heaven full of front porches?)

Perhaps *he* would have liked his wife to have an affair. He might have had a little peace. Her grandfather was full of surprises. He was, according to her mother, the reason Eleanor would have to break off her engagement to a *goy*. If she didn't, it would kill her grandfather. In her family, there was nothing, not even an unwashed plate, that did not have potentially fatal consequences.

Her grandfather called her parents to the porch. He sent *her*, twenty-one years old, to the playground. When she came back, her parents were alone on the porch, hot, red, and miserable. They were also speechless, a milestone in family history, and merely pointed at the front door: *Go inside.*

Her grandfather had an engagement check for her. *You should only be happy.*

Fine, wonderful. Except that she and her ex-fiancé fell to quarrelling about what to do with the money, and once started, proceeded to quarrel about everything else under the sun. A smart man, her grandfather. Perhaps he had intended things to turn out that way. She wishes he had lived to see her marry a nice Jewish man. She married a year after her grandfather died: always too late for everything. Of course, she does not wish he was here to learn about her affair with Toh. Not that she wouldn't like to hear his opinion about it. How wonderful that had been, loving someone who did not punish you.

"Of course he didn't punish you," says her father. "He wore himself out on his own children."

Ah, there they are again, she and Toh, lying on the white narrow hospital bed, arms around each other, legs twined together. She never could lie facing anyone that long before, some kind of claustrophobia. As if the other person was not breathing out air but a poisonous gas. And there she is again, lying in bed, pretending to sleep, while he stands at the window and she watches his naked back (she, always cold, is swathed in two layers of clothing), what a small waist, what a smooth body, so little hair, he is looking out the window and below, crowds pass without ceasing. What is he thinking about, standing there? Every now and then he snakes his head as if to say, It's too bad, but that's the way things are.

Once, when she and her husband and Toh were a happy little band, an odd one, but happy, she used to ask Tom, "Do you think he will stay? Do you think he will stay, or will he go back?" ("If you don't behave," she'd tell Julie, "Toh will go back to China. He doesn't want to live in a country where children behave so badly. Running over your brother's foot with your bike because he wouldn't let you lick his lollipop!" Finally the child's leathery self-regard was breached. But the punishment was worse than Julie's crime and no matter what she told her daughter, she couldn't stop her from crying. It took three days before Julie would accept her apology.)

Finally they concluded that if he found someone to marry, he would stay in their country, but if he didn't, he would go back to China.

"I don't think he knows his way around women," said Tom.

I should have known what was up, thinks Eleanor, when I set about trying to find him a wife. She had done a good job of it. For a while it looked as if he might decide to marry a Chinese girl Eleanor found at the Rockefeller Institute.

During that time, Eleanor was inconsolable. Nothing pleased her. The world had turned mouse-gray. I'll go to the wedding, Eleanor thought, lying in her room, staring at the bare twigs moving up and down in a comfortless wind, staccato in the air; at least I'm not crying. I'm not upset.

Whereas after Toh announced he would have to stop driving in order to study, she had cried so steadily she expected to find mildew clinging to the walls and the floor.

"What is it? What is it?" everyone asked her.

Ten minutes later, she was sobbing.

"I can't get used to these new glasses," explained Eleanor, who was actually quite pleased with them. I'll go to the wedding even if it kills me, she thought. Especially if it kills me, which it will. But then came a blizzard and the wonderful Chinese girl from northern China became homesick and decided to return to China. Eleanor suddenly adjusted to her eyeglasses and came out of her room and noticed the same sun was still suspended in the same sky.

The seagulls cry above the city dump across from Starrett City, that complex of apartment buildings which advertises itself as a world unto itself. Once you come in, you never have to leave, just like a cemetery, and Eleanor looks up at the sky. Snow again. A milk-glass sky turning to lead as she watches. Will she be able to get home from Jane's house? If she can't, she'll sleep on the couch. Jane must have a couch. At least she can call her husband from Jane's apartment and tell him she's there.

The highway is empty, white gauze drifting across the empty lanes in front of her, first clinging to, and then obscuring, the white lines. She drives faster. Will this affair (*why* should she stumble over the word when she doesn't stumble over the deed?) consume all her impulses toward incest? Toh, young enough to be her son, has saved her son from her. Now she will never be one of those black-widow mothers, hanging on to their male first-born as if he were the long-awaited, long-ago-promised groom. Heavier and heavier snow. Eleanor switches on the windshield wipers. Along the blades, miniature mountain ranges travel back and forth, back and forth.

"It's very cold in China," says Toh. "When we were sent to the north, it was just like Russia. They wanted us to die. There were no houses. At night we slept in holes in the ground."

All the time spent together perfects his English. How virtuous of her to have this affair: she has saved her son from incest and taught a helpless foreigner her language.

The bay is disappearing under the thickening snow.

"My uncle was there three years longer than I was," Toh says. "We never told my parents. My father's temper is bad. We had fear he would get into trouble."

What lives, thinks Eleanor, who has often enough tried to imagine sleeping in a hole beneath the earth. Were there worms? What about the little rocks? Did they get in your ears or your mouth? Heroic lives, she thinks; heroic people. They have strength so enormous she feels like a child beside them. Humble, insignificant, inadequate beside them. Can you learn strength? Character? She hopes so.

Toh will see this weather, call the house, ask the children if they want to play Ping-Pong, find out she has left in the car, and he will walk back and forth in front of her house every hour on the hour. She has to call him, but is afraid to get off the road and stop. She drives faster and faster. Even if she skids and turns entirely around, there is nothing to crash into. She, the snow and the seagulls are the only moving things in the landscape. And what, she wonders, does the radio have to say about this, switching on the little man in the dashboard. A traveler's advisory is in effect. Only people with urgent business should attempt to drive. Everyone else should get where they're going and stay there.

Finally, the exit for Cedarhurst. If she didn't know the streets so well, she'd never be able to find Central Avenue.

She pulls up in front of a modern apartment building. What architecture. Someone must have piled a lot of cartons up in his playroom, liked the look of them, and copied them for this building.

She gets out and looks up and down the quiet street. Not a soul in sight. The snow is already lining the bare branches of the old trees and is halfway up her boots. Across the street is the medical building.

How could Jane rent an apartment facing the office of their former dentist, the terror of their adolescent lives? They used to schedule their appointments in sequence. They screamed while the dentist speculated about who was the worse of the two. That question was finally answered when Jane, catching sight of him approaching with something sharp and pointed and trying to fend him off, hit the dentist with her elbow, and the next thing she knew, saw him spitting blood into his dental bowl. She had knocked out one of his teeth. After that, he said they were to come on different days because they were shortening his life. And he died young. Had they killed him? She hopes not, but she still wonders.

Carefully, she climbs up the snowed-under front steps to Jane's building and pauses with her finger resting on the small, black button of the bell. She sees the two of them, herself and Jane, far away, as in a small globe, marble-sized, lying in the deep snow of Jane's backyard. This is their idea of looking glamorous, and they pose for each other until they use up three rolls of film. Eleanor looks at the doorbell again.

She is about to tell someone about Toh. Dangerous, opening the door to that little room and letting someone else in.

Eleanor tells herself that God would not have made doorbells if he didn't want people to use them.

At last, her paralyzed finger moves.

I am losing what's left of my mind, she thinks; it's not much, just a little sawdust and the blue and white bracelet of beads they put on my wrist when I was born, but it's all I have, and inside the bell must have rung because she thinks she sees the doorknob beginning to turn.

SIXTEEN

THE DOOR OPENS, and Jane is there, dressed in a long yellow bathrobe, nubby chenille cloth; it must have belonged to her mother, oh yes, it did. She remembers Jane's mother wearing it during the summer she slept at their house every night, and every morning stole a sleeping pill for the next night. That was the summer before she went to college; she wasn't sure whether life was beginning or ending, or whether her parents would, at the last minute, change their minds and drag her bodily from the plane, a terrible time, as if she were standing on the sharp edge of the horizon next to hers, saying, just take a step, don't worry, there's no way of falling between the two worlds, don't look down, go ahead now, step across. But to her it's not so simple. It is like stepping into a boat that is moving away from the shore. She will spend so long with one foot on each drifting world that she will fall into the black water between them and then the summer is over, and she is safe on the other side.

"You're soaking wet!" says Jane. "What were you doing out there?"

"Trying to remember what the street looks like in the summer."

"Wouldn't it be easier to come back and look in the summer?" asks Jane, opening the door to her apartment,

heaps, heaps everywhere, taking Eleanor into the bathroom, handing her a pile of towels and a blue robe.

"You and your precious snow," she mumbles.

They settle in the living room, Eleanor on the couch,
Jane in a striped easy chair near the door to the terrace.

"Didn't that chair come from your mother's?"
Eleanor asks.

Jane nods.

"How is your mother?"

"Suicidal. She asks the other secretaries which kind of
suicide they think is easiest. Every day at lunch. For a
couple of weeks, they put her in a private office, but no
one could stand the suspense. Could you stand it? They
thought she was in there hanging herself by a carbon ribbon. Drinking Liquid Paper. So they decided to go on
being depressed by her. Now she types and cries, types
and cries. She's a quiet crier. She'll never get over my father's death."

"Never?"

"Never."

The snow drifts by in long white streamers that cross
one another, and then the wind parts them, revealing yet
another layer of snow behind them. The two women look
at each other silently. They are studying each other's faces
for signs of age, change. They are taking inventory of
wrinkles, enlarging pores, graying hair, slackness of flesh,
as if, shortly, they will be in competition with one another,
this time over who will leave the world first, and the sound
of mourning for the unforgivable changes in the body is
high and soft in the air. And then the people they are now
slide away like wet decals and they are two sixteen-year-
olds whose faces they keep preserved in their brittle, identical photograph albums. They are very old friends.

What does Eleanor look like? She doesn't know,

really. She still thinks of herself as a chubby child, awkward, well-meaning, redeemed somewhat by a nice smile. She sits on the couch, her long black hair wet and combed into a tight ponytail which, ballet-dancer style, she wears over one shoulder. She has drawn her long legs up under her, hugs them with her crossed arms, and rests her chin on her knees.

She is just as she always was, thinks Jane, long, beautiful, and tall, an odd aura about her, as if she didn't quite understand she had a body and was constantly trying to get out of it. When she was younger she never sat still. Only her eyes were still, watching. The rest of her was in constant motion. Watching her could make you dizzy. That's changed, Jane thinks now; now she can sit still.

"You look beautiful," Eleanor tells Jane.

"I don't," says Jane. "My hair's getting thin and I'm getting fat and my face doesn't need plastic surgery. It needs major renovation work."

"You look beautiful to me."

For someone so shy, withdrawn really, she has an odd way of coming out with things.

"How's Tom?" asks Jane.

"He's fine."

"Why are you wearing those glasses?" Jane asks abruptly.

"Oh, my eyes," says Eleanor, who suddenly unfolds and stands up. "I've got to make a phone call. Where's the phone?"

"On the kitchen wall. Are you going to call your mother and ask if you can sleep over?"

"No, I'm going to call Toh."

"Toe?"

"It's spelled T-O-H."

"Oh," says Jane. "Now I understand everything."

"I'll explain after I call."

Jane watches her. She's graceful the way an animal is, the beauty of its motion intensified by an almost unbearable suspense: when is it going to look up, startle, and disappear into the woods? Eleanor is like that. She never thought Eleanor would marry, have children, keep the same job for over twenty years. Not in a state of nature, her Eleanor. How is it possible that Eleanor is living the life of *House Beautiful,* while she, the domestic one, owner of two woks, creator of perfect crêpes, is director of mental health in the prisons of Nassau County? Time, she thinks irrelevantly, is a lie.

"Toh?" she hears Eleanor say.

She watches, fascinated, as, in front of her, Eleanor's essential nature changes. Her face is smoothed out by a light which does not come in through the windows, her body is fluid and relaxed.

"I'm perfectly safe," Eleanor is saying now. "No, I didn't come out here because I was upset. She's my oldest friend."

She listens, then laughs.

"No, not in prison, in her apartment. Do you want to say hello to her?"

She turns to Jane, grinning.

"Say hello to Toh," she says, handing her the phone. Eleanor mouths the words, Come on, come on, nodding her head and smiling. Come on, come on.

Who could resist that expression, that evident joy in mischief? Not she, which is one reason she brought home so many notes from the high school principal.

Come on, come on, help me nail shut the doors of the gym. Then we won't have to lie tomorrow and say we have our periods.

"Why don't we want to go to the gym?" asks Jane.

"Because I forgot to iron my gymsuit."

"Oh, come on. Mrs. Tripp never takes attendance in geometry. Come home with me and see the new dog."

"For two weeks?" shrieks Jane's incredulous mother. "You have to stay after school for two weeks?"

Trying to listen seriously, remorsefully, while the principal says he never expects this sort of behavior from two honors students, two *seniors,* while in back of her, Eleanor cackles.

"Go home for the rest of the day," he says, infuriated.

Jane shrugs her shoulders and takes the phone.

"Hello, Toh," she says.

He says hello and laughs nervously.

Jane shakes her head and hands the phone back.

"Does Toh know you're a raving maniac," she asks Eleanor, her voice low, "or am I the only one who knows? Is it a well-kept secret?"

Eleanor nods and smiles. Does she always smile when she talks to Toh? Whoever he is? There's something different about her. What is it? Gentle, she's become gentle.

"Oh, it's a well-kept secret," says Eleanor as she puts the phone back on the hook. "I've been so grim lately people have started taking me for a grown-up."

She starts to walk over to the couch, then changes her mind.

"I've got to call Toh back," she says.

Jane sits down on the couch and watches her, listening.

"Oh, everything's fine. No, it isn't a long-distance call, not really. I don't care what we eat. No, really, anything. *Anything.* No, of course I didn't. There were no cars to hit. I forgot to tell you I haven't called home yet. If anyone calls you, don't say you heard from me. Tell them you heard a weather report on the Chinese radio station and they said the roads to the Island were slippery. Slippery but clear. Okay? No problem? Good. *Fine*. Really." She laughs. "No problem," she says and hangs up.

"Who is this Toh?" asks Jane.

"He's a student who's young enough to be my son and I'm having an affair with him."

"You're having an affair?" Jane says.

Her friend, Eleanor the family dog, that's what she always called herself, whose chief virtue was loyalty so absolute it made Lassie look like a French tart, and whose other virtues were patience, steadfastness of purpose, an ability to finish what she started, all the boring virtues which could have made her the excellent head of a Puritan household. Of course, she can also read minds, appear when you need her, give you what you wanted to ask for when you couldn't bring yourself to ask. Capable of terrifying almost anyone, and then, having done so, collapsing like a small child who wants its mother. Jane studies her. The lost look, that childlike air, all that seems to have dropped from her. As if Eleanor has grown up. But that's impossible. No one really grows up. Then she's grown stronger. How has she done that? Jane would like to do the same thing.

"It's not really a sexual affair," Eleanor says thoughtfully.

"You're not sleeping with him?"

Eleanor says she is. It wouldn't be fair otherwise. He wouldn't understand at all.

"I don't understand," says Jane. "Isn't this an affair of passion?"

"A different kind of passion. Not sexual."

"What kind of passion is it?"

Eleanor says she doesn't know, but she expects she'll find out.

These were the conversations that gave Jane headaches in high school.

"Never mind the affair," she says. "What happened to your eyes?"

"My eyes," Eleanor says, as if she's trying to remember what they might be.

The same person, after all.

"That's a nice dress you're wearing, Eleanor," someone says, and Eleanor has to look down to remind herself of what she's got on. The day they cut geometry must have been the day Mrs. Tripp demonstrated that the shortest distance between two points was a straight line.

"Oh, that's a long story. And boring. Drug-induced cataracts. Jimmy Bergman said so. The doctor gave me drops for an inflammation and forgot to stop me from taking them. I'd still be using them now if I hadn't gone to another doctor."

"When did you start talking to Jimmy Bergman?"

"When I got his number from Eric. He's living in Hollywood now. Trying to write a novel. I never lost touch with him. I used to bump into him all the time when I lived on the Upper West Side."

"I wonder what he's like now," says Jane.

"Larger," says Eleanor. "Not married. Jimmy's taken up snakes."

"Yuk."

"Do people in prisons say yuk?"

"A friend's children say yuk."

Eleanor is silent, thinking that her own children have grown up without once laying eyes on Jane. She can be selfish.

Jane asks again about her eyes, and Eleanor goes over the events of the year. Sketchily.

"What was the worst part?"

"The worst part was before the operation. I couldn't see anything. There was this fog. I was—losing things. My husband, my children. They're still foggy."

She brushes an imaginary hair from her forehead. She looks troubled.

"I haven't seen the children since they were babies," says Jane.

"I have pictures of them," Eleanor says, getting up and getting her wallet. "Here." She hands Jane two school pictures.

"They're still blond!" says Jane. "They're gorgeous." She peers at the photos. "She looks like me, doesn't she?" she says, pointing to Julie.

"Yes," says Eleanor, "she does. I never noticed it."

Jane hands the pictures back as if she wants to keep them. Eleanor knows better than to offer them to her.

Jane shakes her head as if to clear it. "Why were you calling Jimmy and Eric?"

"Oh, I don't know. To find out if there were some things in the world that stayed the same. I felt lost."

Neither of them looks at the other.

"What was the surgery like?" Jane asks.

"Not bad. The worst part was having the eye patch come off and not seeing anything. So I called Jimmy, and he said I had nothing to worry about."

"I knew," says Jane, "there was a reason we were always doing his homework. Remember how many mistakes he made in biology? You got a higher grade on the Regents than he did. Why did you believe him?"

"Because you only lie to your own patients."

She touches her hair. It's still wet.

"It changed me," she says abruptly, surprising herself.

"How?"

"I didn't trust anything. Not myself. How can you trust yourself when you're a malfunctioning machine? *And* I got tired of talking. No one talks to tell anyone else anything. It's patter. It's social glue. To keep the other person sitting next to you when you want company. *I* couldn't say what I meant. It would have been one long wail. You can't do that to other people. Then when Toh started to drive me, I could barely see the car and he could barely speak the language and I thought, fine, now I can just ignore him. And the next thing, we were knotted together, I don't know, like blood vessels. No one has the slightest idea, they don't even begin to suspect. Tom doesn't. He doesn't want to.

"Remember I used to complain that he didn't take illnesses anyone in the family had seriously? I thought it was callous, but it wasn't. It was a loving thing, really. He didn't want to admit how sick we were. He doesn't want to see this, either. Why should he? It doesn't make sense. What would I do with a twenty-seven-year-old Chinese student who doesn't speak the language? Well, now he speaks it fairly well. You'd be surprised how hard it is to get into fights when you don't spend your time talking, or when it's so hard to talk. But that's what they think, anyway: What would she want with him? She's so much older. She's happily married. She's *famous*. What on earth would they *talk* about?"

"Oh, Eleanor," says Jane, "you've fallen in love with him, or whatever it is you've done, to prove a theory."

Eleanor considers.

"No," she says, "the feeling came first, then the theory. If there is a theory. He's the most admirable person I know."

"You idealize everyone."

"I don't have to idealize him. He's the strongest person I ever met. He is, really. The way he came here. The way he manages. The way he *is*. The way he can survive alone. If he has to."

"You'll be surviving alone soon," says her grandmother, "if you don't wake up."

"I think about my mother and grandmother a lot," says Eleanor.

Jane watches her, curious.

"After the eye trouble started, they were the *only* people I heard talking. I knew I wasn't really hearing voices, but I might as well have been. They drowned everyone else out."

Jane sighs. "Everyone's parents were monsters," she says.

"Not Toh's. You can tell by the way he's turned out."

"Trust me. Everyone's parents were monsters."

"They're quieting down now," says Eleanor, "my mother and grandmother."

"If I didn't know you so well, I'd lock you up."

"That's why I'm talking to *you*," Eleanor says.

"Well," says Jane, "I hear from my father all the time."

"He's all you ever cared about," Eleanor says.

"That, I'm afraid, is the truth," says Jane, thinking, that's why I live here alone, unmarried, envying other people their children. "Let's eat something. I'm hungry."

Eleanor smiles. Jane always got hungry when her father was mentioned. The snow swirls outside as if it has intentions, as if it wants to get in.

SEVENTEEN

DOES HE KNOW how old you are?" Jane asks while she beats eggs for an omelette.

"The kids told him the first time he came to a movie with us."

"He's part of the family?"

"Yes."

"What *do* you do together?"

"Not much. We walk, we talk. We look at old family albums: mine. I watch him cook. He teaches me to write Chinese words. I give him books to read and he circles the words he doesn't know and I tell him what they mean. I know how I feel when I'm with him, not just then, but how I *always* felt. Before things went wrong. Do you know what I mean? It's like learning a new language. Or relearning an old one. Words don't matter. They aren't the syllables of it."

Jane stops, a wooden spoon poised in the air.

"And if Tom finds out?"

"He won't find out."

"And if he does?"

"The world would come to an end. He thinks I'm better than I am."

"What about Toh? What does he think will happen?"

"I don't know. We never talk about it. Well, we did

once, sort of. I think he knows it will stop eventually. He tried to stop it once, and when I started to see him again, I asked him if he missed me. He said he missed me, but he could, you know, do without me. But it was empty. Probably he'll find someone his own age or he'll just . . ."

"Just what?"

"Heal."

"Is that what you're doing? Healing?"

She thinks. "It's like going back and starting over as if you could . . ." She hesitates. "As if you could go back into a previous life and repair some of the holes you took with you into this one. Do you think I'm crazy?"

Jane considers.

"You're not obsessed again, the way you were by that crazy mathematician? Remember him? The one you wouldn't let out of your sight for five years?"

"I'm not obsessed. If I don't see Toh, I don't see him. When we go to the country I miss him for a while and then I don't. The mathematician, by the way, wasn't crazy *then*. He is *now*."

"I don't even want to know," says Jane, "how you come to have that information." She takes a comb out of her bathrobe pocket and runs it through her hair. "It's some kind of bizarre transference," she says at last.

"Don't say that!" Eleanor says, jumping up. *"Every-thing* is transference. All our loves are first loves."

"Is that so? When did you become a devout Freu-dian?"

"I didn't. I found that idea all by myself when I de-cided to call Edward, the crazy mathematician you asked about. Do you remember much about him?"

"Who can forget him? You didn't talk about any-thing else for five years. *Five.*"

"I decided to call him, I don't know why. One day I

woke up and it seemed unnatural that someone you were once so close to would disappear from your life as if he were dead, and then I realized I'd been pretending he *was* dead all these years, and I decided to call him."

"Oh, my God."

"There wasn't anything *strange* about it, Jane. I wanted to talk to him. You know, to ask him what *he* thought had been going on all those years we were together, and he said he'd just remarried and his wife was going to China, not permanently, for a visit. So I asked him if he'd like me to get the names of Toh's parents for his wife. It's not easy, managing in a Communist country. I suppose I thought that would put me in his good graces. He's still mad at me for giving the stereo he built to the janitor after we split up. I asked Toh about it, would he mind if this perfect stranger went to his house in Peking and made all the authorities suspicious. At least that's what I was afraid would happen. At that point, I liked him well enough, as much as I usually like people, but that's when it started. We began this *talking,* or whatever it is we do."

"If I hadn't given you a Rorschach that Christmas vacation ten years ago," says Jane, "I'd change my mind about your being sane, call in two friends and stick you in a padded cell."

"Maybe I've gone crazy since you gave me the test."

"No chance, Eleanor. You're perfectly sane, if it's sane to spite Edward's wife by getting so much closer to someone from China than she could, if it's a good idea to want to show Edward how much better you are than his wife after so many years. How many is it? Nineteen years? When you don't care about him anymore, when you're just calling him to make sure he's not dead."

"*All* those things occurred to me. *More* things occurred to me. Take my word for it. It's not analyzable. It's a phenomenon."

"A dangerous phenomenon."

"Maybe."

"But you don't care?"

"No."

"Not even that you might hurt everyone? The children? The short people in the house?"

"*Of course* I care about that. But they won't find out."

"*No one* suspects anything? That's hard to believe."

"Well, maybe Gloria does. She's jealous of Toh. She thinks he's taken her place in our household."

"How's Gloria these days?"

"She doesn't change. It's horrible. You pick up the phone and she just starts. Her gums are bad, she'll kill herself if a front tooth has to come out. *I've* had surgery, but it doesn't show. She'd rather have cancer than gum trouble, because people can see spaces between your teeth but they can't see cancer. If the bathroom's ceiling's coming down, do I think the landlady's doing it deliberately, dripping water through the ceiling so she'll get fed up and move out? Sometimes I answer the phone and she doesn't even bother saying hello. I pick up the receiver and there's this voice saying, A big piece of plaster fell in the tub while I was taking a gymnastics lesson—I could have gotten hurt if I'd been in the bath, and on and on and on. When she stops to inhale, I try to say one word: How about taking a shower, they take less time. But she rolls over you: Oh, no, you know how nervous I am, I need a bath. I never take showers. Now she's found someone, a stockbroker who's a patron of the arts. They're perfect for each other. Completely inflexible, the two of them. *They* don't sleep together. He sits on a couch until four in the morning while she watches television and he studies the stock market report. She's asked him to stay overnight a hundred times, but he always asks why should he? He only lives a few blocks away.

"She got into an argument with him this fall because he wanted to postpone a date with her so he could talk to an old friend whose wife died and she called up to ask me if I thought she was unreasonable to object. She didn't see why she was. So what if the man's wife died. *She* had the appointment before the other man did. For nine o'clock. Breakfast. Very New Yorkerish, those two. He *looks* completely right, of course."

"Does she still stay in your house when you go away for the summers?"

"Not anymore. Every time she comes she fills the house with cockroaches and mice. She traps them and lets them loose when she comes to our house. She says she's always lived with cockroaches and mice. She's used to them. *We're* peculiar because we don't like them. She talks about them as if they're members of the family. This summer, Toh and his uncle are going to stay."

"Gloria knows that?"

"I haven't told her yet. I can wait to face the tears, the pathetic act. She doesn't stay *in* the house anyway. She spends all her time lurking around her own apartment waiting for this paragon she's latched onto to call. He won't come all the way out to Brooklyn just to see her. That's what she says. Who cares? I don't have the patience for it."

"Why do you bother with her"

Eleanor sighs and sits down on one of the high stools near the little counter running the length of the kitchen wall.

"She has one virtue," she says at last. "She never changes. You can count on her to be the same. I can trust her. I used to think she was the only person I could trust."

"I hate to tell you this," says Jane, "but that's a path-
ological friendship you have there."

"I know. But I keep thinking . . . I keep thinking that
I could have ended up like her if things hadn't worked out
well. She's like the Ghost of Christmas Future, narrowly
averted."

"I tell you what, Eleanor. You *better* worry about
Gloria. People like that have a sixth sense. Just threaten
their interest and they become clairvoyant."

"Oh, I don't think so. She wouldn't dare. She's afraid
of me."

"Isn't she still waiting around for you to die so she
can have your husband?"

Eleanor looks at her oddly, gets up suddenly and
walks to the window. Snow on snow on snow.

"She's waiting," she says. "Let's change the subject.
You know what Julie said when we were coming home
from the country last week? She said she wanted to be an
eye doctor, and I told her that was selfish of her. I'd already had my eyes operated on. She should think of something else. You know what she said? She thought a long
time and then asked me: What have you got left?"

"That's not funny, Eleanor."

"It's funny."

"Does Toh know you had a hysterectomy?"

"Yes."

"What did he say?"

"He cried."

"Why?"

"Oh, who knows, Jane?"

Eleanor flops down on the couch, on her back. One
leg is straight, the other dangles over the edge. She knows

why he cried. Because there could be no such things as babies. Because they could never stay together.

"Jane," she says, "you're seeing someone who's married, aren't you?"

Jane nods.

"That's part of the reason I stopped calling you. You can't resist married men. Women are so ruthless."

"And men aren't?"

"No, they're not. Not the good ones anyway."

"Have you ever thought of writing them down, your observations on the differences between the sexes?"

"Oh, come on."

"Eleanor, everyone's ruthless when it comes to something they need. If they need it to survive."

"Men aren't," Eleanor says stubbornly. She sits up on the couch and looks at Jane. She is a blue-eyed blonde, chubby, her hair in curls, a superannuated Botticelli angel.

"Are you sure she's Jewish?" asks her mother. "Blond hair and a name like Jane? I don't think she's Jewish."

"Yesterday," Eleanor says, "my brother called me—"

"Which brother?"

"Robert. The one in California."

"I remember who Robert is," Jane says. "He knocked out my front tooth with a tennis racket. Didn't *you* knock out *his* front tooth with a piece of pipe?"

"I knocked out his tooth. I avenged you before you were injured. Anyway, he called, and it was the usual thing. He was lecturing me about my taxes, how we don't have any savings, we're grossly underinsured, life insurance, that's what he was talking about. Where are our wills? All the rest of it. Then he said something about how he shaved off his beard and now he had to shave twice a

day, the beard grew in so heavily. I was shocked. *Shocked.*
As if he'd said something indecent. I don't think of him as
belonging to another sex. I don't recognize differences between the sexes. I'm not the one to write on their differences."

"Miss Deadly, The Vampire of 1956, doesn't recognize the difference between the sexes? You always knew
what to do with the men who followed you home. You
knew how to *make* them follow you home. You didn't
know whether they were men or women?"

"Until I fell in love with them. Then they weren't
separate anymore. Do you know what I mean?"

Jane does not.

"Then they were part of me, so close there couldn't *be*
any differences. It didn't matter who was what sex."

"After you fell in love with a man, you stopped being
attracted to him?"

"Oh, no," Eleanor says impatiently, "but sex wasn't
the first thing anymore. It was the lack of difference. You
really don't understand?"

Jane really doesn't.

"Well, one day Toh came over to give the kids Ping-
Pong lessons, and they had two friends there, so there were
three girls and one boy, my son David. Toh was playing
with Davey, and the three girls, all seven-year-olds, were
running here and there collecting the Ping-Pong balls that
were hit off the table, and I was sitting in this big wicker
chair on the other side of the porch, watching them, and
outside it was snowing, and I thought, this is what happiness is. You'll never forget this. It happens that way sometimes, even when something's still going on, you know you
won't forget it. Now when I get down, I conjure that up
and I feel better. *That* was one of the most sexual experi-

ences I've ever had. Do you know what I mean now? It was like falling in love with the world."

Jane sighs and folds her legs under her, a Buddha, and just like this, her stomach getting rounder every day. Rounder, she thinks, but empty. She wanted children. She still does. Eleanor has two children and has had one miscarriage and she says she doesn't know the difference between the sexes. What on earth is she talking about?

"In psychoanalytic jargon," says Jane, "we call that the oceanic feeling."

"I know," says Eleanor sadly, "but it's different and I can't say how."

"As to being in love with the world, you've always talked to your furniture. You once talked to a cow and got us surrounded by the herd, remember that? We had to yell for help. You thought if you talked long enough, eventually the cows would understand what you wanted."

"That's what the farmer said the cows were trying to do," Eleanor reminds her.

"How, exactly," Jane asks her, "did communing with the cows differ from communing with the little team of Ping-Pong players on the porch? Aside from the fact that you weren't in danger of being eaten on the porch. *I* thought that was what the cows were thinking while you were talking: What a delicious voice. Let's eat them. I was never so terrified in my life, not even when you dragged me onto the Cyclone at Revere Beach. I came all the way to Boston and you tried to kill me again. How were the two things different?"

"In degree?" Eleanor asks tentatively. "Maybe the same thing raised to a much greater level of intensity isn't the same thing anymore."

She pats the top of her head to feel if it's getting dry.

"I think that's the heart of it. I have to think about that."

"Think about Tom," suggests Jane, "or is Toh the only person you call when you're caught in a blizzard?"

"Oh, God," says Eleanor, jumping up, "Tom!"

Jane watches Eleanor call, Eleanor who could never lie (except to her parents), who got into trouble when she started giving interviews because if someone asked a question she thought she had to answer it truthfully.

"But why?" Jane asked her after the disaster at *The New York Post*. "They don't come with a lie detector. Say whatever you want."

And Eleanor helplessly shaking her head: I can't, I can't, I can't. What is this new capacity for duplicity, guile, betrayal, hypocrisy, all those wonderful things it takes to carry on an affair? Perhaps, thinks Jane, Eleanor has decided to think about all this later. She's capable of that, capable of closing down rooms in her mind the way energy-conscious householders close off rooms in the winter to save on their fuel bills. She ought to know; she's been in one of those closed rooms for the last five years.

"No, I'll stay here until tomorrow," Eleanor is saying. "I don't *know* the number. Jane scraped it off the phone so patients can't get it if they break into her apartment. Her office number's written on a piece of paper taped to the refrigerator. Call it and they'll call here. Toh called? Is he all right? Good."

She listens.

"Well, tell him if he doesn't do his homework, he can't watch the movie about the *Titanic* tomorrow night."

She listens again.

"Put her on the phone," she says.

While she waits, she takes the rubber band off her pony tail and shakes her hair so that it hangs straight down her back.

"No, I am not dead," she says into the receiver, "but you will be if I come home and don't find your room clean. *How* did he get into your room to chew their eyes off? Ask Emmeline to glue the eyes back in tomorrow. She's staying overnight? Good. One less person to worry about. No, Julie, she's not sleeping in your room. She's sleeping on the couch. You called Toh? That's nice. Go to bed. Put your father back on the phone."

She pulls her hair over her shoulder and looks at Jane. When she hangs up, she sits down on the couch, silent. Minutes pass while Jane watches her.

"Julie called Toh?" asks Jane. "How big a part of the family is he?"

"A very big part."

"Who chews whose eyes? What are you running in that house in Brooklyn?"

"Our German shepherd chewed the eyes out of the stuffed animals' heads. All shepherds do it. Julie's supposed to keep her door on a latch."

Jane regards her silently.

"Do you remember when my grandmother was senile?" Eleanor asks. "She thought men were women and women were men. It could be hereditary. Early senility."

Jane doesn't answer, but watches Eleanor as if she is seeing something just behind her. Here, she thinks, is the person in back of whom she sat, day after boring day, for six years. She can make the classroom days run quickly backward or forward, and there is Eleanor, her long braid hanging down her back, and there she is again, hair short, elegant beyond her years, and there she is, hair curly; it's humid. When Eleanor is about, no one needs a weather

report. Very humid, very curly hair. Very dry, absolutely
straight.

And now they are about to graduate, and Jimmy
Bergman is on the other side of the room, trying to catch
Eleanor's eye. He wants Jane to tap Eleanor on the back
so he can make faces at her, or tell her something. Eleanor
can read lips. She can walk around a room with her eyes
closed. She always used to say you never knew when finding your way around in the dark would come in handy.
Even then she was afraid of her senses failing her. Look
how fears come true.

She remembers Eleanor walking through the rooms
of her house with her eyes closed. She remembers the two
of them sitting on the quilted coverlet of Eleanor's bed,
doing their homework, that little room she had under the
attic, shaped like a shoe box, narrow, coffinlike, such a
strange ceiling. Eleanor used to say she was going to wall-
paper it and she did. It was something, sitting in that
room, as if they were sitting on the ceiling and the floor
was above them. She can't have changed.

Jane doesn't believe people change. Still, Eleanor
isn't the same. You can stare at her without first sedating
her. She remembers going up to Eleanor's room, not finding her there, and climbing up the attic stairs to her closet.
There she was, sitting on the cedar chest she'd dragged
over to the attic window, cobwebs everywhere, sitting in
the lotus position ("I'm not showing off. It's the only position I'm comfortable in."), sadly watching the boys from
their school playing baseball in the elementary school
yard. As if she knew she would never be part of life and
was resigning herself to it. Where did it come from, such
hopelessness which fed like snails on warm rocks. Beautiful enough, the snails, in their own way. And then one

day, one of the boys noticed her sitting there, and she never went up to watch them again. If she had a secret ambition then, it must have been to be invisible.

"You're not senile, you're not crazy," Jane says at last. "No one gets off the hook that easily. You're having an affair with a twenty-seven-year-old student. Because he doesn't speak the language or because you knew him in another life. All right, I can understand that. But he's a friend of the family. I suppose he and Tom get on well?"

"Oh, yes. Toh's taught Tom to cook Chinese food and Tom's taught him to cook pasta."

"Then you must have to lie all the time."

"I don't. I don't say anything. It's the usual thing for me to be somewhere else in the afternoons. Unless it's something very interesting, Tom doesn't want to know what I've been doing. He's had enough of the jacket cover wars."

"You never could keep a secret."

"I don't think of it as a secret. It's nobody's business. It's not . . . in this world. Children, they know everything you say or do. They listen at doors with stethoscopes. When they're not up at night filing their elbows so they can keep their mother black and blue, they're pressing wine glasses to the floor listening to what Tom and I say. But they have no idea about this. When Toh and I go into that white room, no one can hear us—there's no one else to hear us."

"Like after a nuclear war?"

"*Not* like that. And I don't feel guilty. You're seeing a married man. Don't you? Feel guilty?"

"Guilty! I don't recommend adultery. After three years, you can start sleeping without a couple of drinks. I'll tell you something. You'd be a lot happier having an affair with one of your photographs or stained glass windows. Sexual relations with a window isn't recognized as grounds for divorce. Not even in the South."

"It may seem strange to you, but Tom's gotten jealous of tables and chairs."

"Don't kid yourself into thinking Toh's another table or chair."

"He was for a while, when he didn't talk. But he talks now. I miss the way he used to say things. 'Snick' for 'snack.' 'Nip' for 'nap.' Things like that."

"You miss the baby talk."

"It's killing you, isn't it? Not being able to analyze this away."

"Sometimes," says Jane, "it's hard to know whether you're awake while these things are going on. You are, aren't you?"

Eleanor nods.

"We're over forty. Going on forty-one, as your grandmother used to say. Maybe he just makes you feel younger."

"*That's* the one thing that bothers me. I look so much older when I'm with him. I look old altogether. Don't I?"

"I'll get a magnifying glass and look for some wrinkles."

"I know I look older."

"Older than what? The Great Wall of China? That's the last thing I'd worry about. In your place, that is. *I* collect the names of plastic surgeons."

"I don't worry. Only about Toh. It's ridiculous, he's so young. When we stop seeing each other, he'll find someone to marry. Men always do. Sometimes I worry about what will happen when we don't see each other anymore. I expect to bleed to death."

"And you say you're not obsessed?"

"Your mother is suicidal and she wasn't obsessed."

"First of all, she never *was* normal. Second of all, she's mourning a real death. Third, she was *married* to my father."

"Married," says Eleanor, as if she's never heard the word before. What can that mean: married?

"You don't sound like lovers," says Jane, "you sound like mother and child."

"Sometimes we are. He cooks. I gave that up five years ago. Some kind of protest against responsibility. Besides, it's easier to stay thin if you're not in the kitchen much."

"Mother and child, a chair, no difference between the sexes, not a sexual relationship," says Jane, turning it over while Eleanor watches her with amusement. There's something she almost gets hold of, but at the last minute, it slides out of view. She looks at her friend, fluid against the couch.

"It sounds wonderful," she says, blinking her eyes fast.

"It is, whatever it is."

"Would you rather it weren't sexual at all?"

"Oh, yes. Then it would be more intense. The sex takes the edge off it. My mind," she says, puzzled, "doesn't seem to have much to do with it."

"Maybe," says Jane slowly, "you should let your mind in on this."

"I'm sick of my mind. I'm out of it, and out of my skin too, all at once."

"You won't be able to stay out forever."

"I know," says Eleanor, who is, in any case, no longer in the room. Her body is there, but she is gone.

EIGHTEEN

THE SNOW KEEPS FALLING. Jane gets up and looks for their high school year book. Eleanor remembers Jane staying home from school, pretending to have the mumps. Every day after school she'd stop at Jane's house, sit at the edge of the bed, and wait until Jane pretended to get up. She knew that under the covers Jane had movie magazines. When Jane would ask her what she was doing there, Eleanor would say she didn't want Jane to think she was fooling everyone.

"What an ugly building," Eleanor says, looking at the year book. "Look at all the poetry we wrote about that monstrosity. I don't know how we did it."

"If we'd told the truth we'd have been thrown out of school. The Nassau Chamber of Commerce would have buried us at the crossroads. Besides, then we thought it was beautiful."

She asks Eleanor if she's coming to the next reunion. Eleanor says no. She still hasn't forgiven the Roosevelt twins. They ruined her childhood.

"Eleanor, it's more than twenty years later."

"An elephant never forgets."

"I hope your husband isn't in the elephant family," Jane says, absently turning the pages. "Look. There we are in Chemistry class."

"They made an awful fuss over that little explosion," says Eleanor. "Is your brother still going to Star Trek conventions?"

"With his wife. They have ten pairs of wax ears in a temperature-controlled case."

And so it goes, on through the night.

In the morning Eleanor gets up first (but then she always did), disappears into the bathroom where she puts in her contact lenses like an automaton. Now the longest part of the procedure is washing her hands. Hello, overly brilliant world. No more having to put them in next to her cordless phone so that, if necessary, she can call her eye surgeon, an ambulance, four friends to carry her in a stretcher should she accidentally remove her cornea. She brushes her hair with Jane's brush. It never occurs to her to ask permission. When they were in high school, their brushes always had tangles of blond and black hair.

"It looks like a dog brush," says her mother, holding one up to the light. "Suppose one of you had lice?"

She looks at her face in the mirror. There she is. After the first surgery, and for some time before that, she couldn't see herself: a cloud, a blur only. She's finished. As long as her face is still there, she doesn't bother with makeup. She puts on lipstick if she's going to meet someone for lunch or if she's going to teach a class.

She wanders out into the living room and sits down, thinking about her old dentist. What was his life like, what was it like looking into people's mouths every day? How small the human mouth is. At least alligators have huge jaws. Working on them would bring a sense of accomplishment. You might even feel as if you were getting inside them. Perhaps that's what he didn't want to feel, using his little drill, his little mortar and pestle, his small, small tools. Perhaps from his perspective white teeth looked like the chalk cliffs of Dover.

In Jane's room, something hard hits the floor. Jane must have fallen asleep with a book. Angry because the night doesn't last forever, she has thrown the book down in a temper.

"Good morning," says Jane, stumbling out of her bedroom, eyes red, on a collision course with every object between her room and the kitchen.

"You want some coffee?" she asks Eleanor, who says no, she still doesn't drink it. One cup sends her up a wall.

Jane says her *heart* doesn't start beating until she's had two cups.

"How *did* we write all that poetry about Northside?" asks Eleanor.

Uh-oh, thinks Jane; she's stuck on a subject again. "It was the only high school we had," she says.

The only high school, the only life, the only husband, the only children, thinks Eleanor, who realizes she's tired of the limits the world sets and then thinks: isn't that too bad, Eleanor; isn't everyone tired?

Jane comes into the living room. The steam from her cup rises straight into the air, then bends at a right angle, reminding Eleanor of her house in Maine where she spends hours contemplating the way smoke rises from the chimneys of the houses across the brook in winter. In summer, you can't see the houses. They're hidden by the leaves.

"It was bad enough when we were kids," says Jane, "the way you could pull a comb through your hair and look as if you'd been primping for hours. At our age, it's obscene."

"I look my age."

"Then you don't look mine. Look at these wrinkles." She points to the corners of her eyes, the corners of her mouth, the furrows over her eyebrows, the loose skin on her throat.

"You look fine. If you'd stop rubbing your eyes. They're red."

They have nothing to talk about, but they're comfortable in the silence.

"I have a patient," Jane says, putting her cup down, "who insists she's adopted. There's nothing unusual in that, all children go through that stage. But this one keeps picking out a real set of parents every other week and she shows up at their doors at all hours of the night. With a camp trunk. Last week she showed up here. I pointed out that I didn't even have a husband, but she said that was all right; she understood. Men were rotten and it must have been hard for me, raising her alone, so she didn't hold it against me for giving her away."

"What did you do?"

"I called her parents. They're going to have to give her away soon. To an institution. God knows whose bell she'll ring next. They can't seem to keep her in the house. She's very bright."

"Maybe," Eleanor says thoughtfully, "a bear trap."

"She'd chew off her leg."

Silence.

"Didn't you ever think you were adopted?"

"Me? There was never the slightest doubt in my mind that I was the children of The Trolls. Oh, no. I knew there was no escape. I was theirs. When I was a child, I thought if I had X-ray vision and could see beneath my skin, I'd find my mother's and father's names tattooed on every bone. Adopted? What a wonderful idea."

"I used to think I was."

"Always unrealistic in a pinch," says Eleanor.

"How long has it been since they died?" asks Jane.
"You always thought they'd die in a car accident."

"Because they were always *having* accidents. Always
the same kind. It took them so long to decide to pull out of
an intersection, the car behind them crashed into their
trunk. Hoping to make up their minds for them, no doubt.
That's always been my theory. Three years."

She looks at her hand on the chair's armrest, starting
to tremble.

"Are you over it?"

"I'll never get over it. That's another of my theories.
No one ever gets over anything. You find some way to
move the pieces around, that's all. I remember everything.
It's a curse. I remember the first day at Northside when
Kevin Miller squashed an orange on the corner of my
desk. I remember running down the street, you know, in
front of the Catholic church. I remember what I was
wearing: a green watch plaid skirt and a white blouse,
seeing his face looming up, and hitting him, and the black
eye he had the next day, except it was blue and green, not
black. I was wearing that blue parka with the red lining,
the one your dog chewed up. I remember the icy light on
the church's stained glass windows, how cold the sand-
stone looked, everything."

Eleanor looks at her watch, gets up and says she has
to go. How has it gotten to be ten o'clock? She drops
Jane's borrowed robe on the floor, stands naked in the living room, and begins putting on her clothes.

"You were so shy about your body," says Jane. "You
used to get dressed in a closet."

"I had to. My brothers were always sneaking into my
room."

"You did the same thing in my house and your brothers weren't there. Mine wasn't either."

"Force of habit."

Your brother wasn't there, she thinks to herself, but your uncle was. She looks quickly at Jane, then away. There was a time when they believed they could read each other's minds.

She asks Jane if she misses her father; perhaps there is an end to it, after all. Jane tells her she is suing her father's doctor for wrongful death.

"Wrongful death?"

Jane explains that her father was treated for asthma, not heart failure. If he'd been diagnosed correctly, he'd still be alive.

"Let go, Jane," Eleanor says softly.

"I can't."

They're both reluctant to say goodbye. Eleanor, with both parents dead, Jane with her father gone, her mother threatening suicide, both of them forty, one with two children, both busy—how can they be sure they'll see each other again?

"Why are your eyelashes so short?" Jane asks suddenly.

"They cut them before the surgery. I should have known better than to brag about how long they were. Tempting fate. Everything looked so strange afterwards. It still does. The world looks gaudy, almost vulgar. I used to sit with a can of diet soda, caffeine-free Coke, the golden can. Anyway, it was so beautiful, a thing of radiance, and there I was, staring at it, thinking, all this beauty wasted on a soda can. I told the eye doctor colors seemed brighter and he said they were. Children see that way, but in adults the lens of the eye clouds over."

"Wordsworth was right."

"Not exactly. It's not our spirits that tarnish. It's our bodies. All physiological, the polluting of the clouds of glory."

They go out the apartment door and down the narrow concrete stairs.

"Are you ever going to visit me?" asks Eleanor.

"Are you ever home?"

"No, but we can work something out."

They hug each other, Eleanor in her sealskin coat (an antique; she didn't encourage anyone to kill animals), Jane in her yellow bathrobe.

"I don't want to go," says Eleanor.

"You never want to leave any place you've been," sighs Jane. "When you get home, you won't want to come back."

Eleanor starts to say something, stops, then pulls Jane toward her and kisses her.

"This time I'll come back," she says.

"Ha."

Jane watches Eleanor march through the snow to her car: a white car. How on earth did Eleanor, so indifferent to mundane things like cars, wind up with a white one? But it is clean and shines like spilled milk. Someone is taking care of it. Perhaps Toh.

Eleanor scrapes the snow from the windows and unlocks the car door. Once inside, she turns the key in the ignition and the motor immediately starts up. She sighs, thinking of the long drive home, the road out of town past the old red brick hospital, onto the highway, the drive along the coast, the turn onto the streets where her grandparents used to live, the drive down Ocean Avenue and

home. She decides not to go home right away. She looks at
the windshield she has just cleaned. Random flakes break
up the white sun like tiny prisms. Jane is standing in the
doorway to her apartment house, her arms folded tightly
across her chest, braced against the wind. The wind does
not come. The sun has polished the snow to a harsh, pure
shine and turned the town silent.

When Eleanor thinks of Cedarhurst, she thinks of her
old house and the noise that filled all its corners. Even
when there was something like peace, it growled omin-
ously, its sound like angry cats who had either just
stopped fighting or had not yet started. Out of the corner
of her eye, she sees Jane gesturing: roll down the window.

"Goodbye," Jane calls.

She waves and rolls up the window.

The roads are clear. Automatically, she makes the
turn which will take her to her parents' old house. It is an
English Tudor house built by the man who later gave his
name to the incomprehensible Levittown.

She parks across the street, inspecting it. The porch
which used to darken half the living room has been torn
down, but as she stares, the porch resurrects itself. The
snow disappears. The heavy green leaves of the oaks form
their eternal, flickering canopy as if, beneath their
branches, a continuous marriage of spirit to spirit were
taking place. Those who were unhappy on this earth are
receiving their second, final chance under these branches.

And there is Eleanor, climbing out of her parents'
bedroom window, hanging on to the wood trim of the
house, climbing in through her brother's window, pursu-
ing the television set he has taken and locked in his room.
A trip through the air for which she will be locked in her
own room after school for two weeks while her friends go
to sweet sixteen parties.

"You can't weaken," her mother is telling her father. "You can't let them think they're stronger than you are. You have to win."

And then there is smoke pouring out the front door because her grandmother has begun to cook something and wandered off, forgetting the stove, and there they are, the two sad-looking policemen, embarrassed by their guns, escorting her grandmother up the flagstone walk because she wandered all the way to the bus stop, boarded the bus, and at the end of the line saw no reason to get off when she was perfectly comfortable, and after that, Eleanor is in the back seat of the Hudson with her mother, while up front with her grandmother, whose white head is motionless, staring straight ahead, her aunt is driving to the home where her grandmother lived until the thinning artery of her heart dissolved her entirely.

And she remembers as if she had seen it herself, because she was told the story so often, of how her grandmother, whom she is said to take after, got to be the first person to enter Radio City Music Hall the day *Gone with the Wind* opened: first carefully packing a lunch in a waxed brown paper bag at home, then tucking it into one of her ample coat pockets, getting on the long line which had already turned the corner of the block, clutching at her chest just as a theater attendant goes by, the man catching her by the elbow while she informs him that it's her heart, her heart. And the horrified man steers her into the theater, all the way down the carpeted aisle to the seat her grandmother is not reluctant to select, under the vaulted ceiling midway to the great stage. He is lecturing her about coming out in such cold to stand in line, a woman with a bad heart, and helping her off with her good green wool coat, and then leaves to patrol the endless, frozen line waiting outside. Her grandmother, alone in the theater, takes out her brown paper bag and proceeds to eat with great satisfaction what she later said was one of the best meals she'd ever be likely to eat: two egg salad sandwiches on rye bread, two sour pickles, and three brownies, one of which (she always said how much self-control it took) she manages to save until after the movie begins and the theater darkens to a blackness almost as rich as the square cake she eats slowly so it will last as long as possible.

And now Eleanor is no longer in Cedarhurst, but back on the porch of the first apartment she remembers in Brooklyn, the door to her bedroom opening out into the second floor porch, standing there in her white nightgown, in her bare feet, eating a Melorol she has just stolen from the refrigerator freezer, thinking, this is how it would be, cold inside, cold outside, through and through, so pure, so pure and cold.

"So, how, Eleanor," asks her grandmother, "did such a priestess of purity come to take up with a Chinese child?"

"Don't you know, Grandma?" says Eleanor. "They say the Chinese are the sixth lost tribe of Israel."

"Are you trying to tell me that Toh is a Jewish name?"

A police car goes by and the driver waves at Eleanor. Does she know him? No, he's just waving at her because she isn't black.

It's too warm in the car and she turns down the heat. All those days, all odd-shaped, all part of a large puzzle in which they play a part, a jigsaw puzzle of a Brueghel painting, and, as with all old puzzles, many of the pieces forever missing. Isn't there more to life? Suppose that seagull circling above came down, turned into an angel, and told her there was nothing more. What would she do? Exactly what she does now. The car's baby blue dashboard is exactly the color of the sky.

She has a white car with baby blue seats because her parents gave her this car when they could no longer tolerate worrying about their grandchildren being driven about in what her father had called The Deathmobile. They bought the car soon after they moved to Florida. They insisted upon a heater that worked perfectly, although they never expected to use it. They were such careful people, thorough, so organized. Eleanor pats the heater switch and her eyes fill. She makes a U-turn and heads for the highway. The sandy shore will be lined with ice. The waves will be slate blue and gray.

A stray puff of wind blows some surface snow across the windshield, like the glitter on the costumes she used to wear in school plays. On both sides of the highway, the snow is deep. The trains and buses must have been slow last night. Wednesday night. On Wednesday night, Gloria teaches her gymnastics class at the same college where Eleanor teaches. Trouble. Gloria, who lives alone, pampers herself as if she were her own, and only, child. When she has a cold, she calls Eleanor every twenty minutes to report on the ravages of the disease.

"But you don't understand," she tells Eleanor. "If I get sick, I don't get paid. I don't have people to cover for me. I don't have rich parents I can run to."

You do. You have everything.

The perpetual subtext.

What started out as friendship has turned, slowly, to hatred. The sound of Gloria's voice on the phone sets Eleanor to considering a new, unlisted number. And how long has this been going on? Eleven years. Almost as long as Eleanor's marriage. And how long has Eleanor been trying to disentangle herself? For almost seven years, during which time their conversations have become ever more poisonous.

"Why do you talk to her?" her husband asks.

"Oh," says Eleanor, "it's easier than not."

Surely Gloria will feel the hatred curling through the miles of telephone wire, long, black, snakelike, through tunnels below ground, through wires wending their way through masses of iced-over branches.

"And if all your hair does fall out?" asks Eleanor.

"I'd rather die."

"Then die," says Eleanor, who used to say, "You always say you'd rather die." Or she says, "For God's sake, get some perspective. None of us *want* to have perspective, but it's necessary all the same."

To have perspective, according to Eleanor, means to know *you* are the vanishing point on the horizon.

When she is particularly vengeful, Eleanor says, "I don't know what to do with my hair. It's so thick. I can't control it. I don't want to go to a beauty parlor; they'll cut all of it off."

Before she can finish that last sentence, Gloria is off, a symphony of self-pity culminating in the great choral movement, during which she transcends herself and becomes sixty people all with the same complaints: hemorrhoids, her broken arm which left her with a scar (visible! visible!), low blood pressure. She has all her mother's ailments, or almost all. She's sure to get the rest soon.

"But you have a father, too," Eleanor used to remind her. "He's almost seventy and strong as a horse."

The truth is, Eleanor cannot part with Gloria because she doesn't believe there are people she can love whom she has not already found. If she shakes her hair more and more brazenly at Gloria, it is because Toh has finally convinced her there *are* others. At night, she falls asleep wondering if there may not be many others. She is beginning to trust the world. Isn't it odd that it should have taken so long? By now, many people her age have died or are dying. Did they know the world could be trusted or did they die before they found out?

Gloria, always aware of danger to herself, correctly estimates the menace Toh has become.

"It sounds as if he lives there," she says again and again.

"Sooner or later, he'll want friends his own age. It's only natural. *You* get attached to someone every time you turn around. You *always* think whoever it is is wonderful, at least for a few weeks. Then you get disillusioned."

Lately, Gloria asks different questions. Does Tom like Toh? Or is it Wu? (Wu is Toh's uncle.) "You spend a lot of time with Toh, don't you?"

"I have to put the kids to bed," says Eleanor, and hangs up the receiver. She stares at it, knowing that at the other end Gloria is still talking, still thinking they're connected.

Last night, Gloria would have seen the snow and decided she could not possibly make the trip back to the Village, and she would have arrived at the house, found Tom, who, like his wife, can never say no to anything, not to an earthworm, not to a vulture in distress, and she would have slept on the couch. This morning, the subject would have been Toh. Was Toh.

Yes, it's terrible to have your own father disown you, terrible to have him look through you as if you were so much empty space, terrible not to be spoken to by him for twenty-six years. A horrible thing, really, but does it justify a lifetime of spoiling oneself, trying to spoil things for others?

Perhaps, thinks Eleanor, I am the embodiment of my

dead mother and grandmother, coming back to haunt me.
It is a horrible thought. Toh's influence. He is so superstitious.

"I felt like there was a ghost around me all day," he
said the day after the car accident.

Does he believe in ghosts?

No, but all the same, sometimes they're around you.
You know they're there when everything goes wrong.

She passes the buildings which used to be the old rid-
ing stables and on impulse pulls over, backs up, and sits
looking out past the water. The familiar caw, caw, caw of
passing seagulls. Flying cats. Eeeyaow. Eeeyaow. Is she
going to delay forever? She looks at the gray-white waves
breaking into foam against the icy sand. Time to go home.
They will all be worried.

She knows, as certainly as if she had been in the room
listening, that Gloria has been talking to Tom. Gloria is
intensely suspicious of Toh because Eleanor so rarely
mentions him. Gloria knows that she has been supplanted.
Not that there is anything to supplant, but Gloria thinks
there is. Hard for Gloria (for anyone) to understand how
resentments build, how Eleanor still does not forgive her
for calling her in the hospital after her hysterectomy and
telling her what a terrible cold she had, her joints were
beginning to ache, she'd call back in a few hours and tell
Eleanor how she was. She thought she'd have to go out
and buy a digital thermometer. She couldn't learn to read
a regular one.

And the phone rang in twenty minutes: "It's a hundred and two, my throat hurts, it could be strep, I don't
want to go to the doctor and give him"—give him!
thought Eleanor; you're *paying* him!—"thirty-five dollars
when it might only be a virus," but if she got sicker, she'd
miss her classes. What should she do? She wasn't very

strong. She might look strong, but she wasn't. Should she skip her gymnastics classes or should she go sweat it out of her system?

"Hold on a minute," says Eleanor. "They're changing my I.V."

She puts down the still-talking phone.

"You can't imagine how bad I feel," the phone says when she picks it up.

The design, but not the nature of the fabric, changes with the years. For the last two, the subject has been Colin, who takes her to the theater, but will not let her meet his friends. It's embarrassing, she's told him so, and what about his apartment? She's never set foot in it, The only person who has is his mother. Is that normal?

Thanks to Gloria, Eleanor is beginning to turn against the telephone, her truest friend, her umbilicus to the rest of the world. Odd, but she cannot really speak to Toh on the phone. She has to see him. If she can't watch his face, she might as well be speaking into a phone that's gone dead. When Gloria finishes asking Tom about Colin (Is it normal? Is it normal?), she will start in on Toh.

Eleanor drives slowly. She is in no hurry to get home, if she still has a home.

NINETEEN

THE SNOW, falling all day, has finally been pronounced a blizzard by the radio, and this gives Gloria the excuse she needs to go to Eleanor's house, five blocks from the college, so conveniently located, instead of to her own apartment, two blocks from the subway station. Lately, she has been hearing little about Toh, and is beginning to suspect that Eleanor has secret plans to have him stay in her house during the summer. Still, Eleanor has not asked her to remove the large drawerful of summer clothing she keeps in Julie's room.

She cannot believe Eleanor is planning to evict her, not when she's stayed there for almost ten summers. Who will forward Eleanor's mail? Not an ignorant Chinese person. Still, she had better find out the worst while she can still do something about it. Summers in New York are terribly hot. Eleanor cannot imagine how hot. Her own apartment is perfectly located. She has a fear of empty time, but then so do a lot of people, a kind of chronological claustrophobia in reverse, that's what Eleanor calls it, whatever she means by that. She has to know, as she's told Eleanor, who still doesn't understand, that she can run here or there *at any moment* or she'd go crazy.

"You're already crazy," Eleanor says to this. "You're out of your mind. Literally. You're afraid to be in it."

Is it her imagination, or has Eleanor become nastier

lately? Whenever she complains about how lonely she is, Eleanor tells her to get a cat.

As she walks down Bedford Avenue, toward the art-deco building on the corner where she turns right, Gloria takes stock of her situation. I'm not stupid, she thinks. I can see what's going on. It must have to do with the roaches.

"There are never," says Eleanor, "roaches in this house until you bring over your bags."

Well, her apartment *is* crawling with roaches, but so what? She grew up with them. Rich little Eleanor, growing up on Long Island, where the only bugs were the ants who came into her mother's fancy pink and green kitchen in the spring. There *must* have been roaches there. Everyone has roaches. She's no fool. Eleanor insists she's never had roaches before just to make Gloria uncomfortable. Eleanor accuses her of finding them friendly.

"You like them," says Eleanor. "They keep you company. Otherwise you'd complain to the landlady or spray them yourself."

"I don't have that kind of money," Gloria tells her.

It must be more than the roaches.

If she stays in her own apartment this summer, she'll have to pay an enormous bill for air conditioning. Her apartment gets so hot. When she stays at Eleanor's, it's assumed that she won't pay the utility bills. Of course, that was the arrangement when she used to take care of the garden and she sees no reason why it shouldn't continue that way even though she doesn't take care of it now because she's too busy waiting for Colin and grading compositions for two professors and teaching classes in gymnastics. And she is afraid of bee bites. She's allergic to bees.

Eleanor may be the one who's always in the hospital,

but she, Gloria, is the weak one. Look at how she's shivering now. Of course, part of that comes from being bone-thin, but part of it is natural weakness, inherited delicacy. She turns the corner: one large Victorian house after another, some turreted, some not, snow filtering down the chasm of dark air between them, snow lit like souls as the flakes fall in front of the street lights, themselves shaped like drooping metal pods. She could never afford a house like these, but anyway what would she do with one? Who wants to live in the middle of the wilderness where there's absolutely nothing to do and all you see all day is families or women pushing baby carriages? Some life those women have.

She sees them in the summer, that's the only disadvantage to living at Eleanor's, red and puffing, the babies in their dark blue enameled carriages, the frozen meat and the vegetables just under the babies' feet, the bottoms of the carriages piled high with groceries, plastic bags filled with fruit tied to the carriage handles. That's a life? She'd rather be dead. She saw enough of that with her own mother.

You can't convince me they like it, thinks Gloria. They say they do, but I know better. My mother used to say how happy she was and then she'd slave away at home and cry. If she'd had more imagination, she'd have drunk the Clorox instead of using it on the sink.

Once upon a time, her mother used to paint backdrops for department store windows—murals, really. Now she sits at the fly-specked window and stares out at the street. The last time she went out she went to the butcher's and fainted in front of the store and had to be carried inside. She woke up and found herself looking at bloody, white-veined slabs of meat. The great adventure of her last quarter century. Gloria's seen enough of it. That's what marriage is: waking up and finding yourself staring at the bloody, hoofless legs of animals.

Of course it's different if you're successful like Eleanor and everyone invites you to give lectures at this college and that, and you can afford a snooty housekeeper and don't have to bother with your children and if your husband puts up with your moods and doesn't try to keep you prisoner in your own house.

"Why in the world," asks Eleanor, "would you marry someone who would keep you prisoner in your own house?"

"Sometimes," says Gloria, "you don't have a choice."

"Unless you're in an iron lung," says Eleanor, "you always have a choice."

The optimism of a rich bitch, thinks Gloria. She decides she shouldn't think about her friend that way until she finds out what Eleanor intends to do with the house this summer. I can be awfully nasty, thinks Gloria; I might become nasty over this business of the house and then where will I be? Eleanor is her only friend. Then she remembers that Eleanor has stopped calling her at night to read her what she's written during the day.

"Well," Gloria's been saying, "I'll read it when you get it Xeroxed."

"Mmmm," is all Eleanor says and doesn't send her a Xerox. It would be easy enough to give her one. They both have offices on the same floor of the college, have olive-drab mailboxes in adjoining offices. Even before they both taught at the same college, Eleanor found time to mail copies to her. Could she be reading things to Toh? Of course not. He doesn't understand English. None of them do. That's why they're all scientists.

She looks at her watch. It's hard to see the dial through the drops of moisture, the falling snow, melting as it hits her eyes. Six o'clock. Tom will be making supper. She doesn't know how Eleanor does it, finding men who like to cook.

She wonders if they resent her eating whatever she wants to eat whenever she stays for the weekend. Of course, she knows Tom can't eat salt, and she ought not to eat their specially bought foods, like salt-free horseradish, but that's what makes them so interesting. Besides she can't resist anything when she's premenstrual. Eleanor ought to understand that, even if she's had a hysterectomy.

"Why did you have to eat *all* the kids' stuff?" Eleanor asks her.

"Because I was premenstrual."

"When you were finished being premenstrual, couldn't you have replaced *some* of it?"

Gloria does not like to think about that conversation, and so she forgets it. She is very good at forgetting things. But an image of the tall, brown-painted metal cabinet in the kitchen, fastened with a bicycle lock, rises up in front of her. She knows the cabinet is not locked when she's not there. She knows, too, that Eleanor can afford the extra food, but would buy a bicycle lock under certain circumstances. For Eleanor, it's the principle that counts. She rings the bell, thinking, Eleanor owes me a dollar nineteen for paper clips. I have to remember to ask her about it.

She's had keys to the house for years. They know they can trust her. Then why is she so worried? She's rung the bell because she wants them to put away that terrible dog they bought last Christmas. Last time she came, he jumped on her. She could feel his nails as if they were going to go right through her clothes.

"You should get rid of him," she always says to Eleanor, who invariably says the same thing: "He's part of the family. Anyway, you don't think he's a dog. You think he's a rapist."

Gloria cannot always argue with the truth, so she rarely mentions the dog. She would poison him if she didn't know they'd suspect her. And of course they'd never speak to her again, much less let her take the children to Radio City Music Hall.

She wonders if Eleanor's figured out why she's willing to spend the money on the children's tickets. She wants to impress Colin with how maternal and affectionate she can be. Thank God she can return them after the day is over. Four hours is her limit. Does Eleanor know? Probably. Sooner or later, she works everything out.

Ring the doorbell again, she thinks. Lock up that disgusting dog. It's too bad she has to ring the doorbell. Emmeline, the housekeeper, will answer it. That battle-ax. She knows Emmeline doesn't like her.

Emmeline, hair wrapped in her eternal scarf, answers the door, looks her up and down. Where, asks Gloria, is Eleanor?

"She's not here, man," says Emmeline, who does not believe in revealing unnecessary information about her employer.

How can anyone stand this woman, thinks Gloria, balancing like a stork on one foot, taking off her snowy boots under Emmeline's severe eye.

"I just washed them floors and no one's tracking up my works," Emmeline says.

Gloria avoids straightening up and looking at her for as long as possible, and when she does, Emmeline asks her what she did to her hair, man.

"I got a permanent," says Gloria. "To give it body."

"Give it frizz, man; that all it did. I born like that. How much money you pay for that mess?"

"Fifty dollars," says Gloria, lying. It cost sixty-five dollars.

"Lord!" says Emmeline. "What some of us have the money to throw it out on!"

"I like it," says Gloria. "Colin likes it."

"So when you marrying this Colin?"

"Where's the dog?" asks Gloria.

"He out in the snow," says Emmeline.

"Eleanor, where's she?"

"She out in the snow, too. Gone to visit her friend and can't get back."

Jane. Gloria had forgotten Jane. The old friend from high school. What is wrong with Eleanor lately, digging people up like a dog after old bones?

"Is Tom home?"

He is.

"You right on time for supper," says Emmeline. "I can set my watch by you. Lord, that hair."

Gloria follows her into the kitchen.

Tom, a big man, distinguished, six foot three, is standing at the stove and doesn't turn around to face her.

"Hello, Gloria," he says.

"I thought," she says, "I'd better stay over here tonight. The radio says it's a blizzard. I don't want to get on a train and have it break down for hours. Not with all those maniacs on the trains these days."

"It's not much of a blizzard," Tom says, "not in the city, anyway. Eleanor can't get back from the Island, though. They closed the highway. If you want a ride home, I'll take you back."

"No," she says, "I'd rather stay here. It will save me a trip back in the morning."

"I hate to keep the dog locked up the whole time," says Tom, who is more direct than Eleanor.

"Can't you let him out once I'm in my room?"

"Which room is that?" Emmeline asks from the top of the stairs.

"The television room," says Gloria, "the one I always sleep in during the week."

Emmeline goes off. She appears to be humming "Col-in, Col-in," to the tune of "Noel, Noel," but that's probably Gloria's imagination. The housekeeper makes her paranoid.

"How are classes?" Tom asks, still not turning around.

What a rude family, thinks Gloria. Why does she put up with them? Then she thinks: to tell the truth, I did force myself on Eleanor. But that was eleven years ago. What difference does that make now? If Eleanor liked her then, she ought to like her now. She believes people don't change; they become more and more themselves. Eleanor used to agree with her, but now she says that's only true if you have a self in the first place. Lately, to be frank, Eleanor has been hateful. This hatefulness is a new development. Perhaps it is related to her eye surgery and will soon go away.

"Where," asks Gloria, "is Toh?"

"Toh?" Tom repeats, turning at last to look at her. "He's at school or he's home. Where else would he be?"

"I thought he lived here." She doesn't like the look she's getting: as if Tom were counting the legs of an insect under a magnifying glass. Silence.

"Did he drive her to the Island?"

"She's been driving herself for the last month. Do you want some chicken or have you eaten?"

"I haven't eaten. It was too early. I can't eat right after I teach a class. I'm too nervous."

From upstairs, a snort from Emmeline.

"Do you have a piece of bread?" she asks Tom.

He points to the top of the refrigerator. She takes down the package, takes out a slice and goes back to the kitchen table.

"Want some butter on it?" Tom asks.

"No," she says. "I only want to swallow a pill. I can't swallow them alone. I break them up and roll them up in bread and chew it all together."

"Why can't you swallow a pill?"

"The therapist I used to see said it was sexual."

"We give the dog heartworm pills that way," Tom says, his back to her again.

"Eleanor's been very busy lately, hasn't she?"

He says Eleanor's always very busy.

"Well, between her teaching and writing and Toh," she says.

No answer.

"I mean," she continues recklessly, "before, even when she was busy, she was home in the afternoons most of the time. Now she's not. Neither is Toh. I've called him in the afternoons but no one answers."

Tom turns around.

"How the hell . . ." He stops. "Who gave you Toh's number?"

"I copied it from the paper on the refrigerator. I thought I'd take Toh's number just in case. I'm all alone, I've got no one to help me, and I could always pay him the way Eleanor did when he was driving her around."

She sees she's made a mistake. Tom is now watching her as if she were a fly he was intending to swat.

He observes Gloria's fluttering, her chirpy voice, her birdlike hand motions, how her hands are beginning to swoop in wider and wider arcs. She used to be merely annoying, he thinks; now she's poisonous.

"Well," she says, "I thought he'd be reliable . . ."

"He is reliable," interrupts Tom.

"Eleanor trusts him completely. To tell the truth, that's all she ever talks about. I was wondering if you still lived here."

She can't stop herself. Tom adjusts the flame on the right-hand burner without taking his eyes from her.

"Eleanor never does anything by halves," he says finally. "When she becomes attached to someone, she's very attached. Anyway, nothing she does surprises me."

"Nothing?" Gloria says, smiling strangely.

"Nothing," Tom says, putting the wooden spoon with its spaghetti-sauce sheen like blood back down on the inlaid antique green tile Eleanor bought on one of her rambles.

"I thought," says Gloria, still smiling, "that maybe Eleanor had another job, but I couldn't think of why she'd need one."

Tom still doesn't say anything.

"She doesn't," he says finally.

"Colin," says Gloria with a laugh, "thought Eleanor was having an affair with Toh, but I said that was impossible."

"Nothing is impossible," says Tom. "Get your coat. I'm taking you home."

Gloria starts to protest, then changes her mind. She's gone too far. She is afraid of him. She's always been afraid of big men. She's so thin, bone-thin, they could crush her by pressing against her. She remembers Eleanor telling her, "Men can be such fools. Try to *catch* Colin. Men never know what you're up to. They can't imagine you'd spend all your time and energy just for a chance to appear outside their doors at odd hours—accidentally armed with a second cup of coffee. Do I think Colin would suspect? No,

I don't. Normal men never suspect." Colin, of course, is suspicious of everything she does.

She is putting on her coat when Emmeline comes down and asks Tom what he thinks he's doing, going out in this sort of weather.

"Call the car service for her, man. You don't have no taxi license."

The phone rings and Eleanor calls to say she won't be able to come home. She watches Tom, as she unbuttons her coat: he looks for a pencil and a piece of paper and writes something down.

"Sometime tomorrow? Fine," says Tom. "I *know* you think you drive better on snow than on anything else, but be careful anyway."

He shouts up the stairs to the children.

"Your mother wants to talk to you."

The doorbell rings, and Tom goes to answer it. She hears a deep voice with a pronounced Chinese accent. He and Tom are laughing.

"It's spicy pork," Toh is saying. "No, not for me. I eat Chinese food enough. I came to give Davey a kung fu lesson. He at home?"

She hears the two of them going upstairs together. She'd like to go upstairs and get a look at this Toh but is suddenly afraid to see him. She goes into the living room and sits there quietly until she hears him going back out.

Tom comes in and asks her if she's called the car service or does she want him to call it for her?

"I'll call," she says helplessly.

He is angry at her because she implied that *his* wife was having an affair. How did it get to be an issue of *her* betrayal? Now it is not a question of infidelity, but of trust in friendship. She is trying to make sense of it when the car service honks its horn outside. Tom opens the door for her and closes it after her without saying goodbye. She hears the cold key turning in the cold lock.

As the car drives off, she feels greater and greater anger until she is so hot she rolls her window down. The driver turns around and glares at her. How can Tom put up with this? If he knows. Is Eleanor crazier than she thinks? Is he afraid to upset her, because, once upset, she'll have to be put away? Is he afraid she'll leave him? Who would leave a prosperous husband, the president of a computer company, and two children for a penniless student? That can't be it. Perhaps he doesn't care what she does. Is he waiting for it to end? She can't begin to understand it.

They're getting rid of her. They've been trying to get rid of her all along. Her mother always said that no one would want her around for long. She should hire a private detective to follow Eleanor and then present Tom with the pictures. It's a good thing she's not sleeping in the house, she thinks, not when she's premenstrual and suffers from sudden, irresistible cravings for sweets. After they'd gone to bed, she'd have come down and eaten sugar with a spoon. But because of the snow Emmeline would have been sleeping over on the living room couch, and would watch her, not like the figurative hawk, but the real one who has sighted a mouse and wants to pull it apart, muscle by muscle, bone by bone.

"I'd kill myself for a piece of chocolate," Gloria says aloud, but the driver does not answer her and at home she has nothing sweet to eat and it's too late to go out.

TWENTY

IN CHINATOWN, Eleanor and Toh are sitting catty-corner at a white enamel kitchen table. She is waiting for Toh to write two sentences in Chinese and then she will copy them. The great sorrow of her life has been her inability to draw, and she has long believed that her peculiarly metaphorical style evolved as a compensation for that inability: word painting. What was the name of the critic who said that about her last book? How could she have forgotten the name of such a wonderful person? She ought to have had a statue of him erected in the backyard.

She looks up at Toh and smiles. In the beginning, it unnerved him, turning to her, finding her smiling at him for no reason. He thought she was laughing at him. *Love, love, love,* says the smile. She does not know she is smiling. Toh is absorbed in his writing. From top to bottom go the characters. She always forgets this when she tries to write without supervision, thus creating new words.

"Nothing to study?" she asks Toh, "no course work?"

She knows how frightened he is of "relationships" with women, those things that sob and cry and wring their hands and distract men from their purpose in life. In her blacker moments, at home, she sometimes wonders if Toh chose her because he knew she was married, had children, a career: in short, little time. She remembers Toh telling her he had a girlfriend in China.

"But," he said, "perhaps I am wrong, but I believe everything has to be subordinated to the main purpose."

Meaning that, when he decided to come here and study, he left the girl there. She remembers the expression on his face as he said that. That must have been the look on Chairman Mao's face when he ordered a long march for two thousand intellectuals during the Cultural Revolution.

She can imagine what the scene must have been in Peking: the girl crying, Toh staring at her with that expression—at the end of it all, once he was determined and no longer crying himself, the girl saying shrill things meant to hurt him while he grimly subordinated her to the main purpose. Who was she? Had she found someone else? Could she be summoned here in case of disaster? What kind of disaster is Eleanor thinking about? She doesn't know.

Toh, whose uncle works in a Chinese restaurant after taking his math classes, is called (by Toh) "a double person." "It's not easy, being double people," says Toh. She is a double person, too. Why isn't she, why aren't they, having more trouble?

"Worrying?" Toh asks her, and when she shakes her head no, he lets the subject drop.

"You remember March eleventh?" he asks her.

She doesn't. When he first asked her that sort of question, she was astonished. Did he think *she* was a computer? She can barely remember what day of the week it is.

"It was day, according to Chinese calendar, when there were to thunderstorm, and on that day, all insects wake up. 'Were to storm'?" he asks. "Is that right?"

"No. *Was to be* a storm."

"Remember it didn't storm? Very strange."

She smiles. He's very superstitious.

"Remember the snowstorm after the Chinese New Year?" asks Eleanor. "Remember you said after that date there couldn't be any more snow, or if there was, it couldn't stick?"

"It didn't stick."

She laughs at him. The city spent a day and a half digging out after that snowfall. But there was no snow on the roads and so Toh pronounced it a snowfall that didn't stick. Suddenly, sidewalks and lawns didn't count.

"Stubborn," says Eleanor. She likes that stubbornness. It means, among other things, that having chosen her, for whatever reasons, he will not easily abandon her. When he came to this country, she thinks, he was like a deaf-mute; no one could hear what he said and what other people said to him meant nothing. Finding her must have seemed like a miracle. That must be why he cares about me, thinks Eleanor, who likes to overlook the many times he says they are so alike in nature he thinks they must have met before in another life.

"I think you are sleepy," he says, and as soon as he says so, she realizes she is. She nods, gets up, stands behind him, then bends over and puts her arms around him. So warm. Always so warm.

"Go to sleep," he says. "I'll draw a picture for you later."

"You *must* have some work to do," she says. She doesn't want to suddenly find herself subordinated to the main purpose, nor does she like to think about the maternal side to this attachment. Sometimes, when he is reading or drawing or silent, in that small space one keeps clear of the past by weeding away memories, she knows he

is the only, the beloved, the perfect child. Just as she is the
child now, ordered to bed by its father, the only, beloved,
perfect father.

"What kind of picture will you draw?" she asks him
lazily.

He draws beautifully, little scenes of the lost Peking,
but he will not draw any of his family. He is particularly
unwilling to describe his mother. She no longer asks him
to try. To conjure her up is to cause homesickness, acute
and pitiable.

Eleanor picks up the leather portfolio she has bought
to keep his pictures in, sits down on the edge of the metal
bed, her feet cold against the bare wooden floor, leans
against the cold metal headboard, opens the portfolio
carefully, and turns, carefully, page after page. People on
their way to work. People in kitchens, cooking. People
climbing a mountain trail. Some villagers from the mountain have clustered around strangers only just arrived.
The figure of the visiting woman is drawn so clearly, but
from the back. The woman cooking at the stove drawn,
also, from the back. His mother, his country, their faces
turned away.

She goes back through the pictures. In almost all of
them, that mysterious figure, its back to the viewer, its
hair black and loose. Seen that way, from the back, it
could be her. She puts down the portfolio, goes over to
Toh and hugs him violently.

"A ghost is hovering?" he asks.

She nods. Yes, a ghost. Not, however, one of her own.
One, perhaps, she is destined to become.

"I was looking at the pictures," she says aloud. He
shakes his head. They have never fought, but when she
bought the leather portfolio, and he woke up and found

her putting the pictures into their plastic slipcases, he was angry.

"So much money for that," he says.

Eleanor says it was worth it.

"How many dollars it cost?"

"Twenty-five dollars."

But look, it is beautiful leather, the color of dark blood, and so beautifully made. The inside covers are suede.

"Twenty-five dollar!"

Toh, who has almost no money, is outraged by the way she spends her own. When he began driving, they went through the Brooklyn Battery Tunnel because that was what Eleanor always did. Then the city raised the tolls, and the next thing she knew, Eleanor's employee was refusing to drive her through.

"If we take bridge," he said, "we save nine dollar a week."

And so they became a "we" and began driving over the bridge.

"I bought it in Chinatown," Eleanor says by way of placating Toh. Everything, according to him, is cheaper in Chinatown. Except rent, which is why he lives in Brooklyn. And where is the friend whose apartment they borrow so often? He is double-peopling in a Chinese restaurant.

"You should let me go with you when you buy," says Toh. "I bargain them. They see a white face, the price goes high."

She says she doesn't care; she is near tears.

"Don't care!" says Toh. "Twenty-five dollars for bad pictures!"

"They are not bad pictures."

"Bad pictures, good pictures! Twenty-five dollar is twenty-five dollar!"

More, thinks Eleanor, with tax.

"They are precious to me," she says at last. "The pictures. Are."

"Oh," says Toh, stopped. "Precious. What means that word?"

"Rare. Special. Worth a great deal of money."

"Oh," says Toh. "Precious to you. I didn't know."

Bedrock. She loves the pictures. There is no arguing about what people love. The argument, such as it was, ends. Now he is only amused and puzzled by her devotion to his foolish pictures. A hobby. No good. They share that: the belief that whatever they do is mediocre.

"But," Eleanor used to say, "you do so well in school. How do you explain that?"

"I begin before the others."

"There are some people," says Eleanor, "who couldn't do the work even if they started last year."

"I think I am only popular."

Eleanor is puzzled. Does he mean he gets good grades only because people like him? No, that's not what he means.

"Intelligence," he says, "is popular. Like everyone else's."

"Oh, you mean average. You're not."

"I think so. In China, we have saying. 'The stupid bird flies first.' "

"What does that mean?" Eleanor asks.

They were in the car, talking. Swish, swish, go the windshield wipers. The windshield beads with little crystals. The Chrysler Building fights free of the clouds. Wonderful building. A cloud ought to be ashamed to cover it up, that magnificent silver wedding cake, that pagan silver temple high above midtown.

"The bird who is stupid," says Toh, "flies first because he knows he will take longer to accomplish his task. The smart bird can sleep later."

"In America," says Eleanor, "we have a saying, 'the early bird gets the worm.' "

"Same thing," says Toh.

"The exact opposite."

"The exact opposite," says Toh, starting to laugh.

("Are you sure he has a sense of humor?" asks Tom. "I roomed with Koreans and the only things they laughed at were sadistic or slapstick." Eleanor tells Tom that Toh has a sense of humor.)

In fact, it delights and amazes her, how he marvels at the world. At small animals. At the way she forgets her keys. At the way she keeps banging into things when she's upset. At her hair, curly when it's wet or damp.

"In China," he says, "you can go for miles and see practically one face."

Her daughter's straight gold hair fascinates him. Too bad she is only six, thinks Eleanor; maybe he'd wait for her.

At times, talking to him is like talking to herself and is dreamlike and strange.

"Maybe we knew each other in another life," suggests Toh again. "You believe?"

She doesn't. For the first time, this life is enough for her. The bad fairy who hung over her crib saying bad, bad world is being beaten back by Toh, for whom she feels uncomplicated adoration. With whom everything is uncomplicated. At first, she thought it was the absence of words which kept things pure. Now she thinks it is the absence of an impulse to complicate. Of course, she does not know which came first.

Eleanor lies down on the bed, the leather portfolio open on her chest. Between her family, her work, and this room, she is always tired. Is it this weekend or the next that she flies to Georgia to give a reading? She really ought to find out. She thinks about having come home from Jane's and learning that Tom had sent Gloria packing. When she called Gloria, she was excessively nervous, even for Gloria.

"How's Jane?" asks Gloria.

"I don't know," she says. "Not drunk."

"I don't understand this obsession you have with people from the past," says Gloria, bitter, bitter, bitter. "There's no one I want to see again. They'd just ask me what I was doing. They don't really want to know. They just want an excuse to tell me about their books and their children and their houses and their wives."

"What's wrong with that?"

"Nothing's wrong with that. Except that I hate it. They ask me what I've been doing, and what am I supposed to tell them? That nothing's happened for the last twenty-five years? That I have nothing to show for my life? People think I'm in my early thirties" (not again! thinks Eleanor). "I don't want to meet the old ones who know. If I'm a failure, I don't want to be reminded of it, that's all."

Eleanor wants to cut the diatribe short. On the other hand, she can't resist prompting Gloria into a characteristic display. *Discredit her,* says a little voice.

"I care about other people, not just what they think of me," says Eleanor, who, in spite of herself, is getting angry.

"Oh, because you care about every pathetic thing who crosses your path?"

Eleanor doesn't answer. She is wondering when they had exactly the same conversation. At her house. One Sunday, about two months ago.

"Do you want to ask Toh and his uncle over for dinner next weekend?" Tom asked her. Knowing perfectly well she is going to Georgia next weekend.

"Oh, yes," she said.

Grateful beyond words. Without him, there is no world for her. Necessary, as Toh is not. Daily, what she feels for him becomes clearer: the sediment of old emotions is settling out, leaving a crystalline fluid, held up to the sun. The catalyst of this process, the filter, is Toh. She has never thought of them—Toh and Tom—together in just this way. As if they were standing next to each other in one photograph and were meant to be compared. Does this mean she will soon be feeling guilt? A sense of peril, yes. That is new. Perhaps it will go away.

The main thing, thinks Eleanor, falling asleep under the comfortable weight of the drawings, is to avoid thinking about trouble. As long as Tom doesn't ask and I don't have to answer, everything will stay as it is.

She feels, rather than sees, Toh leaning over her.

"Ah," he whispers, "you have an investment in sleepiness."

As his English improves, and his excursions into the Chinese-English dictionary become more adventurous, his expressions become more baroque, even hilarious. She smiles and begins to fall asleep again. Did she ever enjoy her own children's murdering of the language? Not so much. She was always too worried they'd go off to college, if they went at all, their sentences tangled like baling wire. His every mistake makes her happy. Although she does teach him. He can't be happy if he can't talk to peo-

ple. The footnote to this text is always the same: Teach
him or he'll go home where he can talk to anyone.

When she wakes up again, Toh is asleep beside her.
Today she is lucky. He has fallen asleep on his side, facing
her, and the sun is streaming in, cold and bright. She can
lie there forever, watching his face. He is no longer surprised to wake up and find her, eyes wide, watching him.
He no longer asks her how long she's been awake. In the
beginning, he did.

"I like staring at you," she said. "It helps me think."

Later, she told the truth.

"I love to look at your face," she said. And then
stopped.

Should she say, I love it more than anything in the
world? It was the one reliable thing, the constant thing, I
saw every day after the surgery? A smoothed-out coin,
worn down by the blinking lids of my eyes which were so
long empty? Like a round page in a round book, that face,
whose pages refuse to turn even in the strongest wind. She
is, even now, afraid of frightening with her intensity. It
has, in the past, frightened so many people. She thinks
often of his determination to avoid entanglements while
he is still a student.

As she watches him sleep, watches that shockingly
dark hair against the white pillow, she thinks how lucky
for her it was that the accident at the airport occurred
after his midterms. Otherwise, they wouldn't be here now.

"Eleanor," she hears her grandmother say (she rarely
hears her grandmother or her mother lately, especially
when she is here), "face it. You're in bed with a child."

The design of the imitation lace curtains patterns the
sheets and walls and his face strangely. A spring breeze is
blowing in through the window. Eleanor pulls the blan-

kets up over her shoulder and over his chest. He does not
stir. Good. Today she will be able to watch him for a long
time. Hoard him up against the time when he will be
gone. When he marries and has children of his own.

"When you are a student," he says, "you cannot do
anything. When you finish, then you have a small place to
stand on."

Eleanor, she thinks, erase those thoughts.

Which she does.

If he had fallen asleep facing away from her, she
would have gotten up quietly, gone to sit in the black
wing chair facing the little iron bed, and watched him
sleep. What sort of love is this? Old. Even ancient. She
waits for his eyes to open as if she is waiting for her own to
open, as if she can see nothing until he does.

"Don't you suffer from culture shock?" Gloria used to
ask. "I mean, he's not like us."

Since the night of the snowstorm, Gloria has been
more careful, almost circumspect. She hardly ever mentions Toh, except to worry aloud over whether or not he
will be able to learn to use the house alarm system (after
all, it took *her* years), whether he won't be lonely for *people
his own age* in such a big house. She does everything but
ask Eleanor if she isn't afraid he'll eat the dog, that rapist
in fur, because the Chinese, if Eleanor happens to remember, eat dogs. *And* cats.

No she doesn't suffer from culture shock. Not until
she returns to her own house, finds one child crying, insisting he has a broken ankle, the other one slamming
doors because someone has hidden her Michael Jackson
button, her husband impossible to talk to because his pro-
grams won't run. Something about bugs.

"We have roaches again?" asks Eleanor, who hasn't

been listening. "How can that be? Gloria's hardly been around this year. Do we have roach spray?"

That perfume, which lingers on so persistently after Gloria's tenancy.

"Not that kind of bug," says her husband, going back into the computer room (once she thought of it as the library, with its oak paneling, its leaded glass bookcases, its glass doors keeping the books free of dust), slamming the door.

Slam! Slam! Slam!

In this house, where no one merely closes a door, in this web of responsibilities, bills waiting in the top cubbyhole of her desk, everyone insisting on viewing her as someone who can cope with them all, *here* she feels culture shock.

Whereupon she sees the housekeeper bearing down upon her with another tale of the children's malfeasance. Oh, she thinks, I'm moving out.

Now she wakes up first, and watches Toh. Oh, she thinks, I wish this could go on forever.

It already has, says a voice she doesn't want to hear, *hasn't it?*

I don't want anything to change, she thinks.

"Oh, Eleanor," says another voice, "you know better." She recognizes that voice: her grandmother, back again.

Toh wakes up and looks at his watch.

"We have to go," he says.

His class, her family. Her head starts to hurt.

TWENTY-ONE

TOM HAS CLOSED his office door and turned out his light so that anyone looking through the office transom will think he has gone home. He knows Gloria is a raving maniac. He knows better than to believe a word she says, but what if his wife *is* having an affair? Should he become violent, shake her, frighten her, shake the truth out of her? Should he begin packing, threaten to move out? Or should he start sleeping *across* the bed, refusing to move over for Eleanor? No, that wouldn't work. She'd just sleep in the space left right under the headboard. When the dog sleeps on her side of the bed, he wakes up and finds Eleanor sleeping, curled like a snail, in whatever space is left. Should he begin criticizing everything she does (Eleanor, there's hair on the sink. Eleanor, the blusher's darker on the right cheek than the left. *Another* parking ticket? This isn't a phone bill; it's the national defense budget.) until she demands to know what's wrong? Or becomes so angry that she blurts the truth out herself? Should he shoot Toh? Shoot them both? Alas, he doesn't have a violent bone in his body.

He thinks back to their first meeting. Eleanor had given a paper at Columbia and was standing in a corner of the room, trying to avoid her own reception. He joined her there.

"Are you interested in problems of translation?" she asked him.

"No, my roommate brought me."

She laughed. What a laugh it was, quiet and infectious. Everyone in the room turned to look at them.

"I'm not either," she said. "That paper exhausted my interest in the subject. I can't translate what people say to me in my own language."

He waited for her and they went to a local bar. He told her she was too pretty to be an academic. She didn't answer but studied him over the top of her glass.

"What do I look like?" he asked, embarrassed.

"Like a man who wants to have children."

Did they say another word that night? He doesn't remember. He remembers driving her all the way back to Brooklyn, the silence comfortable in the car. A week later they were engaged.

Oh, she was impossible to live with. But then so was he. If she was having an affair, what should he do? Go to China. He's always wanted to do that. Eleanor doesn't have affairs. Gloria doesn't know what she's talking about. He'll wait and see. Or wait and see *if* there is anything to see.

It's impossible to think of Eleanor as guilty of any crime. Impossible to think of himself married to a criminal.

Would he let her get away with murder? He thinks of the surgeon, describing how quietly she lay while they operated. He thinks of all the still rooms into which she has gone alone, all the white hospital beds in which she has wakened, alone. When he thinks of Toh, he thinks of him as another doctor, a healer. How would Eleanor have gotten through these months without him? He didn't have the time. He cannot bear to think about her eyes.

If it's true, he'll shoot Toh. Or himself.

But it isn't true.

He'll shoot Gloria, that troublemaker.

He sighs with relief, gets up and switches on his office light.

Immediately, someone knocks at the door.

TWENTY-TWO

I CAN'T," SAYS ELEANOR. "I'm sure it's a wonderful sale. I'm waiting for Jane to come over."

"Jane," sighs Gloria.

She has tried, like an enthusiastic abortionist, to scrape Toh from Eleanor's life and failed. What chance does she have of getting rid of Jane?

"I thought you couldn't stand her anymore."

"Sooner or later," says Eleanor, "I can stand anyone."

She wants to get off the phone before Colin's name induces the conditioned reflex in Gloria which turns her to stone, a granite statue holding a plastic receiver. "Look," she says, "I've got to do something about my hair. It looks like a storm cloud. I should get it thinned."

"I'll talk to you later," says Gloria, who is at that instant, as Eleanor well knows, touching her own thinly covered scalp.

"We ought to sod her head," says her housekeeper whenever Gloria's name is mentioned. The family agrees that grass couldn't look worse than Gloria's hair. There's no question: Gloria has a special gift. She drives everyone around her into a frenzy of hatred.

Eleanor sits in her leather chair, in her living room, watching the white bird dive. Always in the same window:

no freedom at all. And yet he looks like the freest thing there is.

She finishes brushing her hair with the lavender plastic brush her son gave her for Christmas, pulls her hair to one side and braids it.

"Look," said Toh last week, "a silver hair."

"They're all silver," she tells him. "I dye it."

"Die?"

"Dye. As in adding color to cloth. Red or blue or green, I dye mine. Black."

"Oh," says Toh, his expression indescribable. Who knows what it means to dye one's hair in China?

She sits still, watching the dove, so pleased to deliver his message. Why not? An overjoyed world awaits him. *In my father's house.*

At last year's New Year's Eve party, didn't someone from the college try to convince her that the dove was carrying a badly translated and inaccurate message? Originally, the dove flew down saying, "In my father's house are many apartments." That's what the original text said. How very comforting. Did the original version also prophesy the coming of co-ops? Which also have many apartments. Still, it is best to begin small, to begin believing in the little room in Chinatown. Now she is finally beginning to believe in her own house, in which she has lived for over twelve years.

She knows why she is so eager to see Jane. In Jane's eyes, she is always defined, she's a creature in a context, better and more intricately defined than she is in her husband's eyes. Love erases flaws, denies the seriousness of illness, refuses to believe the graying creature one married may lose her sight, sees thousands of flaws which the beloved creature does not have and denies the existence of other more serious ones she does have: fault lines. It hides, somewhere in a suede pouch, as one would hide a precious cameo, the still living belief in the perfection of the woman one has married. Love between women is different, takes a larger canvas, magnifies everything, takes inventory of the flaws, each wrinkle, each gray hair, learns each thin place in the ice and then goes ahead and skates across the lake, taking chances, skating over the dark water, careless, is patient and forgiving, and lasts if the great misfortune does not occur: one man and two women. A misfortune, which, after all, has not befallen Eleanor and Jane. So that now it is Jane she wants to see. What is a good friend if not the Queen's mirror? The only untamed mirror on the wall.

And what does she want Mirrory Jane to tell her? That she is not the woman her family believes her to be: loyal, intelligent, stable? Does she want Jane to punish her with the truth? *Someone* has to see her the way she really is. (*"We* do," say her grandmother and mother together. "You're not fooling us.") Because she no longer knows what she is like, and there are times when she feels dizzy, as if she were seeing one world with one eye, another world with the other.

Jane arrives, coughing, smothered in a black coat.

"I've got bronchitis," she says. "Don't look at my coat like that. Many, many nasty little minks died to keep me warm. They're not mice, like the little white rats we used to work with in Biology. They bite their keepers. Besides, when your hair starts falling out, you're entitled to cover yourself with as much hair as you can find."

"Your hair isn't falling out," says Eleanor.

"Not this minute. Your rug is safe. But when my hair's wet you can count the hairs on my head and you don't have to use the fingers of both hands."

"What's this bronchitis?" she asks Jane. "You have it every other week. Don't you like your job?"

"Every illness is not psychosomatic," says Jane. "Besides, who wouldn't like taking care of ten thousand raving maniacs? How are your eyes?"

"Fine. When I have glasses on. I knew I'd have trouble with contact lenses just because no one else does."

"What's wrong with them? They were working fine when I saw you."

"Now my eyes don't tear enough."

"Oh, come on," says Jane, "you can still cry at the drop of a hat."

"I haven't cried very much since the eye surgery."

"I find that hard to believe," says Jane, who has followed Eleanor into the kitchen.

"It's true," says Eleanor. She is frying onions in butter, waiting until they brown before adding the mushrooms. "The onion is making my eyes tear," she says. "Maybe I should carry one around."

"If you haven't been crying, there's something wrong with you."

Eleanor thinks this over. Usually everything makes her cry. She cries when she's happy. She cries if a dog or a child appears in a movie accompanied by a swell in the music because, in her experience, the music signals the filmmaker's intention of killing the creatures off before the last reel. She's always crying about something.

"Do sniffles count?" she asks Jane.

"No."

She thinks as she stirs the eggs into the mixture of onions and mushrooms. She cried, she says, when she and Toh were driving to the hospital and he asked her how Americans punished their children.

"What did you tell him?"

"I told him that I sent mine to their room for first offenses, locked them in for repeated offenses, grounded them for setting fire to curtains, and when they did something really terrible, I slapped their faces. *He* said that in China, parents beat their children. I started to cry. Not hard. I kept staring out the window until I stopped."

"Did your throat start hurting? Your throat always starts to hurt when you try not to cry."

"It hurt. I couldn't swallow."

"Did you tell him how your parents used to punish you? The leather belt, the wooden hanger, all those nice things they found lying around the house? You didn't let him think that China was the only place in the world where parents were barbarians?"

Eleanor looks over at her, shiny-eyed.

"You're not as badly off as I thought," says Jane. "You're starting to cry now."

Eleanor nods and yanks the frying pan from the stove.

"You're sure this isn't fattening?" Jane asks. "It's all right for you to blow up like a balloon. You're married."

"It's not fattening. I swear to God. Sit down."

They automatically sit down at the kitchen table. That's where they always sat—in either house—unless they went up to each other's room.

"What's up?" asks Jane. "I finally bought that condominium in Queens. Good-bye, Cedarhurst."

"Congratulations," says Eleanor, who does not believe you can say good-bye to anything. "Nothing very new here," she says, picking up a knife.

"Are you buttering that toast or carpeting it?" asks Jane. "Why aren't you looking at me?"

"You sound like my mother. 'Look at me while I'm talking to you.' "

"You always stare at people," says Jane. "You're not even looking at me."

"Um," says Eleanor, "that affair you've been having with a married man? How long has it gone on?"

Ten years, says Jane; no, eleven.

"And his wife never found out?"

"She still doesn't know. She's very busy. You know the thing. The children grow up. The wife goes back to school. She turns out to be very good at what she does. Soon she has a career and her husband feels neglected. He neglected his wife for twenty years, but that doesn't count."

"The guilt . . ." Eleanor begins.

"There are guilts our language doesn't have names for. I told you I don't recommend it."

"How do you manage?"

"I don't. I treat it like malaria. When I have an attack, I get in bed and don't get out for days. I put plenty of food next to the bed. I have a guilt scale in the bathroom. When it goes over one hundred and fifty, I know I'm about to perish. So I get up, wash my hair, hire half of the country's unemployed to clean my apartment, and eat one last cake."

"Adultery," says Eleanor softly.

"That's not what *I'm* committing," says Jane. "*I'm* not married."

"I am," says Eleanor, twisting her wedding ring. "It's as if I swallowed two lions, and they're both comfortable in there"—she pats her stomach—"but sometimes they start menacing each other, and if they get any closer to each other, they'll devour themselves and me in the process."

"Maybe you are a schizophrenic," says Jane. "Or maybe only spoiled. Remember how you used to love tor-

turing your ex-fiancé with tales of your exploits? How are
you keeping quiet now?"

"That was different," says Eleanor. "That was the
only way I could control him. Jealousy was the only emotion he could feel."

"Anyway," says Jane, chasing a last mushroom
around her plate, "it's all because of your eyes."

"My *eyes?*"

"He's *been* your eyes. While you couldn't see. Whenever you fall in love with someone, pardon me, *fell* in love
with someone, you gave them something of yours. When
you're ready to take your eyes back, that's when it will
end. He won't seem so wonderful then."

"Take my eyes back," says Eleanor. "What a disgusting way of putting it."

"Yuckky," agrees Jane.

Eleanor is silent, picking at her omelette.

"Even if that's what it is," she says at last, "even if it
is, why did I pick him? He's the least logical choice."

"He was there. He's nice. Seeing eye dogs don't drive.
If they did, you'd be worrying about impulses toward bes-
tiality."

"That's ridiculous."

"*And* he proves your theory about how communica-
tion takes place best in silence."

"I told you I don't think I had that theory until after
I met him."

"You *always* had that theory. You had it in high
school. You wrote a whole story about how the people we
liked were the ones we talked to without words. The classroom was supposed to be like a barnful of cows. Don't you
remember? Mr. Peru read it to the whole class."

"Nothing of the sort ever happened."

"Oh, yes it did. Ask anyone. Anyone from the class, I mean."

"I had this idea before?"

"*Long* before."

"Let's change the subject," says Eleanor. "Let's look at my old photograph albums for a change."

And they are looking at them when the phone rings. Eleanor says it's probably Gloria. Jane asks why she still talks to her. How much of a masochist can she be?

"Oh, I'm going to tell her off. I just keep putting it off. I'll get around to it."

"And what are you going to say? That's there's a little matter you've been meaning to discuss with her for the past seven or eight years?"

Eleanor puts her finger to her lips and picks up the phone.

There it is, thinks Jane, that same lightness, that same brightening, as if Eleanor had just discovered it was possible for your bones to weigh nothing and still to support you on your long voyage from here to there.

"What?" Eleanor is saying. "*What* man? The man from the accident? *What* man from the accident? I don't understand. You gave him money?"

Jane raises her eyebrows and points to her own chest: *Tell me, tell me.* Eleanor's hand makes a vague, polishing motion, erasing her. Jane sighs and sits on the floor, her back against Eleanor's couch. She's thought of Eleanor's mind in this way for years: a swarm of gnats, traveling in every direction at once, never in a straight line for very long, and then something happens. The gnats are gone. A bee tumbles into the sunshine and heads straight for the new hive. World-obliterating, that concentration.

She listens.

"Is that all, then? Is there anything else you didn't tell me?"

Her cheekbones have become more pronounced.

"I don't know. Don't do anything."

She looks at Jane and shakes her head: Not good.

"You better come over here. No, he's not. My friend Jane's here. Fifteen minutes."

"Trouble?" Jane asks.

"Trouble," says Eleanor.

Did she tell Jane about the car accident? It was a small one. It dented the car, no one was hurt. Toh had the accident the night of the storm, on his way to the airport to pick up his uncle coming in from Peking. It must have been a shock, the first time you have an accident, but he didn't tell her there was someone in the car he ran into. It never occurred to her to ask. Now it turns out there was a man in it, a man with a young girl. Toh paid him forty dollars. He gave the man his phone number and address and now the man is calling him at home and telling him he wants two thousand dollars.

"I don't know why he didn't tell me," says Eleanor.

"He didn't want to worry you."

No answer. Silence. The flight of the bumblebee on its way from here to there, whatever those two points might be.

"You could," Jane suggests, "call my brother and ask him. He's normal except for his Star Trek fixation. He practices law in Connecticut."

"Paul?" Eleanor says as if waking up. "Give me his phone number."

Jane recites it and Eleanor scribbles it down.

"Come with me," she says. "I've got to find the keys. It takes me longer to get in and out of this house than it takes me to get to work. A burglar could come in under the door like smoke. It's ridiculous."

Eleanor's key chain emerges from beneath a pile of papers; it's appropriate for the chatelaine of a very large dungeon, a huge brass ring, twenty-five keys dangling from it.

"Do you need all those keys?" Jane asks Eleanor, who says no, she doesn't, but the key chain is a wonderful weapon, better than brass knuckles; who'd want to get hit in the face with five pounds of jagged keys? You learn to live like this, she tells Jane, when you leave the Island and come to live in the city.

The doorbell rings and Eleanor runs off down the hall and begins unlocking the first of three doors.

"Damn door! Damn house! Damn city!" Eleanor mutters, struggling with the deadbolt which fastens the lower right hand corner of the second heavy oak door.

Oh, this is the Eleanor she remembers, uncontrollable temper, up and down like an elevator that's lost its mind, the black halo around the sun, saying, even in this brightness is the noose of suicide, enraged at the world for being the world. How has she found any peace for herself? How did she find a man who could live with her? How did she find Toh? To stay alive with Eleanor's character for forty years—she couldn't do it. How has Eleanor stayed alive for so long? She must live every day in defiance of herself, that destroying angel, who comes down from the skies bearing long scrolls, all of which tell her this is hopeless, that is hopeless, you are hopeless.

She remembers her own childhood, how often she retreated into bed. When she graduated, she had the school's record for numbers of days absent. She sees herself now, lying in the bed she painted antique blue, and it seems to her as if she has never gotten out of bed, never fought for what she wanted, never fought herself, who was always the real enemy. She doesn't know how Eleanor fought against herself, but she resolves to do the same thing now. After all, it isn't too late. She's still healthy. The women in her family live into their nineties.

She is standing in back of Eleanor, out on the porch, watching Eleanor unlock the last of the locks. Eleanor is pushing aside the white lace curtains and there is the Chinese face of this—child. He looks like every Chinese person she has ever seen. And then she sees him in the transforming heat of Eleanor's concern. That's it, that's it, her strange ability to make her emotions tangible so that even the worst—hatred, envy, greed—are suddenly embodied, *have* bodies, and in that state are as astonishing as demons, materialized for the first time. Near Eleanor, these states, these tenuous emanations, become things. As if one had been blind but could suddenly see what one knows had been there all the time. Living among these states made visible, that's what keeps Eleanor alive: Jane sensed it before, what a thin edge her friend balances on. Now, after thirty years, she sees it, knows it, is even thinking of balancing on it herself.

Toh is making a circular motion with his hand on the other side of the glass—a wave. How old did Eleanor say he was? Twenty-seven? He looks fifteen.

"Tom home?" asks Toh, and Eleanor asks if she should call him.

"What is difference?" asks Toh. "It's exactly the same." Meaning, as usual, I am a man and I am here.

Jane's annoyance at Toh for interrupting her visit vanishes, disappears like steam above a tea kettle. Delight, that's what she feels, delight at being protected. She hasn't felt protected in a long time, not since her father died. Perhaps she never will again. She tends to think of herself lately as a King Lear with long curls, shivering in the storm, tends to think in terms of tragic metaphors. How has she gone through two analyses without noticing that before?

Eleanor does not think of herself in terms of tragic metaphors; she cannot take herself seriously. She says she cannot forgive, is loyal to everything. Emotions and people stick to her as if they were nettles. She is always the center of a storm. The murderous gift of life is what Eleanor turns, this way and that, to the light.

Jane would like to ask Toh: Should she buy a new couch? Is the co-op apartment in Queens she has just bought a mistake? Should she unpack all her cartons and plan on living in Cedarhurst forever? Would he mind looking at her palm and telling her what to expect during the next thirty years? She realizes she is caught up in Eleanor's emotions and beliefs. They are now telling her: Change. She had better get her Coat of Nasty Animals.

Eleanor, who is watching her, smiles and shrugs. *Come back.*

Jane nods. She will come back.

When she looks at Toh again, she is astonished. Now he is an old man; the face at the door has sunk beneath the face of the old man in a movie she once saw—*Ikiru.* An archetypal face of age and pain.

She remembers Eleanor reading over the phone from an article she was writing.

"Under the face is the icon," read Eleanor. "The face of the individual is a transient gift, a thin covering. Each race has its own face. In old age, the face of the race emerges. This is the genetic face, like the face of the world in winter. The face of the old who are slowly dying is always the same face. It arrives as inevitably and as an-

ciently familiar as a season of winter. In that face, one sees
both the end and the beginning of the world because it is
upon that ruined, skeletal face that nature sculpts the face
of the young, who, with their faces of fresh clay built up
over the bones, bend over the powdery plaster skulls the
old have become and fail to recognize the emerging scaf-
folding upon which their own countenances rest. And yet,
when they are tired or ill, or in that strange state in which
thought seems absent, the genetic *face* appears and puts its
seal on the apparently trivial moment, announcing: This
moment is important. There will be few other times so
important."

Poor Jane, who doesn't want to leave, who wants to
talk to Toh. Poor Eleanor. Poor world. As she buttons her
coat, Jane knows she is seeing with Eleanor's eyes. The
tragedy is to be out of each other's sight. She hugs and
kisses Eleanor, is astonished to find Eleanor hugging her
back.

"Don't do anything stupid," she tells her. "Call my
brother. Maniacs are his field. He has a degree in maniacs."

Eleanor says she'll be careful.

She doesn't know what careful is, thinks Jane.

"Call me, tell me what happens," she tells Eleanor.

In the living room, in front of the diving dove,
Eleanor cross-examines Toh.

"*Leave* a stone unturned," says her grandmother.
"Who said it was a virtue to turn over every stone? If you
like worms, *then* you turn over every stone."

Toh says the man who was in the car he hit asked
him for money, and he gave him all he had: forty dollars.
So the man must have thought to himself, oh, this one
is rich. He gives away forty dollars. "I tell him, if he sues
me . . ."

"Sues you?" interrupts Eleanor. "He said he would sue you?"

". . . I go to court and say I'm poor Chinese student and if the judge comes back against me, I go back to China."

Eleanor sees that expression again: subordinate to the main purpose.

"You aren't going back to China," she says. "When did the man say he'd call you again?"

"In an hour."

Eleanor gets up and starts to put on her trench coat.

"Let's go," she says.

Toh says no, she is not coming to his apartment. This is *his* trouble, *his* problem. The man could be dangerous. She is only woman. She stay here until he settles it.

"No," says Eleanor.

"Yes."

"Then come back when you've talked to him," Eleanor says.

"I think I just call you," says Toh. "You think that's good idea?" Meaning: do as I say.

"We'll see," says Eleanor.

Toh warns her not to drive over to his house after he leaves. He won't let her in. The building is never safe for a woman. Now it is certainly not safe.

"I'll stay here," Eleanor says, "if you stop saying you'll go back to China."

Toh leaves and she calls Jane's brother, Paul, who tells her that she is responsible for any damage done by her own car. No, he doesn't believe the man will bother them again. Why not? Because of the young girl he was with in the car. If the man had any kind of sense, he'd have called the police that night. He's a petty crook, garden variety. Don't pay any attention to him. Toh told him

exactly the right thing. Let the man take Toh to court.
They'll be lucky if the man's stupid enough to sue Toh
and not them. He can't get anything from him if he
doesn't have anything. Forget it. *Don't have anything more to
do with him.* Tell the man to call him at the law office.
Don't encourage him by talking to him. Does she understand? Is she sure?

Eleanor says she understands, wondering why she's
listening to the advice of a person who sat quietly on a
living room chair and watched his dog eat the red lining
of her blue school parka. How long ago was that? Thirty
years ago.

Because the car insurance is in both their names, she
tells Tom about the man who is calling Toh. As he listens,
he does not become alarmed or annoyed, only distracted,
as if he is trying to hear something her voice is obliterat-
ing. Eleanor does not like this and gets up from the couch
and sits on his lap. There are things to arrange: confer-
ences with the children's teachers, an appointment with
the accountant; who should fix the carburetor? Their me-
chanic friend won't work in the rain, but is cheap. However, it is raining and is supposed to go on raining and the
car is not running. What about the dealer, who has a roof
over his head, is predictable, but charges a small fortune?
They have a theory that he wants to buy a castle in
England and intends to finance it by overcharging them.
Are they going to the country this weekend? Did anyone
call to get the alarm system checked? Is anyone baby-sitting if they do get to the country? Eleanor has a deadline
to meet. Everything but, Is there life after death?

Eleanor presses her head into her husband's chest. He
is a large, furry man who will not fit into small foreign
cars because his legs are too long, whose smell always delights her, some unanalyzable mix of body and weather

and cigar smoke: her father's smell. Sooner or later, into every good marriage, a little incest must fall.

"We all marry our fathers," Jane once told her.

"Yes, but we don't all start out wanting to do it," says Eleanor.

They don't tell you the truth, she thinks now. A little incest is a good thing. And how much does she love this one? Oh, world without end. Then how does she justify what she's doing? She doesn't. Sooner or later, she will have to make things up, fix things, pay. Sooner or later, you pay for everything. Whenever the bill comes due.

The man does not call. Toh begins studying for midterms again. Eleanor begins driving out to Jane's, her bike in the trunk of the car, the trunk lid tied down. It is spring; she notices that with some regret. No doubt about it. Look how the grass is climbing the dune of garbage opposite Starrett City. In another month, if the smell didn't let you in on the secret, you wouldn't know you were driving past a garbage dump. That's when the real estate agents drag out prospective clients. She hates to see the winter go. She hasn't accomplished enough. When she pulls back her upper eyelids, the veins are still red, the last visible trace of surgery. In another year, even that will be gone. If the winter would only last a little longer. She should have more to show for a year than a pair of redveined eyes.

Soon it will be completely inappropriate to wear a parka anywhere. Spring is about to remove her anonymity, just as the eye surgery has restored the particular identity of the world, room by room, street by street. She will wear her hair loose and pull it forward over her shoulders: such thick hair. Better than a hood. Nevertheless, she resents the exploring farmer's hands of spring. Look, an inch of untilled soil. Take up what covers it. Leave nothing unchanged. Not like the bony, conserving last days of winter during which animals leave no traces and the landscape remains unchanged, tinted only by the changing sky.

On the other hand, once the leaves come out, there is a world of hiding places. Safe in the greenery. And she is shocked to see how quickly she is coming to take the newly returned, never-before-so-brilliant world for granted. How fast the mind strips everything of the exotic, rendering it familiar. They are wrong, she thinks. Familiarity doesn't breed contempt. It breeds domesticity. It stamps out wonder, covering the shining thing with leaves. Familiarity has the instincts of a dog with a new bone. Nevertheless, the thing is there, like a tulip bulb, waiting for the right season to push up its shoots through the heavy wet covering of beige, bleached, veined leaves.

"How will you explain Toh to Tom?" asks Jane.

The two women are lying side by side, collapsed on Jane's unmade bed. Cedarhurst. It never changes.

"Maybe," says Eleanor sleepily, "when it's over. It's not an affair, really. It's a state of mind."

"Most men . . ." says Jane, and then stops.

"We've been over that," says Eleanor. "I'm still putting it off."

She can do that, Jane marvels, put off being afraid, put off worrying. Then, when the danger is past, she lets it all descend on her, a handful of seed thrown out in front of a vigilance of crows.

TWENTY-THREE

SEVERAL WEEKS PASS, and the man calls again.

Eleanor is standing across the street from her own house, as if spying on it, under the boughs of the great Irish maple she sees every day from her bedroom window, waiting for Toh. She rarely waits for anyone on her own porch or in front of her own door. When Tom comes for her, or when Toh does, they begin looking up and down both sides of the street as soon as they turn the corner.

"Can't you wait in one place?" Tom asks her. "Finding you is like looking for a bird."

But the house looks different when seen from different angles.

The autumn Tom first began teaching a course in business administration at college and began walking her home, they would walk past block after block of these great Victorian houses, and Eleanor, more than a foot shorter than Tom, would jump up and down trying to see into the rooms.

"It would be wonderful to live in a house like that," she said, kicking at a heap of dry golden leaves with her shiny black boot.

That autumn. Step, kick. The trees, which just two weeks before had canopied overhead, turning the streets into long corridors of brilliance, in which she and everyone else were part of a majestic procession watched over by giants whose green fluttery hands kept them from the hungry eyes of the night sky, were now ruined columns swaying in a strong wind as it bereaved for all living things, their branches nerve-patterning a gray ice sky.

Next came early winter, heavy snow. The trains would run late, cars would skid; no one knew where anything would end. If she could live in one of those houses, she thought, the snow, the trees, the outside world would fly up, lightly, like startled birds, not to be seen again until the spring. She has always loved the winter, the time when things hatch.

The houses, old, oddly planned, a turret here, a wraparound porch there, windows shaped and paned like spider webs, seemed not to have been built, but to have grown. The houses have their own seasons. Inside, one could age or not. One could age and not know it. One could age and not grow a day deeper in wisdom. To live in such a house would be to assume another form, another skin. In their stained glass windows, flowers bloomed season after season, requiring only light. Lions roared in cement from stoops and backyards. You could, thought Eleanor, go into one of those houses and never come out. It was a great good fortune to live in such a house. Such a house was, in itself, a destiny.

She had lived in one of those houses for over twelve years now and she still believed in it, in all of them, as the Greeks must have believed in their temples. *Offer up your life here and you will be rewarded.* The occasional problems of leaky roofs, of bathroom piping which inundates the dining room table on the floor below, the shock of standing in the bathroom and finding part of its floor gone and the dining room ceiling gone with it, seeing the children's heads moving, from up above, as if one had suddenly been granted a God's eye view: none of it—not coming home to a house in which the furnace had shut itself off and a thin skin of ice was choking the throat of the kitchen sink, the ingenious break-ins through basement windows she didn't know she had—had changed her view of the house as the one safe, the perfect, place.

Of course, she heard the arguments which spiraled out of the neighbors' opened windows when spring came, like long scrolls from the mouths of gargoyles. Of course, she had run from room to room to room, following the unending arguments of the Iusis who lived next door, and it amazed her that the arguments continued when the chill came down in the fall and the windows were closed. She knew it because when she again opened the windows in the spring, there were the voices, as if the Iusis were a book she had put down, marked with a bookmark, picked up and reopened at exactly the same place.

The Iusis proved conclusively that human misery was unending and possibly desirable, because they never learned. The tiny woman next door, Mrs. Iusi, in autumn and spring could be seen, thin as a stick of kindling, staggering under an enormous bundle of sawed-off oak limbs and twigs, while her enormous husband shouted at her: "Not there! Put them next to the cans!" That tiny woman dug the deep holes for the bushes in the yard they tended as if they knew their backyard was part of Forest Lawn and someday they would sleep beneath it, so that the yard was their bed, and beds had to be made daily, without wrinkles.

That tiny woman never complained when, in August, she was dispatched to the store with her shopping cart to drag home bag after bag through the one-hundred-degree heat while her husband, seeing her waver down the street toward him, would lean against the black Cadillac he had been washing, the beads of water still iridescent on its

hood, cool as a crocus pushing its way up through the first
snow, waiting for her to come close enough so he didn't
have to shout: "Did you remember the apple juice?"
When of course he hadn't asked for apple juice in the first
place. Something Eleanor knew because she had listened
when he dictated his order to the tiny creature, who
seemed to shrink with every new addition to the list as she
sat at the living room table in front of the window, writing
each item neatly down.

Eleanor had seen several of those lists, so neat, so elegant, calligraphy, really. But he would shout that she was
getting senile like her mother; she couldn't even write
down what she was told. She better go back and get that
apple juice or she could forget the barbecue she promised
her mother. Why should he get heat stroke for a woman
who couldn't bring back apple juice? What kind of barbecue was it without apple juice? What should he serve,
milk? In this weather? And poison them all?

Inside her own kitchen, whose window faced the
Iusis, Eleanor would hear her trying to fight back, but it
was like watching someone trying to climb a hill of ice: the
higher up she got, the further back she slid. It was her
fault all four of their daughters had run off pregnant. She
hadn't been strict enough with them. When he tried to be
strict, she'd undercut him. There was never any discipline
in the house. Father Murphy, he was sick of Father
Murphy, the way she waved him in front of his eyes. He
was a fraud, a nothing, a trickster. All he wanted was their
money every Sunday. What he said was nothing but what
she wanted to hear. He liked talking to women. He talked
the way a magician waved a handkerchief in front of a hat
to fool stupid people into thinking the rabbit hadn't been
there all the time. He knew all about rabbits and rabbit
tests. Now she was doing it again, their last chance, that

was what she was, their daughter Emily, but she would let her stand outside the house after dark with anyone who wanted to stand there with her. He knew she didn't make her wash off that green junk before she went out.

She was the one who let their daughter go out with fingernails painted black. Emily was a whore; her mother was a whore, her sisters were whores before her. It had to come from somewhere. It didn't come from his side of the family, but her family was always cheating, like her mother, who lay up there in the rental apartment, doing nothing, saying she had a cancer when she had a stomach virus. *If* she had a virus. He wasn't sure about that. Why was her *own* husband dead? Because she'd killed him with her complaining over nothing, and now his own wife was trying to kill him. She was a black widow spider and her mother was a black widow spider. They all were.

What did her mother have to do, screamed his wife, drop dead in front of him?

She could drop dead in front of me, he'd say, and it wouldn't mean a thing. She'd do anything to prove a point.

And of course she died, of cancer, and Mr. Iusi began making plans to move to the house in Florida which his mother-in-law had left them, and Emily cried every night on the front stoop, holding hands with the boy from the house on the other side of Eleanor's, Emily's hands never really clean, but her fingernails the envy of the women on the block, long, beautifully glazed, saying again and again that she didn't want to go to Florida, she wanted to stay here and marry him. Whereupon the front door of her house would open, her father's arm, like an arm in a cartoon, would reach out, grab his daughter by the shoulder and drag her inside, slamming the heavy oak door so the house shook. The daughter remained the whore. The

mother-in-law who had left the Florida house became
"that poor woman."

As the leaves fell, the arguments continued, and before the moving vans could pull up and begin loading the
cartons to be taken to the Florida house, Emily had run
off with the boy on the block and according to her father,
whose opinions roared out the open windows that autumn, she was pregnant and no daughter of his. And
when he stopped, breathless and exhausted, his wife's
high-pitched wail wound itself like torn white strips of
fabric in the naked trees: "You did it! You did it. You
drove them all off! You and your dirty thoughts!"

And after a while, out of pity, no one spoke to her, the
tiny woman who stumbled antilike beneath huge bundles
of sticks while her husband gave her directions: *left, to the
right, left again,* and that was just how her husband liked it.
Why should strangers meddle in their business? And so, finally, the neighbors left her absolutely and irrevocably
alone. Which was how the woman had lived her life: alone
with him. Although before, she'd had her mother.

The women on the block talk about Mrs. Iusi when
they pause before each other's house on the still-warm autumn evenings, on their way to school or back from the
supermarket, women who do not usually stop and talk because almost all of them work.

They are all like birds, Eleanor thinks, who sing loud-
est before the sunset, before the dark, and they talk as fast
as they can and as long as they can before the winter
comes down and shuts them away from one another. It is
something primitive, a reflex, a gathering of the tribes
when they scent the white wolf of winter.

How sorry they felt for Mrs. Iusi, there with him in
Florida, not knowing anyone. He didn't let her know anyone. Whenever she'd stood outside, attempting to talk to

one of them, hadn't everyone noticed how he'd manage to come out with some request: supper—well, at least that was reasonable. But he'd go on to ask for the most bizarre things, or say something was burning, or ask a question. Where had she put the registration? And why did he mind, when they always stood right under the window where he could listen to every word? No, they don't envy her in Florida.

You'd think, Eleanor volunteered, something could be done about someone like that. The other women laughed at her.

Do what? If she didn't like it, she could have moved out. Gone and lived with her mother. He was her cross to bear. No one carried something like that unless they wanted to. No, you had to be sorry for her because of what she wanted to carry.

Eleanor had cut a small dome-shaped entrance into the bottom of her garage door because Mr. Iusi put out traps for the dogs and cats witless enough to enter his yard, and when they ran from his yard, they found themselves trapped in the alleyway between his house and hers. And he bought a gun to shoot at the squirrels and the birds because he was sure the squirrels dug up his tulip bulbs. He had no reason for shooting at the birds. They sang too much, that was all. He got what he deserved for the traps, the women say, laughing softly. All the squirrels went into his yard where they didn't have to fear the waiting shadows with pointed ears and twitching tails which pounced on them with sharp claws and ripped them apart and left some of their flesh as a warning to the others. In spring, if a bulb straggled up in the Iusis' yard it was a miracle, because the squirrels dug there without fear, whereas Eleanor's yard was a constant torture to the man, waving with daffodils and tulips, full of cats and flowers, so many whorish women's tongues flaunting his wisdom, his authority.

You know, one of the women said thoughtfully, the most important thing to decide about a man is whether he likes women. Most men don't.

And a silence fell over them as they contemplated something which was undeniably true and therefore outlandish, something they didn't have time to contemplate just then with winter coming on and storm windows to be put up and oil men to call, something, alas, some of them would have to think about later, propped up in bed on one elbow, looking at the men asleep next to them: Does he like women?

So that this casual conversation, not meant to be about anything, a huddling in front of the fire before it goes out, would, inside the houses, slowly hatch and grow, and when spring came, would have taken on form, become possessed of an appetite, and before the storm windows were taken down, this chance remark would have consumed families. How many one was never sure. Simply counting the *For Sale* signs in front of the houses did not tell you.

And so Eleanor, standing across the street, waiting for Toh, admiring her own three-story Victorian house, its cream color and its chocolate trim, its turret, the little round room in which she types and reads, its long glassed-in porch on which the children play Ping-Pong and pool and learn kung fu from Toh. Eleanor ought to know that the houses had no power to protect their inhabitants from human misery. She ought to know that there is nothing magic about them. And yet she believes that miserable as anyone in the houses might be, they would be more miserable anywhere else, as Mrs. Iusi undoubtedly is in Florida amidst monstrous palm trees with beards.

The houses are here saying, by their very form: We are large and of many rooms and your family should be large and fill these rooms, and just as we are permanent and do not change, so you should be slow to change, and when you do, you should change slowly, a hammock here, a glass-topped table there. Change can be brought about in these small things, but not in your essential natures. Change slowly. Use caution. Build your house so large that you can run away without ever leaving home. Advice which Eleanor has always taken. Until recently, when she began breaking all the laws laid down by the dead architects whose spirits float gently up out of the chimneys all winter.

Toh is walking down the street. She recognizes him by his walk, not by what he wears, which is fortunate, because he seems to have his own sense of weather and will arrive in a sweater, coatless and hatless, on a day when the National Weather Bureau is announcing a weather emergency.

"Warm, huh?" he will say, surprised to find Eleanor bundled in a down coat, snow boots, gloves and a sheepskin hat.

"You're cold?" he asks her, and worried, turns up the car heater.

She has to be the one to turn it off. Toh, she thinks, likes women.

Today, he is coming toward her as if it were the height of summer—not early spring, when the weather still turns cold—wearing jeans and a white shirt patterned with flags: this Chinese shirt. He must have ten of them, all the same. If it were colder, he would be wearing his suede jacket, its sleeves too short for him. Like his reading glasses, far too small for his face, the glasses of a child. At times, she feels herself turning into her mother: "Appearances are important, too." She remembers her grand-mother's comment when she won her first award: "It's a good thing they don't give them for good housekeeping."

She has, in the few seconds he's walked close enough so that she can see his face clearly, turned back into her-self. Up above, her mother is absorbed in sweeping her cloud and has forgotten her. The short sleeves, the small lenses, the shirts from China, what do they mean but con-stancy of purpose? Clarity of heart. From which she bene-fits daily. People like that do not need houses. Like the snail, they carry their own on their back. Unlike the snail, their houses are big enough to allow others in.

TWENTY-FOUR

TOH STARTS UP the car and looks over at her.

"Oh," he says, "that dress is pretty."

An Indian dress, its yoke quilted satin, its skirt full and light in the breeze. A heavy sweater, folded, rests on her lap.

If her mother had put on such a dress, she would have worn a trenchcoat over it to keep it from embarrassing her. Or have found a way of weighting down its hem with small stones. Eleanor has skewered all of her hair to the back of her head. It is spring and windy and a strange man is calling Toh, threatening him, and she does not want to worry about her hair.

"Your hair is very pretty too," says Toh.

"Oh. Dyed," Eleanor says automatically, just as she automatically puts her hand to her hair. Is all of it in place? Is any of it falling down? For once, it is fastened firmly in place.

She asks Toh what the man said.

"He says he is coming to the house to discuss with me. I tell him I have nothing to discuss. He must call my lawyer. But he says he come anyway."

In the face of this crisis, all the endings to Toh's verbs have fled back into his grammar book.

The man is, apparently, coming to his apartment tomorrow afternoon.

"Oh," says Eleanor, "he doesn't work. That's why he's still after us." She thinks it over and says she's coming too.

"I don't think so. It is not good idea."

"If there are two of us," says Eleanor, and then stops because she cannot think of one good reason for meeting this hoodlum, this petty thief, this gangster. Except that he might be none of these things: he might be a murderer or an arsonist. If so, she ought to go and protect Toh. And how is she, blind without her glasses, not in any case the strongest person on earth, to protect him? By her mere presence. By which she means that if something is going to happen to one of them, it should happen to both of them at once, which explains why she long ago decided that her family should always fly together. It would not be worth living if she landed safely and found that half of her family had died on another plane. Better to be the victim of a disaster than its survivor.

But this troubles her: When did she begin viewing her life with Toh as a constant series of adventures aboard the *R.M.S. Titanic?* To see life with her family that way, that's expected.

It occurs to her, briefly, that the two parts of her life are coming to resemble each other more and more, two wings of a bird, herself the body. If that's true, she's made a mistake. Once again she has too much responsibility. She pushes away these thoughts as she used to push back her small dish of vegetables: good for you, no doubt, but she doesn't like them.

"You cannot come," says Toh. "I will tell husband."

"What?"

"I will tell Tom."

That should settle it.

But she feels panic. And she has never been inside his

apartment, which is only three blocks from her house. It seems, suddenly, very important to see it, as if she may never again have the chance. And yet she knows what the apartment is like.

She knows that the rooms are large and high-ceilinged and painted white, that the cracks in the plaster are outlined in gray soot from the furnace because the landlords of those buildings never paint after their tenants move in, and Toh and his roommates, who are always studying, do not have time to paint. She knows that the bathroom is long and narrow, and that its floors are covered with white and black tiles set in an octagonal pattern. She knows the oval shape of the deep wash bowl and the crack in the mirror of the medicine chest right above it. She knows the handle to that chest is pear-shaped faceted glass. The panes of glass in the window next to the tub are frosted and face the frosted windows of the bathroom in the next wing. The floors are oak, as are hers, but they have blackened like rotted walnuts because they were polished with wax for years and then no one polished or washed them again. She knows most of the windows are uncurtained, and the white cracked shades which shut out the street are easy to pull down but almost impossible to raise because the springs in their rollers have rusted. She knows the bottle-green linoleum on the floors of the kitchens, the flat plates of glass covering the ceiling bulbs. She knows the molding on the ceilings, the elegant rectangular shapes inlaid in the closet doors.

There is nothing she does not know about this archetypal Brooklyn apartment, but she has never been to this particular one, never been in it. Too much of Toh's life goes on beyond the margin of her sight. She wants to see these rooms which he has described so often, big empty rooms with just enough chairs for the occupants, rooms so quiet everyone flees from them to the uproar of the college library where freshmen have not yet learned to keep silent. Each bedroom contains nothing but two beds, two trunks, a pile of books near the head of each bed, and readers of those volumes gone, to class, to work in restaurants, to Chinatown for watches, spices, sneakers. In Chinatown, you can close your eyes and believe it's Peking, everything is so much cheaper there, but when you open your eyes you are far from home.

You never knew you could go so far, reluctantly turning back to the apartment on Coney Island Avenue, which is not even a nest, just a shelter from the wind, an animal's temporary lair on its way to its own eventual burrow or cave.

She wants to take possession of that shelter, to make part of it hers. The old, complicated Eleanor, hands sticky with possessiveness, is back. Something has turned. Is it the weather? No longer simply willing to trust, needing to test, to find out how much he will put up with: how much of her he can tolerate. Is she really safe with him?

"You agree?" asks Toh. "It is not a good idea?"

"I agree," says Eleanor, careful to ask exactly when the man is to come. She says she wants to know so she can be home when he calls to tell her what happened, thinking, I should wear jeans and sneakers when I walk over. No sense in provoking the muggers.

She asks Toh if he's sure he'll be safe and he says he is sure. His uncle will be there, too, hiding in a closet. They're both good fighters, he says, which is true. After they first played Ping-Pong, they demonstrated the art of kung fu for her, complaining the whole time that this is a form of exercise, not meant for hurting people. But they can hurt people and will if they have to. On the other hand, what if the man has a gun? What will all the skill in the world do then? She has to go because this is all her fault, because she lent him the car.

"You never know," says her grandmother, "how or when you will find your way out of this world."

More terrible by far than the idea of leaving this world is the idea of someone else's leaving, and leaving her behind, alone.

The man is supposed to come to Toh's house at two o'clock the next day. Eleanor leaves her own house at two fifteen. It will take her five minutes to walk there, her life flashing before her eyes, as they say it's supposed to when you're dying or drowning, she can't remember which.

She remembers skating up and down the block in front of her old apartment house, her scratched knees, leaving school by the back door to avoid the older boy her parents have hired to walk her home from kindergarten. She was five then. She remembers stopping in the playground ("Don't go into those bathrooms," says her grandmother. "There's a man sitting in there who cuts off your braids."), sitting on the green park bench with its black patches where the paint has chipped, each slat a map of some world or other, while on the concrete, the fleshy green leaves of the elms splash their own patterns of light and dark, maps and more maps. Her legs are maps, the roads marked by lines of caked blood. There are so many places to go it's impossible to choose among so many. No wonder she always comes home after her rambles.

There she is, jumping up and down *on* the green Girl Scout uniform, insisting she won't wear it. She doesn't want to look like everyone else. There is her mother, coming home from her school, saying the teacher said she'd grow up to live in a prison or institution. Did Eleanor have any idea of what it was like to sit there and listen to this in front of all the other mothers?

There she is, lying in bed, feeling Toh's hands tracing the many scars of her body, the incision made to allow the surgeons to find the womb and its benign growth, the cut to find the baby growing in the tube, the lost baby, the lost womb, and how his hands erased the scars, so that when she got up, she was always surprised to find them there.

"You'll end up just like her, just like your aunt! Alone!" she hears her mother shouting as she turns the corner and hesitates at the entrance to Toh's building. It's dark and dirty, but there's no one to step over, no one inside asleep over a bottle inside a brown bag. She scurries by the rusted mailboxes, over the black and white tile floor, up the stairs to the second floor, the first door on the right. She asked him which his apartment was long ago. She knows. She stops there, listening for voices, and when she hears them, she knocks.

TWENTY-FIVE

THE DOOR OPENS and Eleanor is confronted with a face so furious she barely recognizes it.

"Ummm," she says, feeling Toh's hand close over her shoulder and pull her into his little hall.

"Not safe out there," he says.

She follows him into the living room. It is exactly as she expected it to be, except for the geraniums blooming feverishly and hugely, their pale green leaves softening the light, their great red blooms electrifying the air, saying to anyone who might enter, I dare you to make small of this. These rooms may be empty and unpainted, but living things grow here, perhaps better than elsewhere.

Watched by the geraniums, she feels foolish for having come. And then she feels someone's eyes on her, and when she turns around, she is astonished to see her Uncle Arthur, who last year, after spending every penny he had on a thirteen-year-old Cadillac, left her Aunt Phyllis, and suddenly it was no longer necessary to put up with his presence at family gatherings. Uncle Arthur has been blackmailing Toh.

"You ought to be ashamed of yourself," she says. "What would Aunt Phyllis say?"

The man stares at her dumbfounded. A thin man whose skin hangs from his cheeks as if he'd just been boiled, who hasn't shaved in several days, whose smell is just beginning to drift across the almost unheated room toward the nostrils of her upturned nose. It is something like the smell of corn beef and cabbage cooking. How can Uncle Arthur, sitting there in a frayed blue plaid flannel shirt, have come to this?

The man asks Toh, "What's the matter, that broad's wigged out?"

Her Uncle Arthur never sounded like that—a thick Brooklyn accent, yes, Brooklyn Jewish, but not Cuban. This man sounds like Desi Arnaz. Still, thinks Eleanor, how dangerous can he be, a man who looks so like her uncle? Her father used to say the only harm he could do to himself was to eat himself to death. Probably this man didn't own the car Toh ran into. How did they know he had a license? Her uncle would have driven forever without one, but her grandfather put his foot down. If Uncle Arthur wanted money from the family, he'd have to get a license and drive like a human being. Driving, Uncle Arthur told them, was no trouble. He could drive in the dark with his eyes closed. At which point her grandfather poured himself another glass of schnapps and made his point again: No license, no funds. Get a job.

Arthur turned out, for once, to be right. When he eventually took the driving test, he had no trouble passing it. His difficulty lay in the written test, which was, he insisted, especially difficult on the days he took it. He was the only person anyone ever heard of who took the written test nine times and the driving test only once.

"The mind of a fruit fly," said her grandmother.

So great was his fear of the written test that he never let his license lapse, although everything else—electricity, telephone, water, life insurance—either lapsed or was shut off.

They would be driving along with him, clutching

each other or the back of their seats because it never occurred to Uncle Arthur to slow down before a stop. He liked to slam on the brakes, skid, and brag he'd stopped on a dime, and her grandmother, who every Thanksgiving announced she wouldn't live to see the next one, said she knew she wasn't long for this world, but for godssake, did he have to kill them all on a *holiday?* Couldn't they die like normal people in their beds?

And Uncle Arthur would say, "You know why I stopped here, in the middle of the block? Because there's a flashing red light. Does anyone in the car remember what a flashing red light means? I told you last time. Let's see who remembers."

"It means full stop, Art, you idiot," says her father, "a full stop."

"Then what about a flashing yellow?"

"Slow down and proceed with caution," says her father, who has gone, without trouble, through law school.

"To make the signs so similar, you'd think they'd have better sense," says Arthur.

"Art, it's two more blocks," says her father. "Give the women a break and let them walk the rest of the way."

Whereupon Arthur would become insulted, demand to know what was wrong with his driving, pull away from the curb as if the police were after him, while her grandmother clutched her stomach and glared at her daughter who had to marry into such a family, and her father shook his head in a silence soon to be broken: no point in irritating the lunatic while he was still at the wheel.

Later, her father rails to his own father about Art's driving, but her paternal grandmother says, "Drive with him, Samuel; it gives him confidence."

"For a smart woman," her father says lately, "she can be a brainless cantaloupe."

"I could have told you that," says her maternal grandmother, whereupon everyone falls to quarreling, the discord to be blamed, inevitably, on Uncle Arthur, whose mere presence created upheavals great enough to cause murder, mayhem, and mass divorce in a non-Jewish family. That's why, thinks Eleanor, we treasured him. He proved what a wonderful family we were.

Perhaps the man sitting in the chair is Uncle Arthur, who everyone knew to be crazy. Not on general principles had they come to this conclusion, a conclusion they automatically came to about anyone who married into the family. In this case, they had specific reasons.

Uncle Arthur liked to talk about his adventures during the Second World War, how the blood had spurted out of the pilot's neck just before he himself parachuted out of the plane, how he had hiked across seventy-five miles of desert to rejoin his troops, this after having sustained a serious bite from a camel who chased him into a ditch full of nettles, for which the peasants, who had to extract the nettles from the camel, blamed him, as if he had anything to do with the camel's decision. All these stories fascinated the children, but the adults even more, especially those who knew that Uncle Arthur had spent the war in Bayonne, New Jersey, selling used cars. For reasons unknown, the army had refused to take him. Probably, claimed her father, because they knew what the family only suspected: that he could neither read nor write.

Uncle Arthur had also sailed out in a rented boat on Sheepshead Bay and been struck by lightning. He himself was struck, not the mast, and he lived to tell the tale—not that he remembered the lightning, but he awoke with his shirt singed and a man bending over him, and that man had told him how the lightning came down, aiming at the mast, but at the last instant veered and struck him instead. On the third button of his vest.

Perhaps this is Uncle Arthur gone mad, his vocal cords clotted with a Cuban accent he has picked up from all those years of "I Love Lucy," first runs and then years of reruns, because Uncle Arthur never worked. It is possible.

"Someday," he would say, "I'll find what I have a knack for."

"He's got a knack all right, a knack for getting fired," said her father.

Impossible not to believe this frayed, smelly man is her uncle.

Alas, Toh is glowering at him, his expression that of a guard dog who sees its mistress menaced.

"Hmmm," says Eleanor, and sits down in a beige and gray tweed armchair, Good Will Industries, vintage 1940, the stuffing under both armrests beginning to emerge. The last owner had a cat. Is it her uncle, or is she confusing the present and the past?

"Who," she asks, "are you?"

If he is going to pretend he doesn't know her, why shouldn't she do the same?

"I'm his lawyer," she adds, pointing at Toh.

Uncle Arthur raises his eyebrows and snorts.

"There are a great many women lawyers nowadays," says Eleanor, "but if you want to speak to my male partner, that can be arranged."

The man looks her over. His eyes are gummy, yellow at the corners. He rubs his left eye until it becomes bloodshot.

"You can cause yourself quite an infection that way," she says.

"Are you a doctor or a lawyer?" he asks her.

"A lawyer."

"Lawyers don't make house calls," says Uncle Arthur. "No one makes house calls anymore."

"You do," Eleanor points out reasonably.

"I could cut you," the man says.

"Oh, I don't think so," says Eleanor.

Uncle Arthur bends forward, pulls up his trouser leg, and draws out a long sharp knife.

"How," asks Eleanor, "do you keep it from cutting you, carrying it around like that?"

"This is one crazy broad," says Uncle Arthur to Toh. He glares at her. "Is she really a lawyer?"

Silence.

"They don't go after lawyer-killers like they go after cop-killers," says Uncle Arthur.

"Just what is it you want from him?" Eleanor asks Uncle Arthur, who gets up, smiles, raises his fist, the knife clenched in it, above shoulder level and advances on Eleanor in her chair.

"There, stop," says Toh.

But the man does not stop.

Afterwards, Eleanor cannot say what happened. She hears a door opening behind her and knows it is Toh's uncle coming out of the closet in which he has hidden himself. She sees Toh moving through the air, flying really, freed of gravity, his foot in its sneaker aimed at the man's head. This, thinks Eleanor, who is there and not there, is like one of Uncle Arthur's stories. She next sees the three of them struggling on the floor, all apparently after the knife. Toh and his uncle speaks rapidly in Chinese.

The man's arm detaches itself from the mass of arms and legs; the knife in his hand flashes, catches the light.

Toh's uncle grunts in disgust, and then she sees Uncle Arthur prostrate on the floor, Toh's uncle kneeling on his chest, the knife in his hand raised high in the air, but when Toh's uncle brings it down, he brings it down gently and then slowly he begins to write something, a character whose meaning she does not understand, on the man's forehead.

Toh and his uncle continue their conversation, of which she does not understand a word. Apparently, as far as they are concerned, she has not yet reappeared from whatever dimension she conveniently disappeared into. Toh gets up, goes into the kitchen, and returns with paper towels which he folds into a large pad and presses against Uncle Arthur's forehead.

"Now," says Toh to the room at large, "we call the police."

The paper towels are already darkening with blood.

"No," says Uncle Arthur. "I'll get out. I'll get out."

His face is gray speckled with pink like a slice of cold ham. More conversation between Toh and his uncle. They take out Uncle Arthur's wallet, find his license and copy down his name, license number and address.

"So we know where to find you," says Toh. "My Uncle's gang, it is fearsome."

Eleanor admires this. She is not the only one in the room with imagination.

"You get out now?" Toh asks Uncle Arthur, "or you wait for the others to get back?"

Uncle Arthur says he will go now. He backs out into the vestibule, one hand clutching the matted paper towels to his forehead.

"We know where to find your den now," says Toh.

They hear the sound of the man's feet running down the stairs.

242   SUSAN FROMBERG SCHAEFFER

Eleanor is as astonished as a child who has seen her first angel. She stares at both of them.

"In China," explains Toh, "my uncle was germinal."

"Germinal?"

"He stole things from the government. Government never caught him."

"Criminal," says Eleanor.

The uncle says something.

"Small time," says Toh, translating.

"I could have sworn," says Elenaor, who is binding up Toh's uncle's arm with gauze from a first aid kit which has emerged from the bathroom, "that he *was* my Uncle Arthur."

Toh's uncle mutters something.

"He says," Toh tells her, translating, "no wonder the man thought you were crazy. Is that right? Were crazy? The grammar?"

"Yes," Eleanor says, bewildered. Does she really have no sense of danger at all? Why was it so important to get in these rooms and inspect their contents? Was it worth the knife to see the geraniums blazing in the window?

It was and is.

Now, however, Toh wants an explanation, and he does not want it in this room. He and his uncle take her out onto the street and the three of them sit on the stoop. Silent. Toh's uncle assures them he's fine. He's going to work in the restaurant. He'll tell them he got mugged on the train. Everyone will believe that. Eleanor thanks him again and again, but Toh puts a stop to it.

"Time to go," he tells his uncle. So unceremonious, the partings of Orientals.

They walk his uncle to the Newkirk Avenue station, watch the train pull away, and Toh asks her again: Why did she come? She tries to explain, but does not really understand why herself.

"Not good," says Toh. "If our lives tangle too much, they choke each other."

"I know."

"It is more serious for *you*," he says. "You have much to lose. I go back to China. I have nothing. But it is serious for you."

Eleanor starts to cry. He asks her why she's crying and she says she does this every time he mentions going back to China.

"Every time?" he asks, amazed.

"Every time."

"If I do it again, you cry again?"

"Please don't," she says. He doesn't.

"How angry are you because I came?"

"Oh. Very angry. Choleric."

She looks puzzled.

"Choleric does not mean angry? In Chinese dictionary it says so."

"God knows," says Eleanor. "I'll look it up when I get home."

She stares down at her hands. She has walked into the house which he did not want her to enter. She might as well have walked, unbidden, into his heart, pausing in each chamber to take inventory. She has trespassed and knows she has trespassed and knew, before she did so, that she would be punished, that she was calling down a punishment.

She opens the front doors to her house and they go in and sit down in the living room. Quiet. Thursday afternoon. Ballet lessons, math tutoring. She still feels the harsh red light of the geraniums on her hands. She looks up at the stained glass window and sees a red light diffusing itself through the drops of rain on the window.

"Has it been raining long?" she asks Toh. He is puzzled. How can she not have noticed? She is always the first one to notice anything.

"You could have been killed because of me," she says at last. "I was an idiot to have come."

"No difference," says Toh. "The danger is exactly the same. You were discretion."

"Distraction," says Eleanor, herself distracted. Her presence was a help, but he is angry.

There are times now when Eleanor suspects herself of wanting to take her own life back, but of not having the courage. She has moved from the text of the page to the glorious emptiness of the margin and the miracle of it is that the text continues to print itself day after day without her, and she knows that if she stopped to read it, she would be one of the main characters of the story. Her defection from the family has not gone unnoticed, but it has been benevolently interpreted. It is caused by a need to heal, to make sense of things. One day it will be over, and when one of the children shouts at her she will shout back and send him to his room, lock his door, issue ultimatums, instead of doing what she does now, sighing merely.

She has been away before: when she is writing or when she goes off to give a reading: The trick, for her, is to kiss them and say, as she always does when she leaves, "Back soon." And they do believe she will be back soon because she always has been. This time she has been away somewhat longer than expected, but even small children know how upsetting it is to have one's eyes cut up, not to be allowed to bend over, to have to ask someone else to pick everything up. What they do not know is that the margin is not a frightening place this time, not an iced-in land where small creatures wait, like baby seals, to be clubbed to death.

No, it has become the safe place, and the blocks of print which mark margin's end are like cliffs against which anything might be smashed: best to stay away. At margin's end is a new country with guards posted to inspect passports, and Eleanor does not even know what kind of passport she needs. She suspects she needs character, courage, all the old virtues, and she knows she has none of them. Although lately, there have been glimmerings.

The last time she and Toh were driving together, the car swerved, and when Toh got out to inspect the wheel, she found herself watching him as if she had never seen him before. She notes his height, five feet seven inches, and how short he really is, only three inches taller than she is.

On the way to the movies with Tom, he tells her that the morning before, Toh was looking out of their kitchen window, and he pointed the crocuses out to him.

"Crocuses?" Toh says. "Isn't that what Gary Hart just won?"

Tom says, no, that was a *caucus*. Eleanor laughs, but wonders if Tom is becoming fonder of Toh, as he seems to be, and if he is more fond of him, might that not be a good thing?

Crocuses, caucuses, the beginning of a new season, spring heating up into summer, the lenses of her eyes removed by a surgeon, but not sitting firmly on the bridge of her nose, a pair of steel-rimmed spectacles. She is beginning to accept them. Her body, that ancient enemy, has been making gestures of friendship, not because she has grown better at accepting time's scarring hands raking across her but because she sees herself, her body, as Toh does. It is as if the lenses of his eyes have been transplanted into her own.

"You're not a prime candidate for an implant," the doctor told her. "if we implant a lens in your eye, the chances are you'll outlast the lens, we'll have to operate to remove it, and then who knows what will happen?"

"Finally," she writes her aunt in Arizona, Lucy, her mother's sister, "I've found something old age is good for. If you're going to have cataracts, it's better to be old. The old people have lenses implanted and see right away."

Her aunt promptly writes back and says: "Growing old is not like turning into a butterfly. You don't shed this wrinkled skin and turn into something beautiful and fly away. You just get uglier and uglier and weaker and weaker. It's bearable only when you tell yourself you've had your day. And since you do reap what you sow, it's best to sow a good crop. Amazing, how the past fills these days with light, handing you tray after tray of the most exotic marvels and all of them only days from your past."

And then she falls back into the familiar scolding. No point in letting her niece sink too far into self-pity: "Your mother wore glasses from the time she was four years old. In our family, it was freakish not to wear glasses. Now that you know you're not losing your sight, be reasonable and adjust. Also get your blood-sugar level checked every six months, because as people get older they develop diabetes and diabetic eyes often become blind ones."

Blood-sugar level! Something new to worry about. She puts down her aunt's letter and smiles. A medical miracle, how she seems to have had new lenses donated to her by Toh. They should write it up, how her impossible mind, which rejects all poultices, all offers of help, has grown psychic lenses to take the place of the ones which were removed.

The phone rings and Toh asks her if she wants to go for a drive. It is a soft, high-domed blue day drifting into summer. She is postponing any serious work ("I may," she writes a friend in England, "make this a chronic condition, like malaria, something that subjects me to sudden attacks, incapacitates me without warning, especially during the reviewing season or the time of selecting judges for various awards.") because she does not yet take seriously the fact of her own health. Surely if whatever it is that hands out punishments finds that she can see, she will be visited with yet another affliction. She has been fighting with this notion for weeks and finds herself staring at a notebook whose cover bears an illustration of Saint George fighting a dragon. How would Saint George feel, she wonders, if he knew he was going to be eaten? If he could feel the white enamel tusked teeth against his skin? The world outside her window has put on its green dragon skin.

She ought to tell Toh she loves him. She never has. There was no need. She knows that she ought to sever her life from his but cannot imagine doing so. Of course, there may be revolutions or earthquakes which will do the trick, but nothing she does will serve.

It is all Uncle Arthur's fault for appearing as he did. That's why she's thinking along these lines. Her grandmother always said that his presence was enough to turn Thanksgiving into the last act of *Macbeth*. Why had she had a grandmother who was arbitrary, irrational, and also literary? It made her arguments so much harder to refute. So many literary allusions, it was difficult to convince oneself that what she said didn't make sense or was simply unintelligent. How like unto a literary critic, thinks Eleanor, who has no immunity against them, either.

She wants to answer her aunt's letter. She had better answer it before her aunt dies, the only one of the family who ever had any sense, and ask her if she knows of any misery more terrible than going through life seeing yourself as other people see you, especially if the wrong kind of people are watching you. Isn't that a form of blindness? How has her aunt managed it, seeing herself as she is all these years? No wonder so many people in the family misunderstood her, dismissed her as smug, when in fact all she had done was see herself as she was.

"Dear Aunt Lucy," she writes without using pen or paper (this is fun, like skywriting), "I know there are famines and starving people in labor camps, but how does this cancel out the misery of any one living soul? Aunt Lucy, it doesn't."

"Don't tell me," says her grandmother (whose voice seems to be getting fainter, bad reception through the ether), "you're comparing your little troubles with the Russian Revolution? Or the Chinese? Or the starving children in Europe? You can't be that egocentric."

"Why listen to her?" Eleanor's aunt asks sensibly.

"I've gotten old enough to know the truth," says Eleanor. "I know I don't have to compare my misery to theirs."

"Old enough," sneers her grandmother. "You're only forty. Going on forty-one."

She adds this automatically, as she always did at Eleanor's birthday parties: "Shame on you! Seven years old, going on eight!"

"I am old enough," says Eleanor. I see how every ten years moves you that much closer to death. I see how many of my friends are already dead, and how many of

Toh's, who died much younger. "You have time, you have time," that great refrain of yours, it's a terrible lie. We're all dying, look at these wrinkled hands, there's so little to hold on to, it goes away so fast, how many people still remember the barber poles outside the barber shops, their red and white spirals twisting, who remembers the chicken farms in Rockaway Beach, who remembers the little chicken eggs the size of the digit of one finger, the ones you used to cook in the soup, does anyone remember what chicken legs *look* like, their scaly skin, their claws sent up to the surface by liquid bubbling in the pot, pointing, like little monster feet, up at the ceiling, does anyone remember any of that?

And there's so little time for mistakes. One mistake can use up ten years before it's fixed, and then you're forty, or fifty, and if you're lucky you may have time to switch trains, get out on the landing, climb up the stairs, go down to the other side, and wait for the train to take you back, but most people aren't lucky, most people die wailing about what they haven't done, what they haven't accomplished, sorry about everything, for not having said they loved this one or that one, for not having closed the door firmly and done their own work, for not having known what work they wanted to do, for envying empty lives and storing their own lives, like out-of-season clothes, in the basement somewhere, not even in the back of the closet where they might have reached in and grabbed them by mistake. It's not a game. There's no stalemate, no checking the king in his position. We all move across the board to the other side, and no one crowns us there.

And wouldn't it be better if we were all preoccupied with our own deaths, as people used to be, so imaginatively stitched by that master tailor, so that no matter whom we have become or what size we have grown to be, that garment always fits perfectly, wouldn't it be better if we thought about nothing but that black suit waiting for us? Why burn anyone at the stake when the stake is already through the heart? Why do anything but keep one's eyes open as long as possible? To keep one's face turned to the light. So little time! Tell them the great tragedy is stumbling blind through life, as I have, following after your voice, and my mother's and my father's. I might as well have had no eyes at all, or an insect's mosaic eye, which sees everything, but so patterns it that what it sees makes no human sense, too many prisms, too many facets.

"You think you're learning to mourn," says her grandmother, "but you're not. You'll never be able to let things go. It's an inherited inability. We all suffer from it."

Eleanor gets up and walks over to the window.

"Dear Aunt Lucy," she says. "I am happy to inform you that there are some skins it is possible to shed. The skins of others."

When she looks down at her bare feet, the blue light pools on the floor as if it were a dress she had unzipped and let fall around her feet.

Is it really possible to mourn the past? Eleanor asks herself, and knows that the mere asking of the question contains the answer.

The bell rings. Eleanor takes her trench coat: mid-May. It can still turn cold. She takes her large key ring and lets herself out the front door. "Back soon," she says to the dog on the bottom step, the cat on the step above.

TWENTY-SIX

THE PARKING LOT in front of the beach buildings is deserted. The white car is parked in the row of spaces nearest the sand, and, as they walk away from it, it looks like an animal grazing on the gritty earth. They walk past the red brick rococo buildings, bathrooms, now shut up because of too many incidents. After fifty years, a vindication of her grandmother's wisdom. The green, short pines look drab now, having provided the only color during the long gray winter. Some of their branches are already bearing red berries. But there is a chill in the air, and Eleanor thinks that if she were back in Chicago, she would be sure it would snow. She tells Toh what she thinks.

"Impossible," he says. "No snow after Chinese New Year."

She has been telling Toh about the beach for some time. Now, as they reach the grayish-beige band of the beach which the sea rhythmically licks, he jumps forward, picks up a clamshell, jumps back and holds it to his ear.

"I hear nothing," he says.

"It's the wrong kind of shell," says Eleanor, peering into a large tangle of seaweed.

Ah, a conch. She picks it up carefully. In past springs, she has picked up large shells and found the original tenant still at home, viscous, mucuslike. This one is empty.

"Here," she says, handing it to Toh.

"Oh," he says, laughing. "Wonderful."

He starts to put it back in the seaweed.

"No, take it," she says.

He hesitates and she holds out her hand for it. The shell is gritty, damp with gray sand, but it is a fine specimen and she puts it in her trench-coat pocket.

They stand side by side, looking down the beach. They can see no buildings, just small dune after small dune, stretching away to the vanishing point. The sand has been patterned to waves by the incoming water. Eleanor turns to look at the water, jade green waves topped with white, the water farther out bright silver, reflecting the sun as the water close to them does not. About their damp sneakers are broken shells, trailing seaweed still alive with little silver bubbles from the last wave to reach this far, logs with toothmarks from dogs who have been brought here to run, and a few feet away, several paper bags and four empty cans of Moose Beer.

"People are already starting to come," says Eleanor.

Too early yet to see condoms, candy wrappings, aluminum pop tops, diet soda cans in the sand. But in another week, they will be there. The unending sound of the sea: *shush, shush, shush, crash.* They are standing by a windbreak, a slatted fence whose brown posts have long since turned gray. The high wind has blown the sand close to the top of the fence, but in some places the sand drops down level with the rest of the beach.

"Rhythms everywhere," says Eleanor, who then has to explain the meaning of the word.

The sound of the sea in your ear is only the sound of your own pulse. Does she believe that now? Finally?

The wind blows. The sky darkens. The whole sea is iron gray and the sun is pulling back like a large jewel on a hand that has moved to a different part of the keyboard.

"Like winter," says Toh, who is starting to shiver.

"It's going to snow," says Eleanor.

"Impossible," says Toh, but by the time they are back in the car, great balls of hail are hammering at the windshield and the roof of the car.

"How do you always know about the weather?" he asks her.

"Experience," she says somewhat grimly, thinking, if they cut me down like a tree, they would wear themselves out counting the rings.

By the time they have pulled out of the great empty parking lot and begun to cross the metal drawbridge back to the mainland, the bridge is coated with an icy slush.

"Slippery," says Toh, his face shadowed again and again by the windshield wipers. Eleanor does not tell him to be careful, as she would Tom, because she knows how careful he is, how well he remembers the accident on the way back from the airport.

"Music from the sky," he says solemnly.

"Oh," says Eleanor, "thunder. What crazy weather."

They drive past the little marina near Kings Plaza, the vast shopping complex that would have pleased her grandmother, the family bargain hound, and Eleanor asks Toh to turn right onto Avenue U. She wants to pass the apartment where she was born.

"Homesick, huh?" Toh asks her, but she says no, it's just the opposite.

He is about to ask her something when a car suddenly pulls out from Knapp Street, a small car, Eleanor will never forget it, shocking green, as if a child had selected the color, a very popular color this year, and Toh yanks the wheel toward her side, trying to avoid it, but the car goes into a skid and begins making a full circle, just as the green car has gone into a skid, and is also traveling in

a circle, but the two arcs, she realizes, are going to inter-
sect. She sees Toh looking at her, *don't worry, don't worry,*
and then the other car hits them with such force that their
doors spring open as if the car, startled, discovered it was
really a bird and was now attempting to fly.

She is lying on the black asphalt, on her stomach, her
hand stretched out in front of her and what she sees is this:
A tide of some kind is coming toward her and while she
watches, her own hand withers, grows thinner, and the
rings on her fingers begin to turn inwards, as if the bands
had now decided to become the objects of attention, and
the sparkling facets of their stones were only to be seen by
people who for one reason or another thought to turn her
hand over and look at her palm. She is looking down on
herself now, from above, as if a seagull had taken her eyes
up for a trip through the air, and she sees her long hair
graying, frizzing, matting into thick strands all of which
end in rats' tails. Her straight back has become humped.
Her long legs are covered with prominent veins, some
blue-black, some pale blue. The breasts she lies on are
shriveling, as is her stomach, which shrivels as if all its fat
were melting beneath her skin and being drawn off.
She is watching herself turn into a crone and knows if
the process continues much longer, even a few seconds
longer, her face will assume the death mask all old faces
put on in their last hours: the hooked nose, sunken cheeks,
the lips which seem to pull in over the teeth so that the
mouth seems toothless. Then the curved spine will press
against her heart. Her lungs will fill with water. The blood
will thicken in her veins, and here on Avenue U, ten
blocks from where she was born, she will drown. She lifts
her head slightly and looks for Toh and sees he is lying
five feet from her, his head raised, looking at her. They

look like two half-dead turtles with their heads up like this, and she sees him reach out his hand toward her and as he stretches his hand out to her, her own hand, of its own accord, pulls back.

Someone is bending over her. He is saying, "You're all right, you're fine," and she says, "Take care of Toh," but the man doesn't seem to hear her. Perhaps she hasn't spoken. Perhaps she is unable to speak.

TWENTY-SEVEN

WHAT SHE NEXT SEES is a brilliant, milky light. The source of this light seems to be two rectangles floating gently above her. They bob up and down. After a while, she turns her head slightly. There is something soft under her. It must be a pillow. She sees a dark red shape floating in the air near her head. It seems to be coming closer.

"Are you awake?" asks a voice.

Jane.

"Where did you come from?"

"They told me to put on your glasses as soon as you woke up," says Jane, bending over and Eleanor feels the cold rim of her glasses on the sides of her nose. The glasses yank the room, the world, out of the mist, into a sharpness cruel to the mind. Eleanor looks at her hand. No more wrinkled than it was before the accident. There is Jane, that beloved face. How did she get here, wherever she is?

"Don't say 'Where am I?' " says Jane, and Eleanor smiles.

Oh good, thinks Jane, her lips aren't broken.

"You're in Coney Island Hospital for observation. It's a good thing you were wearing a seat belt. I wasn't so smart when I got hit by a car. They had to sew up my nose and my mouth. When did you start wearing seat belts?"

"Where's Toh?" asks Eleanor. "What happened to Toh?"

"Nothing happened to Toh. When the car hit you, it hit on his side and he wasn't wearing a seat belt so he was thrown into you. I think he broke some of your ribs. He's asleep out in the hall. Tom's asleep in the hall. They're sleeping against each other and if either of them moves, they'll both end up on the floor."

"Good grief," says Eleanor.

"Yes," says Jane, "good grief."

Eleanor takes a deep breath and discovers it's hard to breathe.

"That's because your ribs are broken," says Jane; "feel your side. You're all taped up. A man pulled you out of the car. He thought it might explode. The paramedics weren't too happy with him. They'll let you go home in the morning if you don't decide to have an embolism or something."

"Make them go home," Eleanor says. "They ought to get some sleep."

"Actually," says Jane, "Toh is sleeping overnight in the next room. He's out in the hall in a hospital gown. They're keeping him here for observation as well."

Eleanor says she's sleepy and doesn't feel much pain. Jane tells her she's had enough Darvon to kill a horse. She won't feel anything for a while. She felt the pain before, though, when she was awake.

"I was awake before?"

"Awake and talking to your grandmother. Something about suffering."

"Oh, God," says Eleanor. "Did I have anything else to say?"

Are the two of them really having this conversation?

Hasn't she heard it before? On "The Guiding Light" or "Days of Our Lives"?

"Come on, Eleanor, even delirious you know how to keep your mouth shut."

No answer. Eleanor is looking around the room, at the plug for oxygen, the sign saying Don't Smoke, the curtains pulled around the other, temporarily empty, bed.

"You thought you were dead?" Jane asks her, and she nods.

"That's what I thought after I woke up, after my accident. Although I can see better than you can without glasses, so I didn't know why there were wheelchairs in heaven. It's a good thing you had that card in your wallet saying you're a contact lens wearer. I thought you'd given up on them. I forgot your eyes started tearing again. When did you start getting so careful?"

"Since I had so many children."

Jane, who has been told not to upset her, as if she were likely to do anything of the kind, doesn't ask her what she means. In any event, she knows.

"Who do you want to see, Tom or Toh?"

But Eleanor has fallen asleep, the sleep of the innocent or the drugged. I'd take either, thinks Jane. Funny, she's always had trouble sleeping, but Eleanor never has, except back in high school. Eleanor's trouble has always been staying awake.

When Jane fails to persuade Tom to go home, she sits on the bench next to him and eventually falls asleep leaning against his shoulder.

Tom wakes up and sits there, between Jane and Toh, staring at the door of his wife's room as if he were looking into the mouth of a beast that had swallowed her whole.

At ten o'clock, his wife still asleep, Tom wakes Toh, sends him back to his room, wakes Jane, who follows him home in her car and then goes to sleep on the couch in the television room. He goes upstairs to his study and turns on the television. He can never get to sleep when Eleanor is not there. He turns the dial until he finds a rerun of *The Thin Man*. He watches it until he falls asleep in his chair, and in the morning his son shakes his arm, saying, "Daddy, it's time to go to school." He follows the child downstairs, tells him to take off the Michael Jackson T-shirt; he slept in it last night. He can't wear it to school today. Tom hears himself telling the boy that Mommy will be back soon. To his own surprise, he believes what he is saying.

Jane wobbles out onto the landing wearing Eleanor's green robe, her hair in hot curlers. She has apparently borrowed them from the absent Eleanor and slept in them, although as his wife has told him frequently enough, sleeping on those curlers is like sleeping on rocks and she believes her skull has been permanently dented by them.

For the first time, Tom likes her. He never did before. A tragedy she wound up single, he thinks. Eleanor was right, is almost always right. For instance, she never thought it was tragic that Gloria didn't marry. Although she did say that Gloria and Colin ought to take each other out of circulation and thus benefit the rest of the human race. He is happy with the children, busy cooking them sausage and eggs. To hell with cholesterol. To hell with the constant arguing of the junior achievers. In a few hours, he will pick his wife up from the hospital, liberate her, as she used to say, from the Coney Island Municipal Hospital Shoe Factory and Concentration Camp.

Jane asks him if he'd mind if she took the children to the circus, and he says of course not, but she'd better ask Eleanor. "It's harder than it looks," he tells her.

When Eleanor next wakes up, the room is still bright white, and everything is sharp, clear, suspiciously clear. Oh, Jane was smart enough to leave her glasses perched on her nose when she fell asleep. She now sleeps with her glasses on, just as she often sleeps in her curlers. What a sight I must be some mornings, she thinks. When she turns her head toward the door, she sees Toh sitting in the chair next to her bed.

"Go back to sleep," she tells him. "You need the sleep too."

"I'm not tired. I start to think, someday I will die in a car. You think so?"

"Nonsense. It was bad luck."

Still, she wonders. Her parents were forever in accidents and they died in one.

"So much bad luck and all of it in a car."

Not inscrutable, thinks Eleanor: superstitious.

"When we get out," Eleanor says, not looking at him, "we have to talk. I'm taking up your time. It isn't right. It's not time you'll have back again. It won't come back."

He starts to protest: She knows he doesn't want to get tangled up with a girl while he's still studying. What good would he be to the girl? He might get distracted and not finish. Besides, he is happy as he is. *This minute.* An expression he has picked up from Eleanor.

"No, no," she says, "it's all wrong. I never should have allowed it. You're not thinking properly. You need to find another girl who's busy and studying. Then everything will be fine. You have to have children. You can't just get your degree and walk outside and bump into a wife. You're getting too used to me. You'll have trouble getting used to someone else."

He tells her not to talk so much; her ribs are broken.

She didn't make him think the way he thinks. He cannot think otherwise.

"We'll see about that," Eleanor says.

Toh begins to cry and Eleanor holds his hand and strokes it.

"Upset about the accident?" she asks, and he says yes, he is. But that, of course, is not why he's crying.

TWENTY-EIGHT

I T IS HOT NOW in the little room they share in China-town, early June, so hot Eleanor no longer bothers trying to hide her face with her hair, but wears it in a tight chignon. In July, she and her husband will leave for their house in Maine—children, dog and cats, all of them—and according to the schedule they have arranged, Toh will move into their city house, watch it, and feed the cat, who is too old to travel. None of this has yet become important, or even real, to them.

But Eleanor, who, when she closes her eyes, sees her body on the black asphalt, her hand outstretched, as the sun tears through the sky dragging her body after it, aging it suddenly, is intent on changing things back to what she likes to call normal. She has gone over it again and again: how young he is, how he can't afford to waste time. It's a new season. They are like the snow that falls after the New Year. They can't stick. She cites every proverb he has ever quoted to her: the stupid bird flies first. Well, then she is the stupid bird. It's time for her to fly first, but nothing alters that mulish exterior, that extravagantly agonized face.

"It is because I bore you," he says.

Bore. Where did he learn that word? She's forgotten how many books she's given him to read and how methodically he's been devouring them. And that he talks to other people when they're not together.

"You don't bore me. Sooner or later, one of us, you or me, was going to say this had to stop. *This*. This life in the room together."

He'll still be part of the family. He *is* part of the family. There's nothing to worry about. It has to stop. She hasn't been paying enough attention to the children. She can see perfectly well now. She has to take back her responsibilities.

"Because I have no future? No money?"

"*You* have a future," she says, "I have more of the same. This was never supposed to have any future. That was your rule."

"Then I continue seeing girl I met in Student Union," he says.

"What? What girl?" she asks, outraged. And decides to postpone her plans to break things off.

It is almost the beginning of July and Eleanor's family is about to leave for the summer when Toh gets out of bed, looks down at her, and says, "After this, we cannot stick."

"Our Chinese New Year?" she asks, looking up at him.

She begins to cry. He gets back into bed and begins stroking her hair. Finally she falls asleep.

He watches her, memorizes the pronounced bones of her cheeks, the long black lashes against the white skin—surely healthy skin should not be so white—the little birthmark above her mouth on her right cheek.

She wakes up and watches him sleeping. Lost in the woods, the two of them. But who is the witch? If there is no witch, it is time to go home.

"Without you," he says later, "I will be empty. There is not another person in the world like you. For you the world spins."

She stops lacing up her sneakers, a new pair of laces, white with red Chinese letters, everything is so much cheaper in Chinatown, and sits still as if paralyzed. She had no idea he thought of her in that way, no idea he could bring himself to say such things aloud.

"It was our two souls," he says. "Together."

She starts to cry agin.

"I will never be without you," she says.

At home, in her own bedroom, the walls of her room around her like another skin, looking back and forth from thing to thing, the gingerbread clock hung with necklaces, the little stuffed pillows impaled with rhinestone pins, the two decorative urns draped with hair ribbons, the warm gold shine of the sun on her newly polished oak furniture, the long gold rectangles of sun on the Oriental carpet, she summons up the room in Chinatown, and when she does this, she begins to cry, not a painful crying, but a kind of breathing in and out.

That little room, empty as air. She thinks of the white walls, their gray dust-streaks, the little metal bed floating like a raft on a very small sea, the child's chest of drawers with the gold and white decal of a lamb skipping, the inevitable battered suitcase in a corner of the room, laid flat, used as a coffee table—that same suitcase she saw in Toh's apartment, in his roommate's cubicle, the sign of the new refugee—the linoleum on the floor, in places worn to expose the gray softwood boards, the paint-spatter design so popular over forty years ago. She is saying goodbye to everything in the room, the lace-patterned curtains at the cracked window, goodbye to those, the world never looked so lovely through the clean seamless panes of any house she ever lived in. Goodbye, goodbye.

She looks up at the ceiling of her own room. The roof has leaked this winter and the plaster above their bed has peeled, leaving greenish-yellow stains behind. Big yellow-white blossoms of plaster are about to fall. Time to call someone to do something about the ceiling. Lucky for everyone she couldn't see it earlier. What a lot of complaining they missed. Now she knows that a bench on the front porch needs repairing, as do two of the bamboo blinds. The dog has trampled some of the bulbs in the backyard and there is hardly any grass left. The children have been tunneling like moles in the back of the house and no one over seven could negotiate that series of craters without breaking a leg. All the holes have to be filled in. Dust has collected above the heat registers during the winter, turning the walls black. Time to wash or paint them. This series of aggravations means that she can see, really see. She never thought she'd be able to see properly again. She turns on her side and looks out the window. Now that she's begun crying, she wonders if she's ever going to stop.

TWENTY-NINE

AT GREAT EXPENSE, Jane has bought a young weeping willow whose slender leaves are now flickering against the windows of her new condominium in Queens.

"How old is it?" Eleanor asks.

"Four," says Jane. "Congratulate me. I adopted it from a nursery. I'm a mother."

"Maybe," Eleanor says after a while, "you should adopt a child."

"At my age? With my mind? Which I'm out of most of the time? I barely lived through taking your kids to the circus. They wanted everything they saw. I couldn't say no to them. I thought I'd bring them home with advanced cases of sugar poisoning."

"They *staggered* in under all the things you got them. They said they had a wonderful time."

"When they weren't asking me how old I was," Jane says, "they kept saying, 'You don't look so old for a forty-year-old person.' They kept asking me if they had cars in my day. Otherwise they were fine. They believed me when I said I watched them build the Brooklyn Bridge."

"Children have no sense of time."

"Oh, well," says Jane, "they made me feel like Methuselah. Or like a three-year-old."

"A three-year-old about to have a temper tantrum?"

"Right," says Jane.

"I feel that way all the time. You're not so bad. Adopt one," Eleanor says. "I raised the two monsters you're talking about and they still haven't killed anybody. Knocked out an eye tooth, given me black eyes, but nobody's dead."

"Is Toh in the market for another older woman?"

Eleanor doesn't answer but begins fiddling with the folds of her yellow cotton skirt.

"Stop that," says Jane.

Eleanor looks at her.

"Stop staring at me like one of your cement lions," Jane says.

"We should find Toh a wife," Eleanor says absently.

"You *are* out of your mind."

"You weren't there. You didn't see what it was like. He was miserable. I was miserable. I never expected it."

"Look, Eleanor, you're the one who wouldn't wear the Brownie uniform because you didn't want to look like everyone else. You *never* agree with anyone else. According to you, Orientals aren't inscrutable. Chicago isn't cold if you know how to dress there. Most parents hate their children more than half of the time. So why do you believe people when they say only the woman gets wrecked when an affair ends? You should hear some of my men patients. Talk about seduced and abandoned. You're intelligent. You ought to know better. He was younger than you were. He didn't know anyone in the country. He always used to talk about how hard it was, not having family. *You* people were his whole family. What did you expect?"

"I suppose," Eleanor muses, "it started because he didn't know anyone else."

Jane makes a face at her.

"Do you remember that cat? Fred? The one you thought was so stupid because he adored you even if you made faces at him? Remember Fred?"

Eleanor nods.

"Remember Flake? The cat who followed you home from school? The one we wound up taking in? Your mother didn't want anything in the house that shed fur."

"I remember," says Eleanor. "So what?"

"An idiot could see he adored you."

"Who? The cat?"

"No. Toh. Remember what happened with Fred?"

"Why are we talking about Fred? Toh's a person, not a cat."

"Could you ever tell the difference? Between people and animals? You couldn't. You can't. I just wanted to remind you. You fell completely in love with Fred. Remember? When he died, you spent a week crying at my house. What if it was all innocent? What if it happened because of your eyes? Which it didn't. You fell in love with him. He fell in love with you. You never do anything halfway. Apparently, he doesn't either."

"*Do* you know any young Chinese girls? Preferably anesthetists. They make a lot of money and they don't have crazy hours. You know a lot of doctors."

"Give it up, Eleanor. Leave him *alone*. You weren't in charge of his life. You're not responsible for finding him a replacement. Leave him *alone*. You said it was over."

"I didn't say that. I said it was changed."

"Oh, God," says Jane. "I've got a box of Godiva chocolates and I'm going to eat all of them right now."

"Get a knife and cut the box in half," says Eleanor. "You're so greedy."

"I'm greedy?" asks Jane, getting the huge pink box, slashing it in half with one of her gourmet knives, each knife only an inch or so shorter than a Samurai sword: "Here."

The sun sets through the large picture windows, making Jane's still unpacked cartons seem radiant with their own light, as if, inside, the wise books were attempting to illuminate the room. The two of them, sitting on cushions on the floor, their backs against stacks of books which in turn lean against a newly papered wall, green bamboo over a design of red blossoms, sit there methodically and hungrily eating their half of the candy.

Oh, it is wonderful here, thinks Eleanor. There's no present here, just the purified past. By what alchemy was this accomplished?

She grins at Jane. "Someday," she tells her, "we'll be sitting here, eating another box of candy, talking about this."

"You think so? I hope someone comes to look for us, because if we finish this box, we'll be too fat to get out again."

"Shut up and eat," says Eleanor. "You'll need your strength if you're coming to play with the kids."

THIRTY

LEAVE AUNT JANE ALONE," says Eleanor. "She's tired. You dragged her all over Alexander's."

"I needed a body suit," whines Julie.

"You got one. Now take it up to your room."

Julie ignores her mother and sidles up to Jane.

"Don't sit on her lap," says Eleanor. "She's tired."

"When you get old, do your bones get brittle?" Davey asks Jane. "I read that in my science book."

"I'm not brittle yet," says Jane, looking at Eleanor, who is beginning to grin.

Davey takes this as a signal to climb into Jane's lap.

"He's heavy," Jane says, patting the boy's hair.

"Don't mess up my part," says Davey. "I like my hair in a part."

"You look ridiculous with your hair parted," says Eleanor.

"Do I?" Davey asks Jane.

"I don't part *my* hair," announces Julie, who has somehow climbed into Jane's lap without being noticed.

"Do I look ridiculous?" Davey asks Jane again.

"You don't look terrific," she says.

"I told you," said Julie.

"*You* look pretty stupid with all your teeth out," Davey says.

"Shut up, both of you," says Eleanor. "One more word and you go to your rooms."

Jane shakes her head, amazed. This is not what is recommended in her psychology books.

"Did you start getting arthritis yet?" Davey asks Jane. "Grandma didn't like my sitting in her lap because she said her bones hurt."

"I don't have arthritis yet," Jane says. "Ouch!"

Julie has accidentally poked her in the stomach with her elbow.

"Upstairs, both of you," says Eleanor. "No arguments. The first one to say anything gets grounded for two weeks."

The two children go upstairs, making faces over their shoulder. Eleanor pretends not to notice.

"I don't know how you do it," says Jane. "I don't know how anyone does it."

"You're getting pretty good at it," says Eleanor.

"Am I?" says Jane, smiling happily.

"Get rid of that married man and marry someone else."

"He says he *might* marry me. Maybe I'll just get pregnant."

"Good idea," says Eleanor, "unless of course you want to adopt mine."

"They seem to like it here," Jane says, sighing. "If they were the same age, they'd look like twins. They look like you."

"They look like Tom."

"No, like you."

"They're not *like* me. I've perfected shyness to a high art. When Davey was small, he used to find the most menacing person in the store and go over and talk to him and he wasn't happy until he succeeded in dragging me over. I expected to be killed about three times a day. But he had good instincts. All those monsters he went up to turned out to be very nice."

"You're doing a good job," says Jane.

"We'll decide about that when they're in their late twenties," says Eleanor.

"Aunt Jane! Aunt Jane!" Davey calls from upstairs. "Come up here and look at what we built!"

"Are you going?" asks Eleanor, grinning at her.

"Of course," Jane says, getting up slowly. "You know something? I think I *am* getting arthritis."

"It's not arthritis. Just a case of exhaustion induced by a day of bliss with those adorable dwarfs."

"Coming!" Jane calls, as she goes up the stairs.

Tom comes in.

"Jane here again?" he asks. Eleanor nods.

"Good," he says. "I like her. She doesn't call me anymore."

"She can only handle one married man at a time," says Eleanor.

Ah, thinks Eleanor, happiness. Peace.

I was right to trust her, thinks Tom; it was only her eyes after all. And she's never been happier. Perhaps adversity was good for her soul. He doubts it. Eleanor would hate that idea. Then it is only the passage of time that has cured her. He sinks back against the cushions of the couch, smiling at her. The dove dives in the window, but he has already received its message.

"Did you know," he asks Eleanor, "that Julie told her teacher you hit her in the eye?"

"I slapped her face when she fell into the foot space between the back seat and the front seat. She wouldn't stop screaming. I warned her twice. I said if she kept it up,

I'd haul her out and spank her. I didn't want to get into an accident. I had to pull over and pull her out."

"Well, that's what she told the teacher."

"I'll kill her," says Eleanor without conviction. "Poor abused child," she says after a while.

"Don't worry about it," says Tom.

"I'm not," says Eleanor. "I'm trying to think up a punishment for lying. One she'll take seriously."

"I don't think there's any such thing," says Tom.

Eleanor shakes her head, gets up, and sits in his lap. "Bones hurt?" she asks him.

"Why not?" he asks.

THIRTY-ONE

A YEAR PASSES, then two.

Jane spends a great deal of time at Eleanor's these days, and so does Toh, who seems to have accepted the return to the old ways as easily as Eleanor. At first Jane's eyebrows go up when Toh arrives, as he frequently does, to baby-sit, a job he not only volunteers for but seems eager to have and for which he will take no money. After a while, she only shrugs one shoulder slightly. Still later, she shakes her head almost imperceptibly, as if to say *who would believe this,* and finally, she begins referring to herself and Toh as the children's stepparents and settles in herself.

She and Eleanor often argue when she offers advice on how children should be disciplined, and when Toh sees them angry he becomes upset.

"Good friends should not argue," he tells them.

"Nonsense," say the two of them together, and so the argument ends.

Jane begins trying to teach Toh the art of analytic introspection, but Tom puts a stop to that.

"Leave him alone," he says. "A person from a dictatorship needs all the luxury denial can give him."

Nevertheless, when Toh listens to Eleanor and Jane discuss their depressions (they have both decided they're

274

depressives), he pays attention, and the next time a book of Eleanor's comes out and is reviewed and Eleanor takes to her bed, he begins to call her every three hours.

"What *are* you doing?" she asks him after the fourth telephone call.

"You were asleep? Good. I will call back in a half hour to wake you up."

He tells her that depressive people are helpless, and that what she regards as inevitable states, triggered by uncontrollable events, are only problems to be solved and no problems can be solved while she sleeps.

"Do you mind if I hang up?" she asks him.

"Why?"

"So I can go back to sleep."

"Go back to sleep," he says, and he calls two hours later. He does not call her during the hours when people usually sleep.

"The thing is," Eleanor tells Jane, "it works. He keeps waking me up. It's infuriating, and he keeps on with these Chinese sayings, how all problems can be solved, and before I know it, I feel better. It's not supposed to work that way. You're not supposed to treat depression by interrupting the symptom. It's too simple."

"Hmmm," says Jane, who has a ward full of depressives to supervise. "*I* should try it."

She issues orders to her staff: Severely depressed patients are to be awakened every three hours, then every two hours, then every hour.

"I think we have something here," she says and looks at Toh with new respect.

"Are you telling anyone what you're doing yet?" Eleanor asks. "Like the administrators?"

"Are you kidding? They'd think I'd lost my mind.

I've got to write it up as a grant proposal first. Then nobody will ask any questions. All grant proposals are for
crazy things. The hospital keeps most of the money for
administrative costs. When you bring in that kind of
money, you can be as crazy as a loon. But I'm bad at
writing up proposals. There's a knack to it, like planning
Watergate."

"Maybe," says Eleanor, "you should ask Colin. The
idiot Gloria goes out with. He's practically knocked un-
conscious by falling grants. Every time he writes a memo,
someone gives him a grant. When he's not in his office on
Wall Street, he writes grant proposals for every department in that college on Staten Island. He's still teaching a
course there."

"Are you talking to Gloria again?" asks Jane.

"A little."

"How often?"

"Every day."

"Why?" asks Jane.

"Some things are inevitable, like death and rela-
tives."

"Do you get to say anything or is it the usual solo per-
formance?"

Eleanor shrugs.

"And you say you can't stand opera," says Jane.

"It's like wolves howling. Wolves like to listen to
other wolves howl. It doesn't matter what they're howling
about."

"If you didn't talk to her so often," says Jane, "you
wouldn't need Toh's wake-up calls every two hours. Are
you going to let her near the house?"

"Not until she stops saying that all Orientals look
alike."

"How is she supposed to know that bothers you? When you don't say anything?"

Eventually, Jane is awarded a Guggenheim Fellowship for what she labels her Wake-Up Call Program, and then she begins to complain about the amount of the award. How can she possibly live on such a small amount? Guggenheim fellows have to stop working for a living. You can only do work of your own. If you can afford the electricity to work by. She hopes there will be bread lines next year so that she can call the papers and have them photograph a Guggenheim fellow standing on the line, while Gloria rants at Colin, telling him that he knows how to get everyone a grant but her. If Eleanor hadn't befriended that idiotic Chinese person and half his family and friends, Jane wouldn't have gotten the idea in the first place. It was Gloria's luck to have a miserable chairman when she first taught. If he'd liked her, he could have kept her on, even though, in the beginning, she couldn't get up early enough to get to class on time. She'd have a permanent position now and not have to worry about health insurance or how to get jobs at five different schools a semester, whereupon Eleanor hangs up, first on Gloria, and then on Jane, who has been telling her not to talk to Gloria. Eventually, she calls them back. She's getting too old to wait for them to recover from being insulted. Still, she is unrepentant about hanging up. People talk too much. The telephone is a wonderful thing *because* it can be hung up. She *loves* to hang up, she tells Tom, who tells her she is becoming worse than her children.

It is a noisier and happier house, thinks Tom, who begins cooking for all of them. The odd way in which cas-

ual visitors become permanent residents is something he's
long ago accepted, as he now accepts the larger scale on
which it occurs. Davey and his daughter seemed to have
moved two children from the block into their rooms.
When there is no school, the two extra children arrive—
one a small blond girl from two houses down the block,
the other a tiny Chinese boy from around the corner—
head down to the basement with arms full of toys and
tape recorders, and put on shows until their parents call
late Sunday and ask for the return of the weekend residents.

He and Eleanor often go out and stand in their driveway, look in through the knee-level basement windows,
and see the four children sprawled out on the floor, reading, coloring, admiring one another's sticker collections.
They agree that children turn into teenagers by the age of
seven these days.

Life is less painful for Eleanor lately, Tom thinks, and
tells her so, and to his surprise she doesn't stop him in a
superstitious fit, trying to convince him that things are
worse than ever.

Until recently, she has claimed that she thinks only
when she's at her typewriter; otherwise, her mind is an
empty shell. But she is beginning to believe that thinking
is no longer a torture to her, no longer a long argument
with invisible departed members of her family. When she
tries to talk to her mother or grandmother, her thoughts
are returned to her, untouched, unopened, return to
sender, addressee deceased. At last. She remembers them
with affection. They are no longer there.

"One must never think about miracles," says Toh.
"*One* must? Is that right?"

He has been reading again, borrowing books from
her library's shelves. He takes them, dusty and yellowed,

cleans them off, puts them in covers made out of brown paper bags, and returns them to her in their new jackets, their names lettered in Chinese on their new covers. She prints their names in English on the spines and puts the books back on the shelves.

However, she does begin to turn the miracle over and over. Nothing has turned out as she expected. She knew and Jane knew and Gloria knew that an affair was punishable, probably by death, death meaning different things to each of them. To Jane, it meant the death of the wife of the man whose life she shared, her suicide, living with eternal guilt. To Gloria, death is living alone or spending holidays alone with her television set because she does not want to be seen alone when everyone else is coupled. For Eleanor, it means the end of her marriage, divorce, unspeakable things like questions of child custody. At the very least, it means punishment and recriminations, suffering occasioned by the loss of one's lover, by the knowledge that one has betrayed one's husband. But she isn't really sure whether Tom knows about the room in Chinatown, or if, in the end, it makes any difference. When she thinks of his generosity of spirit, she cries. She could never have put up with her own behavior.

And what of Toh, whom they usually expect to ring their bell once a day? According to the rules, she and Toh should never see each other again. *Clean breaks are best.* But if nothing is broken? If, instead, something is mended? If it was true that nothing separated them before, not even the impermeable membrane that she has always believed forever seals one mind off from another?

And the children, whose lives ought to have been ruined by their adulterous mother, are becoming healthier every day, out there on the porch with Toh, who is teaching them more advanced kung fu. Afterwards, they kick happily about the house, knocking over furniture and scuffing walls.

All of them go to the movies together nowadays, in two cars, Eleanor's and Toh's, or Eleanor's and Jane's. When she and Tom go away for a weekend, Aunt Jane and Uncle Toh take turns baby-sitting. Jane is no longer depressed by the children's questions about what it's like to be old and doesn't think of herself, at least not aloud, as someone becoming hopelessly more antique with each additional hour. When Toh graduates from school and has trouble finding a job, Eleanor consults Jane's brother, who advises her to sponsor him, and if that's not possible, to adopt him.

"Adopt him!" cries the mortally wounded Gloria, who wants to be adopted herself and sees Toh as the one who took her place in the little wicker basket left on the church steps. "Adopt a twenty-nine-year-old Chinese person? Don't you think you'd better ask his parents first? They may not want their son adopted."

Eleanor sighs and considers hanging up the telephone.

"And how are you going to ask his parents anything? You don't know a word of Chinese. They don't know a word of English."

Eleanor replaces the receiver in its cradle.

"Hanging up on Gloria again?" Tom asks her. "When I first met you, you were always hanging up on your mother. I was very impressed. A pretty Jewish girl, hanging up on her mother. Who knew what you were capable of?"

They are about to call an immigration lawyer when Toh gets a job, not through his own efforts, but through Colin's. Colin, who has listened to all of Gloria's diatribes, knows Toh needs work, makes some phone calls, asks some questions at his alma mater, and tells Eleanor where Toh should go to be interviewed. Colin's helping Toh, Eleanor says, will be the death of Gloria, but Tom says it won't change anything. Colin and Gloria are too locked together to change. Two insecure people, terrified of entrapment, have walked into cement, and when it hardened it did so so slowly that they never knew they were caught, and so it doesn't occur to them to try chipping themselves free.

On a spring day in May, five years after her eye surgery, Eleanor is sitting on her front porch, watching her two enormously tall children play Ping-Pong with Jane. If they get any taller, their heads will go through the planks of the ceiling. They are both taller than Jane, and her son will soon be taller than she is. She remembers when she didn't think she'd live long enough to see them able to cross a street on their own. Now they voyage about the city on buses and trains, and if they're more than ten minutes late getting back, she sits in a chair, shivering with fear. She contemplates the wrinkles on the backs of her hands and wonders if it is really true that intellectuals can't have facelifts. A pile of reviews is under her chair, unread. She is timing herself to see how long it will take her to give in and read them, the ideal length of time being forever.

The little bell on the side of the glass porch door rings. Odd—no one rings that bell with its little rusty knob. She gets up and goes to the door. Toh.

"Come on in," she says, but he seems reluctant, embarrassed, and finally points to someone on the other side of the red car parked in front of their house.

"Come on," he calls, and a small, beautiful girl walks around the car and stops on the sidewalk.

"I'll get her," says Toh. "This is Mai," he says, and

the girl smiles and then moves behind his back. "She doesn't speak much English, but I told her she can come here and learn."

Eleanor smiles, trying to remember: there is something she almost sees out of the corner of her eye. Oh, yes, when her cat had kittens, she disappeared and later at night came back carrying what Eleanor and Tom thought was a dirty sock, which she proceeded to drop on the rug in front of them, staring at them with huge, fierce eyes. The little sock gave a cry and the cat continued staring at them. Finally, Eleanor told the cat the socklike thing was a *beautiful* kitten, whereupon the cat carried the kitten off and refused to let it be seen again. Eleanor could not locate the kittens until they caught cold and then she found four sneezing Brillo pads hidden in the lining of a couch.

Eleanor stands perfectly still, looking at Mai. Toh begins to argue with the girl in Chinese while Mai stares down at her shoes. Finally, she looks up at Eleanor and says hello.

"Hello," says Eleanor.

By now, the children have put down their paddles and are jabbering at Mai: Hi, how are you, are you Toh's girlfriend, are you going to marry him, do you want to get married at our house, are you going to eat supper with us, where do you come from in China, and under this sand-blast of babble, the girl relaxes.

"Marry?" she asks. "Yes."

"Marry," says Toh.

Oh, yes, Eleanor is back on the sleet-covered asphalt, her arm outstretched, watching herself from above, shriveling, wrinkling, entering the sudden land of Cronedom. Toh bends over and kisses her cheek. She does not reach for him, but for the girl, whose cheek she touches gently

with her fingertips. Then she kisses her. The girl collapses
against her and begins to cry. *Far from home.*

She wishes she could tell the children this story because it is about so many things. It is about all the obvious
things, and it is also about herds of gazelles, who signal to
each other by twitching their ears once or twice, the signals governing their mating rituals, but also reminding
them that, whatever they may have been thinking, "We
are all here, all here," all part of one herd, of which the
sun and the moon and the sky are also a part. This, however, is a story she cannot tell them.

"Where is she from?" she asks Toh, but she knows:
Peking.

"You should," Toh once said, when she was having
trouble with Davey, "send him to China for two years. My
parents would care for him. Send him," he went on, not
thinking about what he was saying, "the way I came, not
knowing a word of Chinese. Then he would feel like he
was in jail."

Sentence commuted, safe at last. Eleanor smiles at
the girl with such gratitude that Mai moves closer and
Eleanor hugs her. Mai starts to pull back, but then smiles
and relaxes, her face surprised. She says something to Toh.

"She says it is warm, being hugged," he tells her.
"She likes it. In China, she was not hugged but beaten."

Oh Lord, thinks Eleanor, another girl who was
beaten.

She looks at Mai as if to say she knows what that is,
don't worry, you're safe here, and the girl smiles back and
begins babbling to her. Then she remembers Eleanor
can't understand a word and begins to laugh. Soon they
are all laughing. Except Jane, who, for her own reasons,
has gone to the corner of the porch and is intently watching the new red leaves on the rose bushes.

He is, thinks Eleanor, the illuminated letters of the text of my life. The text will change if only because he keeps changing it, but the illuminations will remain. She looks at Mai, who is very young: twenty-two? twenty-three? Soon they will be having children and the children will be running about this porch and they will call her Grandmother. The little room in Chinatown will rise higher and higher until it is only a sunspot, perhaps too bright to look at.

She and Tom will age together and that will seem natural. When Toh ages, her heart will break. When her own children age, when her young daughter's womb begins to sag like the tired, long-empty wombs of the women who have gone with their husbands to Florida to write a happy ending for their lives, when she begins to look like those heroic women who square dance, wombs sagging or gone, who play golf, breasts resting flat and pleated near their waists, when this happens to her daughter, it will be worse than whatever has already happened to Eleanor. Those heroic women square dancing while death himself calls the steps—and what a good teacher he is, how he keeps them all laughing, how he snaggles them up, how the wrong ones end up partnered, how the corners never face each other, how the couples are severed and reunited, how tired they all get, how they pretend to clutch at their chests—such grand dancing in elastic hose, such royalty in blue blood of their protruding veins, such trust in the world, leaving their true faces at home in old photograph albums, pretending they recognize the faces they see staring back at them from the mirror. Will she have it, such trust, such heroism? She remembers the reviews under her chair and doubts that she will.

But it is time to usher Toh and Mai inside, to find Tom, to unglue him from his computer, to prepare for a small horde of plump Chinese children, every one of whom she will wish she had borne, to prepare for years of envying the girl, in whose place she would like to be.

"We are only given one life," says her grandmother, whose lips have suddenly been freed of their celestial adhesive tape, "and now you see why. Who has the courage to live even one?"

His little children are already running down the hall, pulling sleeves of coats dangling from the coat stand, threatening to topple it. Toh is going to see to it that she does not end her life asleep in a dream of immortality. His children will polish the magic false words *we live forever* from her windows until they are clear and she can see the bony, hard landscape beneath the greenery. They will polish the indisputable facts of this life until they shine white and glorious like bleached bones struck by sun on sand. So there was a price to pay after all. In this way, Toh will be her particular punishment and her joy.

The gazelles, thinks Eleanor, the gazelles.

ABOUT THE AUTHOR

SUSAN FROMBERG SCHAEFFER is the author of five previous novels, *Falling, Anya, Time in Its Flight, Love* and *The Madness of a Seduced Woman*, as well as five collections of poetry and one book of short fiction. She was educated at the University of Chicago where she wrote the first doctoral dissertation on Vladimir Nabokov. She has written many scholarly articles and is a frequent book reviewer for the *Chicago Tribune* and the *Chicago Sun Times*. She is Professor of English at Brooklyn College and a founding member of its Master of Fine Arts Program in Poetry. She lives in Brooklyn and Vermont with her husband and two children. A Guggenheim fellow, she is now working on her next novel and next collection of poems.

Look for the SUMMER IN PARADISE SWEEPSTAKES entry coupon where these bestsellers are displayed:

On May 14

On June 18

Summer in Paradise